D0616387

TRUTH
BEHIND THE
MASK

by

Lesley Davis

2008

TRUTH BEHIND THE MASK
© 2008 By Lesley Davis. All Rights Reserved.

ISBN 10: 1-60282-029-5
ISBN 13: 978-1-60282-029-6

This Trade Paperback Original Is Published By
Bold Strokes Books, Inc.
New York, USA

First Edition: September 2008

THIS IS A WORK OF FICTION. NAMES, CHARACTERS, PLACES, AND
INCIDENTS ARE THE PRODUCT OF THE AUTHOR'S IMAGINATION OR
ARE USED FICTITIOUSLY. ANY RESEMBLANCE TO ACTUAL PERSONS,
LIVING OR DEAD, BUSINESS ESTABLISHMENTS, EVENTS, OR LOCALES
IS ENTIRELY COINCIDENTAL.

THIS BOOK, OR PARTS THEREOF, MAY NOT BE REPRODUCED IN ANY
FORM WITHOUT PERMISSION.

Credits
Editors: Cindy Cresap and Stacia Seaman
Production Design: Stacia Seaman
Cover Design By Sheri (graphicartist2020@hotmail.com)

Acknowledgments

My greatest gratitude goes to all at Bold Strokes Books and especially Radclyffe (Len Barot) for welcoming me into the fold. Thank you doesn't begin to cover it for all your support and encouragement.

Thank you, Sheri, for a cover I am thrilled with beyond measure. It served as inspiration in my final editing and is such a beautiful work of art. I am delighted to have my words wrapped in it.

Thanks to my editor, Cindy Cresap, for teaching me so much and for editing my story with humour and 'Brit Speak' alerts! You guided me to a much better realisation of this story and I appreciate that immensely.

Thank you to Stacia Seaman, my copy editor, for helping put the final touches on my story and making it such a joyful process.

Wayne Beckett for encouraging and supporting me in everything.

Beth Mitchum...Just because.

Dedication

Always for my Cindy
You are my all and everything.

Chastilian's many great towers rose high into the night sky, daring to touch the stars with their majestic height. They stretched to fill the seemingly endless skyline, illuminating it in a myriad of lights. A Sentinel stood atop one such structure, keeping watch from her vantage point. Dressed all in black, her face hidden behind a mask, she embraced the shadows on the roof and used them to her advantage to watch over the city unnoticed. Using her night vision binoculars, she focused her attention on a figure on the street below.

Shifting suddenly as her quarry made a move, she climbed onto the roof edge and for a brief moment was silhouetted against the full moon, revealing herself to the night. Then she stepped off the edge of the building and disappeared into the darkness.

CHAPTER ONE

Pagan Osborne maneuvered her van through the wild and manic early morning traffic, marveling at how many commuters were still racing to work as she tried to cross at a busy intersection. Pagan squinted at the bright sunlight that spilled through her windshield and hitched up her sunglasses to try to cut out the light that threatened to blind her tired eyes. She drove with gritted teeth, trying not to let the erratic maneuvers of the other drivers test her patience. She was relieved when she finally saw the ornate gates of the Ammassari Dealership, and she steered the van into the designated parking bay and got out. She looked over the endless rows of cars and vans laid out for the lucky buyer to peruse. She gave a quick glance at her own vehicle. The black van was decorated with a lighthouse motif on both side panels, its beam of light highlighting the words *Ronchetti Security.*

"Finally!" A small, rotund man barreled his way toward Pagan and clapped his broad hand on her back. "I thought you'd never get here."

Pagan looked at her watch. "You only came and saw us yesterday, Mr. Ammassari, and you are the first call on my rounds."

"Yes, yes, but things happen in a busy city like ours." Tito Ammassari leaned forward and whispered, "I'm hearing all sorts of things from all sorts of people. I need this place wired and alarmed pronto. A man in my line of business needs to be secure."

Pagan nodded, intrigued by his almost palpable unease. "I'll start with the offices first, then we'll work our way out." She scanned the lot with an expert eye. "You'll need plenty of cameras out here. This is a big lot to cover."

"Anything, any cost. It doesn't matter. Just keep me safe!"

Pagan nodded and gestured toward the office building attached to the main car lot. "Can I set up in there?"

"Yes, yes, go see Erith. She's our new girl. She'll show you anything you need." Tito nudged Pagan with a meaty elbow. "She's very smart. She's mended half the antiquated machines in our office, and she's very fast on the computer."

Pagan was bemused as to why he would be sharing this information with her.

"She also fixed the coffee machine." From the awe in Tito's voice, this was some miracle of science.

"It sounds like you have found yourself a good employee, Mr. Ammassari."

"She's pretty too." He gestured to his own sparse hair. "And all fire."

Pagan was a little mystified at his description but paid it little heed as she grabbed her case from the back of her van. "I'll just go get started, then." She watched as his attention was caught by potential customers arriving on his lot, and he dismissed her with a distracted wave.

She jogged up the steps that led to the main offices that housed the car lot business, then meandered through the series of short corridors until she found the office where visitors were sent. Pagan stuck her head around the open door first so as not to startle the office's occupant. The greeting Pagan was set to utter stuck somewhere in her throat.

A young woman stood by a filing cabinet, and when she turned to see who was entering her work space, Pagan was pinned to the spot by the greenest pair of eyes she had ever seen. She was doubly arrested by the color of the woman's hair. Pagan removed her sunglasses to better appreciate the vibrant colors she was seeing. Ammassari had not been exaggerating. This woman was indeed *all fire*. A rich red mane of hair streaked with highlights of orange framed her face.

Pagan realized that the woman was waiting for her to speak. She had struck a pose against the cabinet and was regarding Pagan with an amused look.

"You're Erith, right? Mr. Ammassari told me to just come up…" Pagan began, but her voice cracked like a teenage boy's.

"Ronchetti Security, yes?" Erith filed away the paperwork she had in her hand, then slid the cabinet closed with a nudge of her hip.

Pagan headed for a flat surface where she could lay down her case. It clattered loudly, making her cringe. She flipped open the lid, and a coil of wire snaked out in a bid for freedom. She stifled a sigh and began to wind the wire back up again.

"Got out of bed just a little too early this morning?"

Pagan looked over her shoulder. "It's always too early. I'm more a night person."

"Do you need coffee to start your day more smoothly?"

"I honestly can't drink the stuff."

"There's a pop machine just outside if you're in need of a different caffeine fix."

Pagan nodded, grateful of the excuse to escape. "Can I get you anything?"

Erith tapped a black painted nail on the side of her mug. "I drink coffee. I'm made of sterner stuff."

Pagan grinned at the delightful drawl of Erith's soft voice and left to find the drink machine. She fumbled with her money, trying to get it into the coin slot, and was amazed to see how slick with sweat her palms were. She jumped as the can fell with a loud clatter into the tray, and she removed it before it made any more noise to startle her edgy nerves. The coldness did little to stop her hands from sweating. Pagan was drawn back toward the office. She chuckled at the thought that entered her head: *like a moth to the proverbial flame.* She was surprised to find Erith waiting for her at the door, all but barring her entry.

"Just how tall *are* you?" she asked as she tipped her head back to take in Pagan's full height.

"Six feet, give or take an inch." Pagan looked down at the much smaller Erith. "And you're what? About five foot in your biker boots?"

"Five foot four, if you must know."

Pagan bit back a smile at what was obviously a touchy subject for Erith. "What are a few inches between friends?"

"So quick are you to make friends with the office girl?" Erith walked back into the office to lean against her desk. "For all you know, I could be a mass murderer who wanders from office to office seeking my next prey amid the paper clips."

"I'll bear that in mind, though I think you might need a touch more black to carry the whole murderer thing off with any panache. I'm Pagan Osborne." She held out a hand politely.

"*Pagan*? Is everything about you so unusual?"

"You have *no* idea."

❖

Erith Baylor. Pagan let the name roll around her head as she meandered from office to office, marking off every door and window on her plan. She wandered back into Erith's office and tapped further instructions into the small electronic notepad that held her virtual map. Seated across from Erith, she pretended not to watch her work.

Pagan was fascinated by Erith's clothing. She was dressed in a black wool sweater that hung from her shoulders to reveal a dark-colored T-shirt underneath. Jeans that had seen better days were held up by a studded belt. Black biker boots added a touch more menace to the ensemble. The brightness of Erith's hair was at furious odds with the darkness of her clothing. She understood the draw to the darkness of attire; black was a color that could be very intimidating. She wondered why Erith would feel the need to warn people away. Pagan looked down at her own clothes, starting with a pair of black boots that were polished and shiny. She also wore jeans, but high-quality ones that were smart yet practical. A dark blue sweatshirt bearing her work logo finished off her attire. Pagan reached up to check if she'd at least taken the time to comb her hair before she'd grabbed the keys to the van and set out into the day's early light.

Her movement caught Erith's attention. Pagan sensed Erith's sharp eyes traveling over her like a physical touch. She lifted her head from her notepad to find Erith watching her, looking straight into her soul, it seemed. Erith smiled, and Pagan smiled in return. She shifted to try to ease her long legs out across the floor before her and not slip out of the chair that was too small for her. She caught the smothered grin Erith tried to stifle at her predicament.

"Damn plastic chairs aren't built for comfort."

"Not for the giants among us, no," Erith said. "So, Pagan Osborne, what draws you to the world of security alarms?"

"It's a family business."

"Do you like your work?"

"Who wouldn't want to keep the city safe from harm?"

Erith chuckled at Pagan's obvious party line. "So you're fitting the car lot with cameras and such?"

"It seems Mr. Ammassari feels the need for an eye on every corner of his business. We're here to fit whatever he requires for him to feel his business is secure."

"How long do you think that will take? To get everything set up and alarmed?"

Pagan pursed her lips a little as she calculated the work necessary. "A couple of days and then we can start on his home too."

Erith's head lifted slightly. "Tito's having his house done as well?"

Pagan nodded. Erith flashed her a cheeky grin.

"Guess there is plenty of money to be made in selling cars."

"His business is keeping me in business, so I have no complaints. I'll be loitering around here on the lot until further notice." She took a healthy swig from her drink. It stuck somewhere in her throat like a leaden lump at the soft *good* she heard whispered from Erith's lips.

"I'll make sure the pop machine is stocked for you." Erith studied Pagan, unabashed in letting her eyes wander over Pagan's face.

"How old are you?" Pagan blurted out and cursed her lack of social etiquette. "I'm sorry, I just…" She could feel the redness of her cheeks burn like a beacon to her stupidity.

"I'm twenty-two."

"I've got a year on you."

"Checking I'm old enough to be out of school, eh? Please don't put me back through that torture." Erith held up her hands to ward off the unimagined horrors.

Pagan chuckled at her expressive face. "School wasn't so bad, unless you happened to tower over all of the kids by the age of twelve. Adolescents take umbrage to that, for some bizarre reason. The boys see you as a threat to their manhood, and the girls think you're just plain weird for letting your hormones make you grow *up* instead of *out*!"

"Ouch. Bullied much?"

Pagan shook her head. "More left alone than singled out once I gained the muscle to add to the height." She saw Erith look her over and tried not to react to the obvious glint in Erith's eyes. Her body flamed to that look. She shifted once more in her seat.

"Made you more the strong and silent type?" Erith rested her chin in her hands. "I'd have probably been drawn to you at school. All that tall, dark, and brooding air you exuded would have called to me. And I like the sound of your voice. It's kind of low and edgy. You have a very strange accent going on there. I'm sure we would have hung out together."

Pagan was intrigued by the light dancing in Erith's bright eyes as she ignored the comment about her voice. "Doing what?"

"I'm guessing you are the brainy type, so I'd have had you help me do my homework so it was in on time. And maybe I'd have even had the incentive to stay in class."

"You hated school that much?" Pagan had loved her years of schooling.

"Let's just say the motivation wasn't there for me to stay. And we moved around a lot, so I never got to stay in the same seat for very long."

Pagan wondered at Erith's sudden stillness and where her thoughts had taken her. It didn't look like a happy place. "And now you work here."

"Yeah, the office is all mine and the guys are great." She rolled her eyes. "If a little overprotective."

"You're the only girl on the lot; it's to be expected." Pagan stood to put her calculations away. She stretched to try to dispel some of the nervous energy she could feel building up inside her. She couldn't explain what she was feeling, but it intensified when she looked at Erith. She felt like her stomach was filled with a thousand butterflies all taking flight at once.

"Time for me to head back to the office and work out a plan of action." Pagan drained what was left of her drink. She smiled at Erith, still seated behind the desk. "It was nice meeting you, Erith."

"Same time tomorrow, Pagan?"

"I expect so, or at least before the lunch rush hits."

"I'll try to find you a bigger chair."

"I'd appreciate that." She gathered up her case and waved good-bye. Pagan wondered at her own haste as she left the offices and headed back for the van. She saw Tito Ammassari busy herding a client around a more expensive range of vehicles and pantomimed he'd get a call later. He nodded and went straight back to business. Pagan settled back in her van and purposely did not take one last look at the office window where she could sense Erith stood.

❖

Pagan drove back toward the business that was also her home. Ronchetti Security was a shining beacon in the middle of the city, quite literally when the building's famed lighthouse shone its gentle beam across the city advertising its presence. The light was not so bright as to cause problems for the dwellers in the high-rise buildings surrounding the out-of-place lighthouse on land. The lighthouse was a lasting reminder of what used to be there by its side. The Last Port in the Storm restaurant had been in Pagan's family since before she was born. On the night her parents died, the restaurant had been set on fire, and the building, including their home, had been lost. The lighthouse, miraculously, survived the blaze. It continued to be a welcoming sight, tall and proud amid the noise and bustle of Chastilian. The restaurant was long gone, but in its place stood a new building, the home to the Ronchetti Security offices. Now the lighthouse was used to advertise alarm systems and personal protection for the citizens of Chastilian. The company's motto paid tribute to what had gone before: *Ronchetti Security, your first and last port in a storm.*

Pagan parked the van and took a small detour through the back door of the building where she spotted her older sister making a pot of coffee in the small office kitchen.

"Pagan!" Melina Osborne's cheerful voice greeted her. "Everything go okay?" She set cups on a tray, along with a jug of milk and sugar. Then she arranged a small plate of cookies.

Pagan smiled at Melina's finishing touch. "Ammassari's lot is a huge place to cover, Mel. We should get a good few days' work out of it."

"That should keep Rogue happy." She handed Pagan the plate of cookies and then poured her a glass of milk. "I think you need these cookies more. Go eat. You skipped breakfast again. Rogue is out in the shop meeting with a new client. I thought I'd win them over with some old-fashioned hospitality."

Pagan accepted the plate gratefully and opened the door to let Melina pass by. Pagan was struck by just how different she and her sister Melina were, for all their shared genes. They had the same jet-black hair and dark blue eyes. Melina, however, was quintessentially feminine while Pagan had heard herself described as handsomely androgynous. She peeked through a small window into the shop where she was able to spot Rogue Ronchetti walking around with the new customer, showing him what was available and what she recommended for their security. Rogue was attired in jeans and a white shirt, her hair already slicked down in a vain attempt to tame its natural curl. Pagan looked upon Melina's lover as someone who was as much a parent to her as her blood sibling was. Rogue and Melina had brought Pagan up when the sisters' parents had been killed. She watched as Rogue demonstrated a particular product in her no-nonsense manner. Pagan grinned as she watched her. It was no secret she worshipped Rogue. She was a quiet woman, solid as oak, butch to a fault, with a wicked dry humor that very few were privileged to witness.

Melina was her perfect foil. She stood nearly as tall as Rogue's intimidating six foot two, but had hair that curled almost to her waist. She was vocal, temperamental, passionate, and loud. Rogue was all calmness, possessing an almost zenlike quality, but was passionate when her temper got riled.

Pagan thought Rogue and Melina made a striking couple, and she loved them for taking on the parenting roles they had been forced into so young. As role models went, they could not have been a more loving couple whose ideals spread far beyond their lives together or the security business.

Juggling her milk and plate of cookies, Pagan climbed the stairs that took her to the living quarters above the office building. She went through the living room and down a corridor to climb more stairs that led to her bedroom. She wandered over to a poster of a film heroine bedecked in shiny leather and dark glasses and ran her hand over the print. She pressed a small hidden button, and the wall before her revealed a door cleverly hidden by the line of wallpaper covering it. Pagan opened it and stepped into a secret set of rooms, accessible only by a spiral staircase that ran inside the lighthouse tower. The lighthouse held a hidden lair that was known to a select few and used only by Pagan and her family. Pagan sprinted up the staircase and checked the screens off one of the landings. She reached for a keyboard and entered in her codes. The screen sprang to life, and she was greeted by a familiar face.

"Hi, Uncle Frank." Pagan began reading the messages that ran along the bottom of the screen.

"Hey, Pagan, you're on the screens early."

"I had a new job to price. I just wanted to see if there was anything you've heard happening in the city. It's got our local car dealer shaken up so much so that he's having his entire lot and home alarmed. He seems frightened rather than merely security conscious. It just struck me as odd."

"I'll run it by our man in the police force. They might already have a lead on what's going on around there. I heard they've been busy with some thefts. They think it's kids because it's primarily money being taken and the burglaries are sloppy, a lot of mess and little regard for alarms. As for the car lot, have you seen the prices that guy sells his vehicles for? Might just be a disgruntled buyer wanting payback and terrorizing him. But otherwise it's quiet so far. Chastilian is just gearing up for the day. But, as you know, when night falls it can all change in the blink of an eye." Uncle Frank winked at her and shooed her away from the screen. "Go do your other job. You have people to protect out there. Be sure to give my best to Rogue."

Pagan turned the screen off to end their conversation. She swiveled around in her seat to look at her black leather suit hanging from its pegs. Pagan ran a finger across the collar.

"And welcome to the *other* family business," she muttered before padding back down the tower's steps to reenter her bedroom. She closed the connecting door between the rooms, hiding away her other identity and life.

Chapter Two

Pagan pulled on her pants and felt the snug black leather mold to her body like another skin. She tucked in her T-shirt and fastened the zipper. Sitting on a small bench, she reached for her boots. The thick soles were heavily ridged, the steel toes encased in tough leather, and the boots reached to mid calf. Pagan laced up the boots and made sure they were comfortable. Lastly, she donned her thick leather jacket. Lined with Kevlar to act as body armor, the jackets were the Sentinels' main protection against those who meant them harm. The lean lines of the jacket fitted firmly to Pagan's broad shoulders and fastened with a hidden zip.

Pagan fastened the last catch on her jacket collar and reached for her mask. She slid the molded material up to cover her eyes and protect her nose. She grinned. Out of all the clothing she put on to pursue what she did, the mask was the one thing that made her laugh. *"If you don't wear a mask, people will know who you are, and none of your family will ever be safe. Family is the most important thing. You have to keep it protected at all times and at all costs."* Pagan could still hear Rogue's voice from years ago explaining why the mask was a necessary tool. She adjusted the settings to keep the mask in place.

The mask also housed a tiny microphone and a sophisticated camera lens, both used by the Sighted to keep contact with the Sentinels. While the Sentinels were the ones who watched over the city, they in turn were watched over by the Sighted. The Sighted were the unseen force that the Sentinels employed. But for all the technology the Sighted had at their fingertips, a Sentinel had to rely on her strength alone in a fight.

Pagan gathered up her utility belt and fastened it about her waist. She ran through each pocket and over every clasp to make sure everything was in its place. A dual flashlight, small but with a powerful two-headed beam, dangled from an iron clip. An army knife with a myriad of attachments was nestled in a pocket. There were plastic bindings for tying up hands and feet. In another pocket were a pair of night vision binoculars, another housed a cell phone, and then a small first aid kit. A breathing mask and a small Taser finished the equipment list. Pagan attached her collapsible escrima sticks in place by her side, then slipped on her gloves and walked across the room to where Rogue was sauntering around the lighthouse, her own mask dangling from her fingertips.

"Any chaos out there tonight?" She cocked a head toward the police scanner that was announcing what activity was keeping the local law enforcement busy that evening.

"Nothing yet, but the night hasn't started. Give it time. Chastilian never seems to disappoint."

"Keeps us busy, that's for sure."

Rogue fastened her mask in a brisk, no-nonsense manner.

Melina entered the lighthouse and made straight for her seat in front of the mass of computers and screens. She entered a password and the screens flickered to life. Uncle Frank appeared onscreen.

"Good evening, Melina."

"Hi, Uncle Frank. Do your boys have their territory covered?" Her fingers flashed over the keyboard.

"Affirmative," he said as he looked at a screen on his left. "Casper and Earl are out there on their watch. Nothing has been reported as of yet. We may have the beginnings of a quiet night ahead."

Melina grinned. "You do that just to stir up the elements and jinx us all." She continued tapping at her keyboard, bringing her systems up. "Uncle, we are online and active." Two screens showed the inside of the lighthouse, courtesy of the small cameras secreted away in Pagan's and Rogue's masks. Melina turned up the volume on the police scanner, and the soft chatter buzzed through the lighthouse.

"Good hunting, Rogue, Pagan." Frank's image cleared from the screen to be replaced by a spinning graphic. Pagan smiled as she watched the animated lighthouse shed its light over an animated night sea.

Rogue leaned over Melina's shoulder and read the information that had begun scrolling on a screen.

"We'll head out into the city. Maybe tonight we can just sit back and watch the police arrest those burglars that have everyone so antsy." Melina looked up at her, and Rogue placed a kiss on her waiting lips. "Keep an eye on us."

"Always." Melina put her hand to Rogue's cheek and received a kiss pressed in her palm.

Rogue smiled the smile she reserved for Melina alone. She cocked her head at Pagan. "Come on, kid, time to scope out the city."

Pagan waved to her sister as if she were just heading out for a stroll.

"Do as Rogue tells you!" Melina said as if instructing a child, knowing all too well that it would get a rise out of her.

Pagan made a face at the comment.

With her attention still fixed on the computer screens, Melina continued, "And don't you roll those baby blues at me."

Pagan sighed at the admonishment. "It's true. You *do* have eyes in the back of your head."

"She sees *all*," Rogue said, adjusting her mask over her eyes.

"She's wasted at the keyboards."

"You got the muscular physique, Pagan, whereas I got all the super brain power," Melina said with a superior air.

Pagan snorted. Rogue swatted at the back of her head. "Which is why she chose me as her love."

Pagan shook her head at them both. "I need my own sidekick, someone I can bully you two back with."

"That would have to be some sidekick," Melina said from her station.

Rogue pulled Pagan into the elevator after her, effectively cutting off the siblings' war of words. Pagan's startled "Hey!" was muffled as the doors slid shut. Her stomach shifted as the elevator powered down from the lighthouse to open up into an underground garage. All manner of vehicle were housed there. Pagan's gaze lingered on her treasured motorbike. Rogue's twin was beside it, then a large black van used strictly for Sentinel work, and then Melina's small car.

"Let's stretch our legs tonight. We might see more from above than on the streets themselves." Rogue keyed the combination that opened up a small door in the garage and let them into the dark alley behind the Security offices. As soon as they were in view of a tower, they both removed a wire gun from their belts and aimed for the building above their heads. Pagan's gun, shaped like a fat pistol, shot out a long stream of a high-tensile wire that was tipped with a finely pointed dart. Whenever the dart struck its target, whether concrete or steel, it would open to reveal a set of barbs that secured the line. With a swift movement, Rogue was suddenly whisked upward. Pagan felt the bite of the wire being attached, then fitted her own gun to her belt clasp and released the button to race up the building as well. She marveled at the ability to ride the wire and traverse the city from rooftop to rooftop. At the top she scrambled over the ledge of the building and unfastened her gun, the wire shot back in its casing with barely a sound.

"Ammassari seemed more than a little spooked for someone who just wanted to update his alarm system," Pagan said, leaning against the lip of the building and looking down at the city below.

"Then we'll make sure he can rest easy knowing that he is protected by the best alarm system we can offer." Rogue's grin was bright in contrast to the darkness of her mask. She stood on a higher part of the roof. "You did a good job with all the details you brought back today."

"The woman at the lot made a comment about my *accent*."

"I'm guessing you didn't explain it?"

"I don't announce it to everyone when we first meet. I don't want to be seen as some freak of nature."

"You are no freak." Rogue leaned down and dragged Pagan up beside her. "Don't ever let me hear you use that word again to describe yourself. We've had this conversation way too many times before, and you are never going to win."

"She said she liked how low my voice was." Pagan tried to appease Rogue's ire.

Rogue took a deep breath and seemed to relax. "Did you tell her that's what attracts *all* the girls?"

"I don't attract girls, Rogue," Pagan said with a soft snort of derision.

"You do, but the right one hasn't come along yet to attract *you* back."

Pagan considered this. "So when the right one comes along, I tell her what? I'm a security specialist by day, and at night I watch over the city from its rooftops, seeking out the bad guys?"

"When the right one comes along, you tell her as much or as little as you can trust her with."

Pagan leaned against the railing that ran along the edge of one of Chastilian's highest apartment buildings. "Who's going to believe there's such a thing as a *deaf* vigilante?" She reached up a hand to touch where one of her hearing aids was attached inside her ear. The mechanical brilliance that was housed in the tiny casing gave her the unique ability to hear despite her hearing loss. Each lay hidden behind the hair that fell over her ears in a concealing cut. Her ears were in turn covered by the fashioning of her mask to protect both her aids and her identity.

"Who would believe? The one who will recognize you as more than just what your life entails. And the one who will love you no matter what."

"Do you think she's out there?" Pagan cast her eyes over the bright lights of the city.

"It's a big place, kid. I think she just might well be."

❖

From her vantage point high above the city, Pagan could look down at the city streets where her parents had met their fate. She had been rendered deaf as a result of the horrific catastrophe that had befallen her family. In the madness that swirled below, Pagan remembered all too well what had changed her destiny.

Pagan had been four years old when her family was driving home from a rare night out at a competitor's restaurant. Melina, then a studious eighteen-year-old, had left her studying behind to join them on their trip. Alexis and Camillin Osborne had been laughing about something in the front of the car, making Pagan laugh with them as she watched the city lights sparkle in the dark. The first sign that there was trouble was when her father cried out as someone jumped into the road in front of them, and he had to swerve hard to avoid hitting him. The car banged up the pavement and skidded to a halt, shaking up everyone inside and knocking Pagan to the floor of the car. Then the car doors were wrenched open.

"Mr. Phoenix says you should keep your nose out of his business," a deep male voice grunted, and Alexis was ripped from the car.

Another male dragged a screaming Camillin from her seat.

Thick hands grabbed at Pagan, but Melina snatched her up and clutched her to her chest.

"Gimme the brat!" The man tried to pull Pagan out of Melina's grip. Melina was manhandled out of the car by another man.

Pagan managed to take in the confusing scene before her. Her father was fighting with a young man dressed all in black. In the darkness it was hard to see who her father was trying to fight off. She was surprised at how well her father could fight. He was landing as many punches as he received. Her mother was not faring so well in trying to go to her husband's aid. Pagan squirmed in Melina's arms to go help her. Melina was pinned around her shoulders by a man twice her size and girth, and no amount of kicking was freeing her older sister from the man's grip.

"Keep that up, girlie, and I'll have to hurt the kid."

Melina subsided and clutched Pagan closer, whispering for her to keep quiet.

Pagan watched as another man arrived and joined the other to beat her father down. The whole time she could hear a man's voice screaming at the men to hit harder, not to let him up, and to shut the damn woman up. When they couldn't stop her from screaming for help, the man silenced her himself. Pagan could feel Melina's chest hitching with silent sobs. Her mother stopped screaming, and Melina let loose a tortured wail. Pagan began to cry at her sister's torment, not quite understanding what was happening. All Pagan knew was that her mommy had stopped moving and her daddy was on the ground being held down by two men while a third began furiously beating him.

Melina began yelling and tried to get away, but the man who held her punched her and knocked her down. He ambled off with a cocky lilt to his step to go join the much larger fight. Pagan was stuck under Melina's dead weight. She squirmed and twisted to break free of Melina's confining arms. She crawled out from under her sister and was finally able to see what the men were doing. Her mother had been placed back in the passenger seat of the car, her head lolling against the headrest at a very strange angle. Pagan began to wander in the direction of the vehicle as her father was dragged into his seat and left there, head placed against the steering wheel with a solid bang that set off the horn. She watched as the five men were told to spill liquid all over the car. The man who had been issuing the orders stepped forward. He lit a match, watched it flame for a moment, and then flicked it on the car's hood. The car burst into flame. The other men all started to edge away. The man with the matches then tossed a shiny piece of metal into the carnage.

"Here's your tip, Osborne." He watched the flames for a moment, then waved to his men and they started to leave.

The metal piece twirled in the air, then fell to the ground, still spinning. The men's retreating footsteps as they ran away sounded muted over the roar of the flames engulfing the car.

Pagan wandered over to where the coin spun on the pavement. She flinched at the heat from the car that licked at her skin. She halted the coin's twirling by putting a foot on it, then picked it up and held it in her small hand. The head and tail sides were visible in the light from the fire. She started to walk toward the car.

"Daddy, what's this? Daddy? Mommy?" she called, stepping closer to the car. She was intent on reaching her parents, giving no thought to the danger. She didn't know why her parents weren't answering her, why they weren't cautioning her away from the fire. So she figured it was all right and just kept on heading toward them.

The car exploded with a furious roar. The blast threw Pagan across the road, cracking her skull against the pavement where she came to land, knocking her out cold.

When she came to, she was left with the barest minimum of hearing in both ears. The force of the explosion had shattered her tiny eardrums and rendered her deaf. The coin had still been clutched in her hand, another tangible memento.

For Pagan, that night had brought about many changes with each loss she had endured. Her parents had been killed; their family restaurant had been destroyed. The coin became just one more souvenir left from that fateful night. Both she and Melina had vowed to find Phoenix and his gang and avenge their parents' deaths, no matter how long or what it took to gain justice. It shaped their whole lives and those they touched.

"Hey, what's got your attention so bad?" Rogue asked, coming to stand beside Pagan and looking down at where she had been staring for so long.

"Just remembering stuff," Pagan replied with a soft shrug.

Rogue was still for a moment, then nodded. "Remembering is good, but I need you to put that on pause for a moment while we go see what's happening down on Cater Street. Word's coming in of a disturbance down there. The police have already been dispatched." Rogue put a hand on Pagan's arm. "You up for it?"

"It's what I was born to do." Shaking off the memories of the past, Pagan brought her attention back to the present. She took off behind the agile Rogue as they ran for the edge of the building and dove over it with silent stealth, ready to face whatever the city had in store for them that night.

CHAPTER THREE

The Past...

The headquarters to the Vigilante Council were hidden deep within the bowels of Chastilian. Ironically, it was nestled underneath the city's police department and accessed from a tunnel leading from the building next door. The innocuous tailor's shop had beneath its floors a whole series of tunnels that branched out across the city, many left over from the modernization of the sewer system. The Council Chamber had dark gray walls lined with crumbling statues striking heroic poses and dominating the corridor leading to the main meeting hall. Red lights illuminated each figure in a blood-red glow, casting shadows on the walls behind them, making them appear larger than life. Rogue Ronchetti walked down the hallway with a tempered arrogance. She knew every inch of this hallway, from the light fixtures to the less-than-tasteful decorations. She personally had had the Council wired for every intrusion, be it an eavesdropping device or an actual physical break-in. She was the best at her job. The Council knew it, and false modesty aside, Rogue knew it too. She was twenty years old, her body honed from the martial arts training she performed every night. She purposely threw off a brooding air that kept most people distant. She tried to smooth down her unruly curls. *If I could just tame these blasted curls I would be much happier*, she thought as she toured the long corridor. She drew to a halt as she passed a photograph, newly hung and draped in black, of Alexis and Camillin Osborne, founders of the Sentinels. She shook her head as she remembered her father breaking the news of their death to her. Reagan Ronchetti was another founding member of the small band of citizens who had decided enough was enough and they were taking their city back from the thugs that were ruling the streets. They had feared nothing, felt that right was on their side, and had set to reclaiming Chastilian. But Xander Phoenix and his men had gotten to their members first, and what the Osbornes had learned had gone up in flames that night with them. Losing the restaurant as well had been a double blow that many feared the Osborne girls would never recover from.

Melina had been able to identify the name of the ringleader, but the darkness of the raid had hidden the other men's faces from ever being recognized. Rogue had gone out that same night with her father, and they gathered their people to search for Phoenix. They asked the vagrants living in the alleyways, bumped into old friends and questioned them—soon the whole city was alight with the need to find the man who had ordered the deaths of the Osbornes. The police were more than aware that there were people who were tired of being held captive by those who wanted to bring Chastilian to its knees. Instead of trying to shut down the self-appointed Sentinels, they enlisted their help and in turn helped them. Chastilian was a big city; what transpired during the day only intensified when darkness fell. The city needed all the protection it could get.

Xander Phoenix was found rolling dice in a local gambling den. This time when the Sentinels faced him, they did so with more care. They waited well into the early hours for him to leave the building. When he finally came out alone, flushed and happy at his good fortune that night, they grabbed him. They wore scarves and balaclavas to hide their faces and were careful not to give away their identities. With the deaths of the Osbornes, the Sentinels had learned that to be the silent force against evil, you had to protect *yourself* first.

Rogue took in the framed newspaper clippings that captured the moment when Phoenix was apprehended. He had been delivered to the police by the elder Ronchetti, who had handed him over to the chief of police, Aaron Cauley. Rogue had watched from beside him, with the other Sentinels gathered nearby. The chief watched his officers manhandle the murderer away and then gave Ronchetti a curious look.

"Hiding your identities now?"

"We need to protect our families as well as the city. This way we can do both." Ronchetti nodded respectfully in the chief's direction. "With your help, of course."

"The Sentinels are a great help to us. I just wish the city didn't need you."

"As long as there are people like him killing innocents, Chastilian will have need of us all."

"I'll help all I can."

Rogue was amazed that was but a few days ago. Since then her whole world had shifted and turned upside down. Now the Sentinels were going to rebuild, grow stronger, and make sure that nothing like the loss they had suffered that night would ever happen again.

Shaking off the weight of the past, Rogue finally entered the main hall. She scanned the room for the two people she knew were due to come before the Council that day. She straightened her crisply ironed shirt nervously, wanting to look her best. She sought to find the woman who had captured her heart, and when her eyes finally fell upon Melina Osborne, the room disappeared and all that remained was the woman she loved. Melina's long hair was wild and untamed, falling over a somber dress that bespoke her mourning. For all the pain that was etched on such a young face, Rogue still thought Melina was the most striking woman in the room.

And with her was Melina's little sister Pagan, who held her own special place in Rogue's heart. Her clothes were more befitting a child, blue dungarees matched with a bright T-shirt. Rogue knew Melina was determined for life to go on as normal for her younger sister, whether they were in the hallowed hall of the Council or not.

Pagan was the only child allowed to enter the rooms that housed the technology center that watched over the city and kept the peace. She had been called along with Melina to meet the Council to discuss what direction the Sentinels were to take next. It was thought that Pagan, being but a child and rendered deaf, would be no security risk. Also, Melina refused to be separated from her sister and had made that point very clear when summoned to the Council. Rogue smiled as she watched them both. No one messed with Melina Osborne where her sister was concerned. She was highly intelligent, almost frighteningly so, and a marvelous match to Rogue's own intellect and intense demeanor.

Rogue had met her two years previous at another such Council meeting and had been caught staring at her. Melina had called her on it after the meeting, much to Rogue's chagrin. Rogue had apologized and then was amazed when Melina invited her to the family restaurant where, she was told, she could stare all she liked in much less stuffy surroundings. Rogue had set to courting her, treating her with the respect she deserved. As their courtship lengthened, only Melina got to see what the Rogue behind the stoic face was really like. Now, two years later, fate had dealt Melina a cruel blow, and Rogue was more than ready to aid her in whichever way she could. That was what Sentinels, and more importantly, women in love, did.

Rogue watched as Pagan followed Melina into the huge room, the small child made to seem even smaller by the vaulted ceiling and towering walls. Pagan clutched Melina's hand, clearly trying to make sense of what she was seeing. Rogue recognized the particular frown that appeared on the little girl's face. She knew that Pagan was well aware that her parents had been special. The little girl had seen inside the lighthouse that housed screens with so many views of the city. Rogue knew that Alexis had even set one up to play Pagan's favorite cartoons. Pagan, for all her age, knew her family was more than just a restaurant business. She had seen more things in her short lifetime than many other children, and her parents had chosen not to hide anything from her. Pagan was destined to be a part of the wider family, one built from trust, not blood.

Rogue hastened over to them and saw Melina's face light up with relief as she drew near. Her heart tripped at the look she received.

"Rogue." Melina let go of Pagan's hand and quickly hugged Rogue to her.

Rogue held her tightly, feeling her shivering with nerves at being called before the Council. "It's going to be all right, I promise," she murmured.

"How can you be certain, Rogue?"

Melina's breath warmed Rogue's ear and she shivered at the caressing touch.

"Because I fix things. That's my job."

Melina pulled away and studied her intently. "Not everything can be fixed so easily."

Rogue shrugged. "Then we do what we can to repair. You have nothing to fear here. You're among family."

"My family were killed." Melina's voice trembled and tears welled up in her eyes. Rogue wiped away the tear that fell across Melina's soft cheek.

"Not all of them," Rogue reminded her and then bent down to Pagan's level. "How are you today, Pagan?" She watched as Pagan studied her intently, watching her lips form the words.

"I'm okay, but I'm hungry," Pagan replied, displaying a gap-toothed smile.

Rogue picked the little girl up easily. "I promise we will all go out for lunch after this meeting and then you and I can work on your lip-reading skills. Would you like that?"

Pagan nodded and nestled her head in the crook of Rogue's neck. "Rogue's here, Mel, it's gonna be all right now," she mumbled and tightened her arms about Rogue's neck.

Melina shook her head. "What is it about the Osborne girls that just draws us to you?" She took Rogue's hand in her own and squeezed it.

"For you, it's because you know I love you with all my heart." Rogue leaned down and planted a tender kiss on Melina's lips. "For Pagan, she knows I love her because she's a wonderful kid, one who's going to make a marvelous Sentinel some day."

Melina bristled immediately. "She's deaf now because of that blast. What kind of Sighted would I be to send out a Sentinel who is impaired?"

"One who will know that if we hold her back she will never realize her full potential. She's just hearing impaired, Melina, not living impaired."

Melina sighed after a moment. "You love her because she's cute too." She ran her hand down Pagan's back as she snuggled into Rogue's arms and watched everything going on around her.

"Just like her sister," Rogue said.

Melina looked about the room as everyone began to take their seats. "Do you know what is going to happen here today?"

"I have a good idea."

"Have you been speaking with your father?"

"Yes. So you have nothing to worry about. The Council have no idea what strength you possess. The blast did not render you weak. The blows you received did not break you. And you have me by your side."

She looked down at Melina. "Nothing is going to happen today that you don't wish. I will personally see to that."

"I love you, you know that, right?" Melina wrapped an arm about Rogue's waist and hugged her.

"I both know it and feel it." She smiled at her. "Let's go see what the Council has to say."

The Vigilante Council was suitably reverent in their dealings with the loss of Alexis and Camillin Osborne. There were five men and a woman who chaired the top table, ones who had worked alongside the Osbornes, the elders of the Sentinels. Reagan Ronchetti sat among them.

"We have lost great people from our midst." A voice from the inner circle of tables spoke. "But now we must decide what is to become of those left behind." The man's voice echoed about the room. "There is first the matter of the young child. She has to be considered now that she has been left deaf."

Rogue stood from her seat beside Melina and Pagan and addressed the Council. "She's just deaf, not incapable. We should hone her abilities while she's young, not cast her to one side because she cannot hear."

"How do you know she would become a Sentinel?" another asked.

Rogue looked down at Pagan, who had been watching everything. She was aware she was being talked about and looked to Rogue for explanation.

"She's still here," Rogue said bluntly. "The blast, by rights, should have killed her." She looked down and silently asked permission to take Pagan into her arms. Pagan immediately reached up to be held. Rogue took Melina's hand and helped her to her feet. "Chastilian has lost two of its most brave," she said as she looked at Melina, "and I'm not the only one who mourns their passing. But until the time is right for Pagan to step forward, should she so choose, we have others who can take their mantle and keep the streets safe. Our numbers are growing. Your children are following in your footsteps. Now we need to turn our attention to whatever comes next to test us and be better prepared for it."

"I know how to run the computers that the Sentinels rely on," Melina said. "The lighthouse need not be shut down as a base. I know what my mother, as a Sighted, did. It's the Sighted's job to watch over the city and keep track of all the chatter so the Sentinels are kept aware of what is happening when they go out. I can direct whoever is sent; that was my mother's legacy to me." Melina stumbled over the last few words, and Pagan reached out to her. Rogue handed her over and Pagan clutched at her sister, obviously sensing something was wrong and wanting to comfort her.

Rogue faced the Council. "The Osbornes were killed not because they weren't vigilant, but because they allowed themselves to be recognized outside of the dark that the Sentinels work in. If the Sentinels are to continue, then we need to be bigger and better than the ones who mean us harm. We need to be stronger, harder, more determined to stop the rot before it spreads across the city like a disease. We need to be better equipped, to be a force to be reckoned with. We have to befriend the dark because that's where our enemies hide." She looked at everyone in the room, then finally at Melina and Pagan. "And we must never, ever, let the dark follow us home."

"The child could be put with another family," a woman's voice said.

"No!" Melina roared, startling Pagan, who drew back in her arms and stared at her wide-eyed. Melina's grip on her intensified. "I have had my parents taken away from me. You are not taking Pagan too."

"But she'll need a family environment. Her home was destroyed too," the woman continued.

"She has family," Rogue said and stepped closer to Melina. "With Melina's permission, I will move into the lighthouse with them while we start to build a new home. The insurance will cover for a new home to take the place of the old. Melina has already told me she doesn't want another restaurant where the old one stood. I have my own money to start my own business now. We can build something that's ours on old foundations. You are all aware it will be only a matter of time before Melina and I commit to each other. Pagan *will* have a family who will care for her."

"You'll need help," a gentle voice said from the circle.

"Then we'll request it when we do," Rogue replied. She addressed Melina formally, her heart pounding at what she was suggesting. "Do I have your permission?"

Melina nodded furiously. "They're not taking Pagan away from me," she whispered, her voice quivering.

"No one will. I promise. They'll have to go through me first," Rogue said. She directed her speech to the Council once again. "Do what you have to do to make sure Pagan is safe with her sister. The lighthouse will be lit again. The legacy of the Osbornes will not be lost. It has merely been passed to their children now."

"The child is too young," someone said.

"But she will grow, and in time, she will fulfill the destiny she was born into." Rogue stared at the Council. "Whether she actually hears its calling or not." Rogue guided Melina from where they stood and made it very clear they were leaving. She put a gentle arm about Melina's shoulders. "Let's get you both home," she whispered and began to lead them out.

Melina looked up at her. "You're coming with us, yes?"

Rogue smiled shyly as her heart swelled at the look she was being given. "I thought you'd never ask."

Melina blushed. "It's a good thing my mom and dad approved of you."

"They had to. I have been courting you properly for the past two years. I showed them how serious I was."

"I'm only eighteen. What if they can still take Pagan—"

"No one will take her from us," Rogue interrupted her. "We're both old enough to look after her. If they have to assign me as legal guardian, then so be it. I will fight with all I am to make sure that this child stays with you…and me." Rogue ran a hand over Pagan's soft hair. "We'll make our own family. It's something I have dreamed of."

Melina smiled softly. "Big bad you wanting a family?"

"You, of all people, know I'm not so big or bad."

Melina's eyes twinkled. "True, but you carry it off so well I'd hate to ruin the illusion." She smiled at Rogue. "I can't believe you just announced to the whole of the Council that you and I are going to be married."

Rogue shrugged. "We've talked about it. I just thought I'd warn them they would have a fight on their hands if they tried to take my family away from me." Rogue's head was swiftly pulled down to receive a very passionate kiss that, given their surroundings, caused many whispers to rebound off the exalted walls. Once released, Rogue tapped Pagan on the arm to gain her attention. She signed something rapidly. Pagan's eyes lit up, and she wriggled excitedly in Melina's arms. Melina stared at her sister.

"What did Rogue say?" she mouthed carefully to Pagan's smiling face.

"We're going for pizza!" Pagan crowed loudly, unmindful at that tender age of propriety and reverence, blissfully unaware at what had just happened in the Council chambers.

❖

Rogue was amazed at how swiftly Pagan had gotten used to utilizing her other senses to make up for the one she had lost. Pagan had never been fitted for a hearing aid because the doctors said that her hearing was so negligible that it was pointless. With Melina and Rogue's help, she had learned sign language and how to read lips. The rebuilding on the lighthouse proceeded quickly, and Rogue's security business was born. They moved out of the lighthouse to a comfortable apartment built above the main shop front and offices. Melina finished her schooling, trained in accounting, and helped Rogue run her business. By day, Rogue and Melina set to keeping Chastilian secure with their security plans and alarms. By night, they had a wholly different method for doing exactly the same thing.

Rogue's laboratory was a mass of technology with endless shelves full of wires and machine parts. Pagan was often found with her, sitting on a high stool pushed close to one of the tables that ran along the wall of the lighthouse tower. Rogue had brought all her equipment to the lighthouse and commandeered the very top of the building to house her apparatus. Pagan had spent many a long hour watching Rogue twist dials and work with electricity as she fashioned gadgets and gizmos that aided the Sentinels on their nightly sweeps. Now eight years old, Pagan was growing up fast and proving to be strong and highly intelligent. She watched Rogue closely, learning from her example.

"What are you doing now?" she asked, twisting a spare piece of wire between her fingertips.

Rogue finished what she was working on, then lifted her head so Pagan could see her face. "I'm trying to boost the range for this communicator. I want to see if I can have the Sighted hear what the Sentinel hears." She turned the diode a little and smiled with satisfaction as it set neatly into place.

"Mel's a Sighted," Pagan said.

"Yes, she is. She commands those screens and sees all."

"Do you feel safe knowing she's watching you when you go out in the dark?" Pagan asked, innocently referring to the fact Rogue had taken over her parents' Sentinel role.

"I feel very safe. It's almost like she is beside me wherever I go," Rogue said. She snapped the casing into place and fiddled with a tiny set of dials on the earpiece. She frowned a little.

"What's wrong? You've gone all frowny," Pagan asked, leaning closer to watch Rogue's fingers setting up the dials.

"I may have the settings wrong," Rogue admitted. "I won't know until I hook it up to the computer and we can see the tones across the screens. Then, maybe, I can fine-tune it." Rogue held the small earpiece out for Pagan to look at. "What do you think? Does it look okay? I'm going for a different style this time."

"I like the colors." Pagan turned the black and silver earpiece over carefully in her hands. "How does it fit?"

Rogue removed the magnifying lenses she had been wearing. The unusual pair of glasses had been keeping Pagan silently amused while she had watched Rogue work. She walked around the table to join Pagan.

"Like this." Rogue slipped the much-too-large communications device into Pagan's ear.

Pagan sat very still as it filled up most of her ear. She touched where it was positioned and her little fingers caught at the dials.

Rogue was working at switching on the computer screens she needed to test frequency and range. She typed in the codes to start her experiment running. A pattern emerged on one monitor, a series of peaks and lows ran across the screen. She typed in some variants, her back toward Pagan as she calculated what she needed. Then she turned back around and watched as Pagan continued to touch the aid in her ear. Rogue was aware it was too bulky and cumbersome for her. She watched as Pagan trailed her fingertip over the dials set on the earpiece. The computer behind her beeped and Rogue turned back to her findings. She typed in more equations and codes and tuned in her dials. For a long, silent half hour Rogue tapped in her calculations while Pagan watched the screens with rapt fascination.

"What was that?" Pagan asked suddenly.

Rogue turned to face her. "What was what?" She was concerned by the look of fear on Pagan's face.

"*There!* Can't you hear it?" Pagan whipped her head around, and the overlarge device slipped from her ear. Pagan held it in her hand as she stared at a point in the room behind her.

Rogue looked to where Pagan was staring. She frowned, moved forward to go investigate, then she realized what Pagan had said.

Can't you hear it?

Rogue moved into Pagan's eye line. "Did you hear something?" she asked, half fearful and half astounded.

Pagan opened her hand from around the communicator. "I think I did," she said quietly. "Like a whisper. It made my ear tickle inside."

"Put it back in," Rogue instructed and Pagan complied.

They both waited a moment. Rogue repeated what she had previously punched into her computer. Pagan instantly reacted.

"There it is again!" she said, holding the earpiece more firmly, straining to decipher what was happening.

Rogue typed something else in, her face deliberately away from Pagan's sight.

"What's your favorite ice cream? Who's your favorite cartoon character? What's your favorite color?" Rogue asked aloud, clattering on her keyboard, praying to all the deities that what she had done might be the key to unlocking Pagan's hearing.

"Blue," Pagan replied and then just stared as Rogue faced her and they both came to the same conclusion.

"You heard me!"

"I heard you!"

Pagan's bottom lip began to quiver with emotion, and Rogue gathered her up in her arms. "It's going to be okay. We can work on this together."

"I want Mel," Pagan said.

"Let's get her up here right now," Rogue said and leaned over with Pagan still firmly attached to her to press an intercom to call Melina.

"I heard you, but you sounded far away and muffled. Am I getting better now?" Pagan sniffled, pulling back a little to see Rogue's face.

"I don't think so, sweetheart," Rogue said, "but I think this earpiece might have triggered something left in your senses that might let you hear some things. I'll have to work on this for you."

Rogue removed the earpiece again and looked it over intently, her mind working overtime on calculations and ideas. She heard someone inside the lighthouse and handed Pagan the earpiece back. They shared a conspiratorial look.

Melina came into the room and smiled at them both. "You called?" Her eyes instantly fell on the brightly lit screens. "Have you gotten the communicator working?"

Rogue nodded. "In a way, yes, just not how I expected it." She moved to turn Melina's back to Pagan. Melina gave her a very strange look. "Tell me what's for dinner tonight."

"Rogue, honey, you could have just called down and asked me what I was ordering in for supper!"

"Tell me, nice and slowly," Rogue said. At Melina's look, Rogue softly added, "Humor me, please."

"I was thinking about ordering in the chicken bucket, with fries and an extra two corn on the cobs for Pagan," Melina began and stopped when she heard a little voice behind her falteringly repeat every word. Melina twisted around and stared at Pagan.

"Rogue's comlink thing helps me hear stuff!" Pagan told her with a big, toothy grin.

Melina spun around to Rogue. "How is this happening?" Tears began to fall.

"She's apparently hearing on a totally different frequency than what the rest of us do. I'm going to try to refine it, get her hooked up with two earpieces and not just the one." Rogue looked at Pagan. "I promise you, Pagan, I'm going to do my best to help you hear again."

"I know you will."

Melina hugged Rogue to her tightly. "You are a genius and I love you! Thank goodness you're our technology expert. The Sentinels are truly blessed."

"It had to be for a reason that I excelled in gadgetry," Rogue said. "Maybe this is why, to help Pagan."

"I'm so glad you are in our life," Melina muttered against Rogue's cheek.

"Are you two gonna kiss now?" Pagan asked, watching with great interest. She held the earpiece against her small ear, as if straining to hear more.

"If we do, is that okay with you?" Rogue asked politely, daring her to disagree.

"Sure, go ahead. It's nice. It's like what Mommy and Daddy would do," Pagan replied innocently.

"You took on a great deal more than you bargained for when you decided you wanted to court me, Ms. Ronchetti." Melina draped her arms about Rogue's neck.

"It was all worth it." Rogue leaned closer to Melina's face. "You were worth every lonely day until I found you and then every day spent in your company until I could make you truly mine."

Melina blushed. "Do you really think you can help her?" She nodded toward Pagan, who was swinging her feet against the stool and laughing as she could obviously hear her boots clattering against the wood.

"I'm going to try," Rogue said.

"I love you." Melina sighed and pulled Rogue closer for a kiss.

Pagan chuckled at them.

"Hey, you!" Melina said, looking over at Pagan. "Can you hear me?"

Pagan nodded. "I will hear you better too," she said with certainty and laughed as Melina scooped her up in her arms and hugged her. Pagan looked over Melina's shoulder to catch Rogue's attention. "We're going to need more wire, Rogue, because you have to remember, I have two ears. And it has to be smaller because I can't walk around with my fingers in my ears holding the things in place!"

"I'll see what I can do," Rogue said.

CHAPTER FOUR

The Present...

Pagan tried desperately to ignore the silent chuckling coming from Rogue as they rode the elevator back to the lighthouse.

"I can see you shaking," Pagan muttered. "Stop it!"

"I can't believe you let him hit you," Rogue said with a sigh as she once again surveyed Pagan's bruised face.

"Yeah, I purposely let the only piece of my face left uncovered run into his well-aimed fist!" Pagan growled. "It was a slow night; I obviously needed the thrill."

"Mel will know what you need," Rogue assured her.

Pagan took a step back, suddenly nervous. "I can't let her see me like this! She'll stop me from going out, she'll..." She wound down her tirade at Rogue's patient look. "She'll think I'm weak if she sees this." Pagan dropped her eyes from Rogue's.

Rogue tipped Pagan's head back up. "She won't think you're weak. You have proved yourself anything but weak. She'll be worried you are hurt." Rogue ran a gentle finger along the swelling of Pagan's jawline. She winced a little in reaction to Pagan's flinch at the slightest touch. "He got in a lucky punch. You more than made up for it."

Pagan grinned and yelped as her smile pulled on her face. "I did, didn't I?" She remembered how, after the one hit that she had foolishly allowed to land, the man behind the fist had never gotten up from the ground. She'd regained her balance and poise quickly and made sure he had not hit her again. Rogue had then tied him up securely after kicking him swiftly between his legs for his audacity.

"The police were informed. They can deal with him now. He's all theirs." Rogue began to undo her mask.

"Think the lady will be okay?" Pagan remembered exactly what they had come across down one of Chastilian's endless alleyways.

"She might learn that walking alone at night down dark streets is not the safest of choices."

"He was going to do more than just rob her, wasn't he?"

"I'd say he intended to take more than what she had in her purse," Rogue said. "Chastilian by day is a wealthy, frenetic metropolis where the rich and lazy bask in its beauty. But by night," Rogue leaned back against the wall of the elevator, "by night the underbelly exposes itself and hell slips out from the cracks in the pavement to roam the streets."

Pagan carefully took off her own mask and adjusted the hearing aids in her ears to switch off the communications she needed when out on the rooftops.

"That's where we come in." She rubbed gingerly at her jaw. "I think hell got a little cocky tonight."

"But we can beat it back down again tomorrow night, and the night after that." Rogue spared Pagan a look. "You're scheduled to go back to Ammassari's place tomorrow in between the other jobs we have lined up. You'll be too busy to worry about your jaw."

Pagan let out a breath. "Then it's a good thing I am highly skilled in the art of multitasking. Everything is finished in time for me to go battle the underbelly."

"That's what I love about the Osborne sisters, super-smarts in every way." Rogue pulled Pagan to her to place a kiss on her head. She sweetly maneuvered Pagan in front of her, almost like a shield. "Now go let your sister deal with your jaw," she said as the door to the elevator opened and they were both faced by Melina standing there with her arms folded.

"Am I going to have to fit you out with a cowl so you don't get hurt?" Melina asked, her bright eyes furiously looking over Pagan's face.

"It's hard enough wearing the mask. You wouldn't believe how much they chafe sometimes."

"Come here. Let's get you sorted." Melina fussed over getting Pagan settled at a corner of the lighthouse after exchanging a welcome-back kiss with Rogue. There was a wide variety of paraphernalia set up for tending to cuts and bruises and other ailments. Melina frowned as she helped Pagan remove her armored jacket and finally got her seated. She shook her head. "Okay, Pagan Osborne, while I tend to this I need you to come up with an idea as to how you're going to explain *this* away to our customers tomorrow."

❖

Pagan hoisted the small basket from the passenger seat of the truck and ignored Tito Ammassari's curious stare as she smoothed down her shirt under her denim jacket and checked the creases in her trousers. She'd already run the gamut of Rogue's comments about dressing so smartly for an outdoor estimation. "I'm here to measure your lot for the cameras you require." She noticed his eyes never wavered from the basket. "I brought my lunch. Thought I could share it with Erith while I'm here."

"That child in the offices needs a good feed. She has very little meat on her bones."

Pagan nodded. She had noticed the same thing yesterday. One carefully placed word with Melina, and a local shop had delivered sandwiches.

Tito crowded a little nearer to Pagan. "We had a break-in last night."

Pagan's eyes narrowed. "What was taken?"

Tito's arms lifted in exasperation. "My pride and joy! My own car. Now you know why I need the security your firm sells. Forget the estimates, just fit me with the best!"

"They knew what they were doing, then," Pagan said, scanning the car lot with its barbed walls and heavy metal gates. She nodded toward the office building. "Who was last to leave?"

"Erith was working late in the office, so I left her with the keys and the codes to lock up. She never saw a thing. They must have waited for her to go and then broke in. I'm just thankful they didn't do anything to her." He nudged Pagan in her side. "Where were my protectors of the night? They say this city has ones who keep the thieves and looters at bay."

"That's what we pay the police for. Have you contacted them at all?"

Tito snorted. "They came and filled in a report. It will get filed away and lost in time. I want my vehicles kept safe by Ronchetti Security, not the police who treat me like some low-life car trader. I've worked hard to get where I am today. I'm not prepared to lose it." His tirade over, Tito waved Pagan on her way. "Go. Measure the place for cameras and detectors that will tell me if a mouse dares to set foot on my property. And tell Erith to leave the phone on answering machine; it will field any calls we get. Get her out into the sunshine, feed her, and get some sun on her skin."

"I will," Pagan said and took the steps a few at a time to enter the offices. Walking through the corridor, Pagan grinned as a voice carried its way toward her.

"That van of yours barely makes a noise. I only knew of your arrival thanks to Tito's loud voice."

"So much for me making a discreet entrance." Pagan pushed the office door open wider and stepped inside.

"Discretion is overrated," Erith said, but her smile faded as Pagan lifted her head and Erith saw the angry discoloration marring her face. She closed the distance between them and stopped barely an inch away from Pagan. She touched a spot that was unmarked, mindful of where Pagan's jaw was hurt. "What happened here?" she whispered, her hand shaking as it stayed on Pagan's cheek.

Pagan was surprised by the tremors she could feel from Erith's fingers. "I had an accident—" Pagan began and was interrupted by Erith's snort of derision.

"That's what they all say! Don't 'accident' me, Pagan. I know a fist mark when I see one. Who the hell did this to you?" Anger colored her voice, and her face darkened.

Pagan's eyebrows lifted in surprise at Erith's furious tone and her more-than-obvious ire. "I was about to explain," Pagan started carefully, curious as to Erith's reactions. "I got caught between two guys outside the restaurant next door, and in my trying to point them elsewhere to brawl I got punched in the face by an unlucky swing." Pagan grimaced ruefully.

Erith took a shaky breath and moved her fingers from Pagan's face. "I see, I just…" She leaned heavily against the table behind her, lowering her head to look at her shoes. "I thought someone might have hit you," she finished weakly.

"They did! But it was an accident. My face got in the way of me trying to help and assist." She chuckled a little and leaned forward conspiratorially. "Rogue nearly beat them to a pulp for what they did."

"Who's Rogue?"

"My sister's partner. They raised me after my parents—" Pagan stopped as she realized she was telling Erith way more than she usually told anyone. She looked up to find Erith's eyes on her and saw nothing there but genuine curiosity staring back at her. "My parents died when I was very small."

"I'm sorry to hear that," she said. "So this Rogue, is he a big guy to beat the living daylights out of men that punch you?"

Pagan laughed. "No, but *she's* big enough to bounce anyone off the sidewalk, no matter what they do."

Erith's eyes grew wide. "Rogue's a she? And she and your sister… they're…*together?*"

"They were the last time I saw them, yes," she replied cheekily. "Do you have a problem with that?"

"No, God no! I don't have a problem with that. No problem at all," Erith said enigmatically and then leaned back a little. "You work in security and were brought up by lesbians." She rested her hands on the top of the table behind her and leaned back, completely unaware of the seductiveness of her pose. "What else is there about you I don't know, Ms. Osborne?"

"There's not much else to know," Pagan said, too busy staring at the pale flesh unintentionally revealed by Erith's stance. She wondered how soft it would be and could feel her fingers itching to reach out and test her theory.

Erith's eyes roamed over Pagan's face, considering. "Guess those guys won't be eating out for a while, then?"

"Not for a long time," Pagan said, satisfied in the knowledge that the real culprit was behind bars after the police had found him trussed up like a turkey in the alley he'd been stalking. A call from one of the Sighted had secured his arrest. The man had been off the streets in moments.

Erith stood again and broke Pagan's inner thoughts. She blinked as if an actual connection had been deactivated. Pagan looked up to be met by Erith's stare. Her body immediately reacted to the almost physical touch of her eyes.

"What?" she finally asked, curious about the intensity on Erith's face.

"I find that I don't like the thought of someone hurting you."

Erith had spoken so quietly that Pagan almost didn't register the sounds. Only her habit of watching a speaker's lips let her know what Erith had actually admitted. She opened her mouth but was at a loss for what to say.

Erith shook her head "So, what you got in your basket?"

Pagan was thrown off at the swift change in their conversation. She was still trying to sort out the sudden feelings that hung silently between them. "I brought lunch," she said. Erith favored her with such a beaming grin that Pagan felt her heart melt on the spot. *Oh God, I am in so much trouble!*

"Are you asking me out on a date, Pagan Osborne?"

Pagan felt her face flush and her heart begin to race in her chest double time. She held up the basket. "I'm asking you to join me for lunch." She frowned at Erith's amused expression. "Why do I get the feeling you are laughing at me?"

Erith shook her head, her hair instantly catching the light. "I'm not laughing at you. You're such a contradiction, Pagan. You're able to jump into a brawl and get smacked in the face for it, yet you blush like a girl when I mention the word 'date.'"

"You're going to give me more trouble than a whole gang of brawlers, I can tell."

Erith hooked her arm in the crook of Pagan's and led the way out of the office. "I'm no trouble at all, Pagan. I am sweetness and light personified."

"Yeah, right," she muttered, and chuckled as Erith backhanded her in her stomach.

"Geez, Pagan!" Erith rubbed at her hand. "You have a gut made of steel." She shook her hand out and flexed her fingers.

"You must have hit a bony bit," Pagan said.

"You intrigue me, Pagan."

"I'd have to say the same about you, Ms. Baylor."

Erith tossed her head and fixed her sights firmly on a place for them to sit outside. She tugged Pagan toward her designated spot. "I hope you brought plenty of food to share. I'm suddenly feeling ravenous." She ran a soft hand along Pagan's arm. "I may be small in stature compared to you, but I have a big appetite."

The look in her eye gave Pagan cause to pause. She swallowed against the lump in her throat. "I'll consider myself forewarned," she replied and tried not to watch where Erith's hand lay on her arm. She could feel the heat burning her skin at the soft touch. Pagan wasn't used to being touched by members of the fairer sex. She had known at a very early age that she would be drawn to females just as her sister had been. Between her shyness and her silence, Pagan had effectively set up walls around herself that few had managed to penetrate. Pagan also had her mind set firmly on her destiny. The life of a Sentinel was very demanding, and she had a score to settle with the ones behind her parents' deaths. It didn't leave much room for anything else. She had rarely been distracted from it. She feared that this distraction would prove harder to dismiss.

Though the view from behind the office building was less than impressive, it did afford a secluded seat away from the noise of the main car lot. Pagan's gaze drifted to linger over the towers and skyscrapers in the distance, visible over the wrought iron fencing that surrounded the lot. She knew that tonight she'd be seeing the imposing towers from a totally different perspective.

"Tito says his car was stolen last night," Pagan said.

Erith nodded. "I don't think he remembers the right code to enter on the main gate keypad. If he didn't lock up right last night, this place was wide open for any takers. I even reminded him to be careful of that when I left early yesterday."

"Tito said you locked up last night," Pagan said.

Erith stared at her a moment, then shook her head. "Silly man, I locked up everything the night *before*. He's so stressed he can't keep his days straight."

"Only *his* car was touched, though, right? That's a little strange, don't you think?"

"Life *is* strange." Erith shifted her head to again check out Pagan's bruised side. "How's the face feeling?"

"It's throbbing like crazy. I have some tablets I need to take to try to keep the swelling down and the pain at bay." Pagan opened the basket and started to take out the food. "Hope you don't mind if I have the egg salad. That was my mood for today, and I can't really chew meat at the moment. I got my sister to order us a few sandwiches to choose from, so take your pick."

"What did your sister say?"

"About what?"

"You carting extra food to the car lot."

"Nothing. Why would she say anything about that?"

"Because you're feeding a stranger."

"I'm getting fed in the process, and it never hurts to treat someone." Pagan touched Erith's arm to get her attention. "It's no problem. I needed a quick meal today, and I thought you'd like the surprise. Is it so wrong for me to want to share?"

"I'm no charity case," Erith grumbled, her shoulders hunching as she hunkered inside the black jacket that hung from her frame.

"I don't see you as one," Pagan said. "Come on, Erith. Look at me. You're the first person I have spoken to properly in ages outside of the business. I'm comfortable with you. I enjoy your company. I don't picnic with just anyone, I'll have you know."

"Really?"

Pagan nudged her. "Yes, *really*. Now can we eat? Because I'm starving and I need to keep my strength up to walk around this lot and see what is needed where."

They ate together in a companionable silence, enjoying the food and the sunny day. Pagan lifted her head to let the sun's rays warm her face and Erith leaned toward her.

"I never noticed you wore earrings before, Pagan," she said and brushed back Pagan's hair.

Pagan flinched from her touch. Erith paused, her hand in midair, until Pagan resignedly put her head within reach. Carefully, as if not to spook Pagan any further, Erith leaned closer and pushed back the hair that covered Pagan's ears.

"This is like no earring I've ever seen." Erith carefully traced the hearing aid that curled about Pagan's ear with its unusual ornate shape.

"It's not an earring." Pagan waited for the condemnation she feared would follow Erith's realization. She tried not to jump at the tickle of Erith's soft finger.

Erith moved her finger. She just looked at Pagan until Pagan finally lifted her head.

"And here I was thinking you were looking at my lips because they held some fatal fascination."

Pagan swallowed hard. "That's just one reason," she said.

"Are you deaf, Pagan?" Erith finally asked.

Pagan nodded.

Erith frowned as her mind obviously was working overtime. "But not completely, right? Hence the aid."

Pagan nodded again and lifted up the hair covering her other ear. "Two of them," she said. "I have some hearing. I hear enough to get along without people realizing I am deaf." She looked pointedly at Erith. "Usually, that is."

Erith wrapped her arms about her knees. "I saw the shine of silver behind your hair. I'm inquisitive, I wondered what was there. I thought maybe you had some weird and wacky piercing going on."

"I'm not pierced anywhere," Pagan said. "Or tattooed."

Erith gave Pagan a very mischievous look.

"*You* have a tattoo?"

Erith nodded, suddenly tight lipped.

"Where?"

Erith's mischievous look only deepened. "I won't tell you that until we're much more…friendly."

"Oh, I see, or…not, I guess." Pagan stumbled over her words, intrigued by what Erith was hiding. "Did it hurt?"

"Kind of, but I've lived through worse and come out unscathed. I figured I needed a mark to celebrate that fact. When I hit nineteen, I treated myself to it."

Pagan blinked at her, and Erith laughed.

"You have to be the least inquisitive person I have ever met. You never ask questions, you just wait until you are told something. You're an unusual woman, Pagan Osborne."

"So I've been told."

Erith uncurled herself and leaned into Pagan. "No, not because of your hearing. I don't care about that. Well, I do, of course, but it obviously doesn't impair you in any way, so why should it matter to us?" Erith took a deep breath. "Do you know what I'm trying to say here?"

"Yeah, I know exactly what you mean. Thank you."

"For what?"

"For not resorting to raising your voice to me once you realized that I don't hear perfectly. For not making me feel like a freak."

"You are no freak. So you don't hear so great. It doesn't make you any less who you are. It doesn't make you any less *Pagan.*"

Pagan smiled, feeling suddenly lighthearted and equally light-headed.

"Do many know?" Erith asked.

Pagan shook her head slowly. "Not many. My family do, of course, but it's not something I need to announce when I'm fitting alarms."

"I won't say anything. It's not my disclosure to make," Erith said, then chuckled. "After all, who would I tell? You're the only one who talks to me. I'm new to the area, and still regarded as that weird goth chick."

"You're not gothic. You don't paint your face enough. I'd say your more rock chick if anything."

"I wear a lot of black. It tends to frighten people."

Pagan regarded her seriously. "You don't frighten me." *You just make me nervous of what I feel whenever I'm around you*, she thought silently, her stomach doing flip-flops at the way Erith looked at her.

"You're obviously made of strong stuff, Pagan." Erith squeezed Pagan's bicep. "You're very deceptive, Pagan O," she added, staring at Pagan's arm.

The sound of Tito yelling something to an employee rang through the backyard where they sat.

"I'd better go get started on my job here." Pagan carefully let her arm slip from Erith's grasp, and she got a thrill seeing disappointment momentarily color Erith's features.

Erith put a finger under Pagan's chin and made very sure Pagan could see her face. "One day, there will be no such distractions to cut into our discussions, Ms. Osborne."

Pagan feared that would never be the case. The city would always demand her fullest attention, in whatever guise she served it.

CHAPTER FIVE

Rogue held up the pads that covered her hands to deflect the blows Pagan threw at her. The solid-sounding whomps echoed in the lighthouse's training room.

"So, she knows you're deaf?" Rogue said as Pagan battered away at the fighting blocks while Rogue stood her ground. "What is it about this woman, Pagan, that lets down your guard? You've only met her twice, yet she seems to have found a way to reach under your skin."

Pagan punched harder in a faster rhythm, managing to push Rogue back under the onslaught. "I don't know. It's more than just her looks." She finished her volley and let her hands hang limply at her sides. "Did I tell you she has this amazing red hair that seems to radiate fire from within? And she has such a pretty face too, almost impish with a smattering of freckles here." She lifted up her bound hands to brush them over her nose awkwardly.

"Does she now?" Rogue replied, trying not to let her amusement show at Pagan's unwitting adoration. Rogue held up the padded blocks in a less-than-subtle hint that Pagan needed to keep her concentration on her training.

Pagan smiled sheepishly. "Sorry," she muttered and began to pound away at Rogue's defenses. After an hour of training, Pagan's shirt and shorts were sticking to her, and her breaths were escaping in short, ragged pants. In stark contrast, Rogue's gym clothes still looked immaculate and her breathing was barely labored.

"It's about time," Rogue said after they completed the set routine.

Pagan was panting harshly, her arms dangling by her sides as she rested from her exertion. "What is?" she asked before collapsing to the floor in a heap and attempting to unwrap her hands from their binds.

"That someone caught your eye."

Pagan held out a hand for Rogue to help her unwrap. "There's just something about her that draws me to her. And it's not just the fact that she's pretty. Which she is. Seriously pretty, in fact." Pagan chewed at her lip thoughtfully. "She's also smart, funny, and sharp as a knife." She then added conspiratorially, "She even has a tattoo."

"And you know of its existence how?"

"Because she *told* me! We haven't...I haven't...She probably wouldn't...*Rogue!*" Pagan's face flushed.

"You are a shy one, Pagan, for one so mighty," Rogue teased her, tugging on the bindings on Pagan's hands to get her to look up at her.

"Around her I don't feel so mighty. I feel lost and unsure and uncertain."

"Does that scare you?"

Pagan nodded.

"It's okay to feel like that." Rogue finished unwrapping Pagan's binds and freed her hands. "That's how I feel around your sister all the time. She can render me as weak as a kitten or make me feel like the strongest woman on earth."

"That's a good thing, right?"

"It's the best thing," Rogue assured her.

Pagan flexed her fingers with a reflective air. "So what do I do?"

"Do you want to get to know her better?"

Pagan nodded.

"Then do just that. Seek her out, talk with her, and listen to her. Find out who she is, what makes her tick."

"It sounds so simple."

"It is, once you get the hang of it. You can do it. There's nothing to be nervous about."

"Why do I feel it might be easier to face off against a gang of thugs?" Pagan flung herself spread-eagle on the floor, her arms covering her face.

"Because you are more than aware that when it comes to feelings, it's a hard battle to win against your own self-doubts," Rogue replied. "Tell me again about the freckles."

Pagan lifted a hand from her face and peered at Rogue suspiciously. "Why?"

"Because you got this really cute look on your face when you were describing them to me. It was kind of sweet. I want to be able to memorize it so I can describe it properly to Mel."

Pagan sat upright. "You can't tell Mel about this!"

"Why not? These freckles might become important in your life, and that, in turn, affects our lives." Rogue enjoyed watching the multiple emotions race across Pagan's face. Terror seemed to be taking the lead, judging by the look in Pagan's expressive eyes. Rogue relented and waggled her eyebrows comically.

"Rogue!" Pagan said, realizing she was being teased. She lowered her face into her hands. "How cute?" she mumbled.

"Really cute, to be honest. Something akin to the cute you had as a little girl when we caught you doing something you shouldn't and you tried to wheedle your way out of it."

Pagan groaned. "I can't be cute. I'm a Sentinel, for crying out loud!"

"Hey, Sentinels can be cute. That is why we get all the neatest uniforms." Rogue stood and then helped Pagan to her feet.

"Do I display this cute face often?"

"No. But I for one am very happy to see it." She put an arm about Pagan's shoulders and hugged her close. "Go shower, then we can eat. We have a busy night ahead." She bumped Pagan along with her hip. "Think you can be cute out there tonight while we go patrol the city?"

Pagan sighed. "I'll try, but I'm not promising much. I was aiming for the mean and menacing look this evening."

"Whatever works for you, kid, whatever works." She steered Pagan in the direction of the shower. "Now, about this tattoo business and you getting any ideas…"

❖

Briskly toweling off her hair, Rogue went in search of Melina. She found her in the security office, sitting before her work computer but working on something from her laptop.

"Am I interrupting?" Rogue leaned over to brush a kiss on

Melina's forehead. Melina leaned back to press her body into Rogue as she wrapped her arms about her.

"Never. Hmm, you smell nice. Have you two finished sparring?"

Rogue nodded against Melina's hair. "Yes, we—" Rogue saw what Melina was researching. "Why have you hacked into the Department of Motor Vehicles database, sweetheart? I thought you were working on the payroll."

"I was, but this is a whole lot more interesting. Pagan said that Ammassari's car was taken last night, even though the lot was full of vehicles just as easy to steal. So I contacted our friends on the force, and word along the police vine is that it wasn't the only car taken last night. Now normally, that wouldn't raise any alarms for me, but I heard some interesting gossip from our man in blue."

"Have you been flirting with the Sentinel insider at the department again?"

Melina just laughed at her. "Considering he's as old as your father, flirting is all that Chief Cauley can handle!" She checked her computer screen and directed Rogue's attention to it. "I just ran the license plates to see if there is any rhyme or reason to their all being stolen." Melina printed out the computer's findings. She placed the four registration details on the desk for Rogue to see.

"These are all very fancy and expensive high-performance cars."

Melina's finger underlined something else for Rogue to see. "And they were all taken from the same car lot."

"Now why would five cars, all linked to Ammassari, go missing on the same night?"

"Coincidence, maybe?"

Rogue snorted. "There's no such thing as coincidence in Chastilian."

"Is this why Tito has been so anxious to get alarms set up at his premises? Is he another victim, or is he using his own car as a smokescreen to deflect us from what he's doing?"

"Maybe he's stealing the cars back to change their appearance and sell them again." Rogue mused for a moment. "But his reputation is a solid one. What do we honestly know about Tito Ammassari?"

Melina flicked between the windows on her laptop and began typing into the police database. Rogue shook her head at Melina's audacity to just hack into wherever she pleased.

"Do the police know you can do that?"

"I'm merely putting into practice what you set in motion. You got the Sighteds hooked up to the city's CCTV cameras so we have a view on the street. And you furnished us with high-tech computers so the Sighteds and Sentinels can all keep in touch. Admittedly, not all the Sighteds hack. That's my domain thanks to you rubbing off on me, Ms. Cyber Genius!"

Rogue laughed at her impudence. "Just so long as you play safe and leave no footprints."

"I take all necessary precautions. I'm a little cyber Sentinel, slipping in and out like a shadow." She typed in a password and opened up the criminal database for Chastilian. She quickly entered Tito Ammassari's name. A teenaged Tito dolefully stared out from the screen.

"This says he has a record for misdemeanors, thieving and vandalism, all with a gang of other juveniles." Rogue read the rest silently. "And then…nothing?" She frowned at what she was seeing. "What? He just started on the road of hoodlum only to suddenly see the light and become a model citizen selling cars?"

"You don't buy it?" Melina printed off the report sheet and then backtracked out of the system.

"It sounds too good to be true."

Melina shut down her laptop and turned to face Rogue. She tugged Rogue down by the towel that still hung over her shoulders. Melina's fingers speared through Rogue's hair. "It's a good thing I like my women tall, dark, and cynical."

Rogue let Melina's fingers work their magic against her scalp.

"Try to be home at a sociable hour tonight?"

Rogue laughed. "Ever the optimist!" She brushed her lips over Mel's, waiting for her to open her mouth, and when she did, Rogue ran her tongue inside. She felt Melina tug her even closer as their kiss intensified. It was with some reluctance she pulled away. "I'd better go before you distract me any further."

Melina slipped a few buttons on her shirt free and opened the fabric to reveal tanned skin.

Rogue groaned. "You do not play fair."

Melina smiled seductively at her. "I have to have some way of competing with the others in your life. The city is a harsh mistress. I can't afford to let her take you away from me."

Rogue tugged Melina up from her chair and into her arms. She kissed her with a passion that was almost bruising, their exchange heated and raw. Rogue wrenched her mouth away from Melina's neck. "I'm yours alone. Not the city's, nor anyone else's. *Yours.*"

Melina cupped Rogue's face. "I know. That's why I'll let you go now, because I know you'll come back to me."

"Right back to your side, sweetheart." Rogue nuzzled at the sweet point that pulsed in Melina's neck. "That's where I belong."

CHAPTER SIX

Pagan always felt the slightest hesitation when she climbed over a roof edge to prepare to fly from tower to tower. No amount of training prepared her for the split second of sheer terror before launching herself into the air. She eased herself out onto the ledge that skirted the rooftop, watching as Rogue threw herself off with a graceful dive. Rogue swiftly swung from the wire that was attached to the wall behind Pagan and firmly embedded in the wall of the building she was heading toward. Pagan marveled at the mechanics and the machinery that Rogue had fashioned that allowed them to traverse from building to building on a single length of wire. She toggled a button on the gun and shot the wire into the concrete behind her, then aimed for the tower across. Pagan knew that to the untrained eye it appeared that the Sentinels flew from one skyscraper to another, able to climb untethered, like spiders drifting on their invisible thread. She snorted softly. *Were that it was that easy. It's all done with sheer guts and endless wires.*

Pagan watched as Rogue's wires drew her to the tower directly opposite the one they had been standing on, pulling her with great speed toward the wall. With another slight movement, Rogue was able to slow her descent. The tether beside Pagan disengaged from the wall and shot across the divide. Rogue detached the wire keeping her close to the tower and dropped, coming to land on a fire escape, agile as a cat.

Pagan secured her wire gun to a strap on her wrist and palmed the machine. She stepped off the ledge without another thought. Pagan could feel the rush of air as she dove down. She calculated her own landing on a small ledge that could easily take her body weight. Setting down with a gentle thump, she felt the wall's coolness when she found her face pressed almost too close for comfort against it. Pagan patted the wall in gratitude as she caught her breath. She really had to work on being quicker on depressing the button to slow her descent. She could hear Rogue's soft chuckle nearby and knew that was a lesson to be repeated by her mentor.

As Pagan half listened to Melina's broadcast, she thought back to her first flight. She remembered Melina's utter horror as Rogue had strapped Pagan to her chest and climbed out onto the roof of an apartment building.

"If she's to be a Sentinel, she needs to know how to fly," Rogue had said simply.

Pagan could still remember the excitement of the silent fall, all the time safe in Rogue's grip, the moon lighting their flight.

"What are you grinning at?" Rogue asked.

"Just remembering our first flight together and how quiet it was, even more so than usual to me then."

Rogue smiled. "You needed to learn. No better way to learn to fly than to take that first jump."

"I think our Sighted would have preferred you had jumped from a lower-floored window for my first experience," Pagan said, and chuckled as she heard Melina fervently agree over the comlink.

"You loved it." Rogue shared a conspiritorial grin with her.

"I knew I was safe with you," Pagan replied seriously. "I never doubt that."

Rogue knelt down to put her gloved hand over Pagan's. "You ready to see what the night has in store for us?"

"Are we going high or low?" Pagan asked, looking down on the city. The tops of the street lamps were burning a path along the roads leading to wherever the city would direct them that night.

"Let's climb a few walls," Rogue said. "If we go too high we'll miss the fun, too low and we'll be easily seen."

"Middle ground it is," Pagan said. "I need to break in these boots a little more on the walls. They're kind of noisy."

Rogue pulled Pagan up beside her in an amazing show of strength. "Race you up the wall, *squeaky*."

"You have a better grip," Pagan grumbled, climbing up onto the metal fire escape to stand alongside a waiting Rogue. Pagan aimed her wire gun into the air and shot out a seeking wire. When the device signaled it was attached, Pagan suddenly launched herself into the air.

"Hey!" Rogue called after her. "What happened to a countdown?" She sprang after Pagan.

"I decided on a competitive edge," Pagan called back as she rode the wire up the tower wall.

"Sighted, we have spawned a shrewd Sentinel here," Rogue muttered in her comlink for Melina's ears. Pagan, linked into the same frequency, heard every word, as she was meant to.

"She gets the shrewdness from me. The sneakiness she undoubtedly gets from you," Melina replied sweetly.

Pagan burst into laughter at the blustering she could hear from beneath her, laughter that was swallowed into the night by the noise of the city below.

❖

"Rogue, I think you and Pagan might want to head over to where Casper and Earl are situated," Mel said over the comlinks half an hour into their watch.

"Where are they?"

"According to their Sighted, they are currently watching four cars racing around the Do or Dice Casino parking lot."

"I didn't know those boys did traffic duty on the side." Rogue took out her handheld screen and tapped out the directions for the casino.

"They thought it was just another case of youthful exuberance until they recognized the license plates as the ones belonging to Tito's stolen cars," Melina said.

Rogue and Pagan traded looks and then raced across the rooftop.

"Tell them we're on our way." Pagan readied her wire gun and once again took to the air.

❖

The Do or Dice Casino was ostentatious and richly decadent. The gold brickwork was lit up, marking out its territory as Chastilian's number one gambling palace. Huge pillars framed the entrance. Above

LESLEY DAVIS

a canopy, two dice were affixed, rolling and tumbling in endless gyrations. Above them, the casino name beckoned in neon to those who wished to be parted from their money. The casino occupied the first two floors of the building, while the exclusive hotel stretched high above with forty floors of rooms for those whose streaks ran lucky.

Pagan shielded her eyes against the glare of the lights that ran like searchlights up and down the building.

"Sighted, we are in position," Rogue said, then took out her high-powered night vision binoculars.

"Hey there, glad you could join the party," Earl called in his deep voice as he and Casper joined them. Earl was broad-shouldered and imposing, while Casper was slender and wiry, and appeared almost too slight to be a Sentinel. Both wore the customary leather suits, as well as masks that covered most of their handsome features.

"We thought we'd come see what has caught your attention over here." Rogue clasped Earl's arm and then nodded toward Casper, who returned the greeting with a grin before he went to join Pagan at her sentry point.

Pagan was enveloped in a warm hug. "Long time no see," she said.

Casper, mute from birth, signed to Pagan. *I think you and Rogue will like what we have spotted.* He gestured for Pagan to follow him and they both hunkered down to watch what was happening in the parking lot below.

"Can you believe it? From small gambling dens to a casino worth millions. Louis Miller certainly exceeded his humble beginnings. Not all thieves get to become multimillionaires legitimately." Earl gestured to the grand casino. "I wonder if he stole someone else's luck to make this place so successful." He leaned over the wall to point down toward the car lot. "We were watching the parking lot on our rounds and were surprised to see your stolen vehicles come driving in. They started out just circling the lot, but that soon escalated to a more dangerous game of excessive speed in a small area." Earl leaned against the wall Rogue was peering over. "The police can't stop them. They're dodging every spike strip employed to shred their tires." Earl pointed to another vehicle. "And while we have four cars using the lot as a speedway track, car number five seems to be waiting for something."

A bright red car, with huge wheels and a body to match, stood idling. Even from their position, Pagan could hear the engine roar, a deep, guttural sound.

"Mel, any word out there from the other Sighteds?" Rogue asked, training her binoculars on the parking lot.

"Nothing yet. We're all watching you four."

"Then I hope we're keeping you all entertained."

Pagan's attention was fixed on the red vehicle. She watched as someone got out of the car and stepped away. The engine, however, kept on revving. She took out her binoculars and focused on the driver. Pagan was surprised to see that the man was much older than she'd expected. His hair was thinning, but in the garish lights from the casino, she couldn't make out what color it was. In his hand was what appeared to be a box with control rods.

"I think we have a problem," Pagan said. "Mel, warn the police down there. I think our idling driver has a remote control system in his hands. The other cars must be distractions. I think he is our primary target."

The words had barely left her lips before the red car's engine revved to a high pitch, the tires squealing at being held back. Pagan could see the car shake against the restraining brake. With a spin of its tires, the car was suddenly set free.

"It's heading for the casino doors," Earl said.

The car hurtled forward, scattering people in every direction as it headed for the casino entrance. The bouncers who flanked the doors scrambled to get out of its path. The car mounted the pavement and smashed through the doors with a deafening crash. It came to a stop wedged in the door frame, the casino design effectively barring it full entrance.

Pagan immediately readied her wire gun to swing over to the stricken building, but she was rocked back by the explosion that ripped through the car and blew out the front of the casino.

"Rogue, we need to get down there. People will be trapped."

Rogue pointed toward the casino, directing their flight. "Aim high and then lower yourselves to the fifth-floor balcony. We'll get in through there."

Pagan heard the screams of the injured in the parking lot and the accompanying wail of sirens as fire trucks were called to the scene. She shot her wire and felt it snag into the casino's golden tower. She fixed the gun firmly to her wrist catch and let it pull her off her feet and across the divide from tower to tower. She followed Rogue's lead, Casper and Earl behind her as she reached the building's side and then lowered herself to the balcony. They recoiled their wires and moved on to their next task: getting inside the building. Earl kicked open a service door, and they were in.

Rogue opened another door that led to the hotel rooms and heard the chaos below.

"We need to split up. Casper, you and Earl get everyone out of their hotel rooms. They'll have to use the fire exits. We can't risk them in the elevators or inside the casino itself. We'll go below and see what damage has been done. It's the only chance we'll get to see for ourselves."

Casper and Earl banged on the hotel room doors to get as much attention as possible over the wailing of the hotel's fire alarms. Terrified people stumbled out of their rooms. They were quickly gathered together, then steered toward the back of the building and to safety by the two men. Pagan and Rogue ran down the stairwell in silence until they reached the casino's upper floor. There was a terrible roaring coming from behind the door. Rogue looked at Pagan.

"You ready for this?"

"As ready as I'll ever be."

Rogue pushed the door open, but the sound made them step back. The fire alarms in the casino had activated and the sprinklers were on, for all the good they did. The fire from the floor below was licking up through the huge gap in the front wall of the casino. Most of the upper floor was still intact except for a huge chunk of the front wall closest to the blast below. Through the thick smoke Pagan could barely see out the windows into the parking lot. The contrast between the dark of night and the furious fire raging below seemed almost surreal. She edged forward carefully to a spiral staircase that was still miraculously intact. The hole, however, was much bigger after the explosion.

"Oh my God, Pagan. Who would do such a thing?" Melina asked over the comlink.

Pagan didn't answer; she was too busy looking down at the ground floor and wondering where to start.

Rogue appeared by Pagan's side. She removed a small breathing mask from her utility belt and gestured for Pagan to do the same. They then attached their flashlights to their wrists to light their way.

Her breathing mask in place, Pagan gingerly picked her way across the room, treading over smashed tables and chairs. She spied a fire extinguisher and wrenched it from the wall. With a swift twist, she prepared it for use. She looked around curiously. "Rogue, why are there no bodies up here? The place is decked out with every poker table imaginable, why weren't they using this floor?"

Rogue directed them to the stairs below. "I don't know. Maybe casino security saw what was happening and evacuated the floor. Or maybe the fun doesn't start up here until later in the evening." Rogue made her way down the stairs.

Pagan was still able to hear her through the comlink they shared.

"Or maybe everyone was herded down here for the party and that's when the bomber struck."

Pagan stepped onto the staircase and could barely take in the sight of the ground floor carnage. The casino floor was a tangle of broken furniture and glass. Pagan could make out the charred remains of bodies buried deep beneath the wreckage. She closed her eyes to the sheer horror of what she was seeing. In her years as a Sentinel she had never had to witness such carnage firsthand. Pagan looked at her extinguisher and then at the burning car.

"I don't think this is going to touch that."

"The fire trucks are here. They can deal with the car." Rogue set off across the floor. "I think we're too late for many of the people in here. The fire doors are back there, though." She nodded toward the back of the room. "Maybe the rest of the partiers got to safety. I'm going to check it out."

Pagan picked her own way through the wrecked roulette tables, her flashlight reflecting through the smoke. She looked up. The floor above was creaking ominously. She found it was easier to keep checking the ceiling than to watch where her feet were treading.

"Keep moving, Sentinel." Rogue spoke softly in her ear. "It's not going to get easier. Some bastard locked the fire doors back here to keep everyone in."

"There's nothing we can do," Pagan said. Broken slot machines flashed erratically, their reels racing wildly. The gaming tables were destroyed and multicolored chips were scattered everywhere. The mournful sounds of the trapped began to filter through over the roar of the fire, and she tried to pinpoint their locations. She spotted Rogue gathering up a few people who were hurt but mobile. Rogue got them to another exit at the back of the room.

Through a shattered window Pagan spotted a team of firefighters trying to get over the rubble outside. She quickly made her way over to help them in. Smashing more of the window out with the help of the extinguisher, she called the men over and helped them enter the casino.

"What the hell happened in here?" a female firefighter asked, accepting Pagan's hand as she scrambled through the debris.

"A ram raid with lethal intent." Pagan saw a small fire start to take hold nearby and sprayed it out quickly. She then handed the extinguisher to the firefighter. "You might have a better use for this."

"How many Sentinels are in here?" another firefighter asked.

"Just the two of us down here. Two others are helping to evacuate the hotel above us."

"You'll need to leave for safety reasons."

"We will. We won't get in your way."

The firefighter nodded and rushed off to help his teammates find anyone who had survived. Other firefighters came in through the window and started checking out the structure while others fed through hoses and began tackling the blaze from inside.

Pagan wiped at the water that was stinging her eyes. The sprinklers were doing very little to put out the flames that still raged at the casino's door. The smoke was thick and cloying, the air hot and scorching to breathe. She stumbled over the debris and then heard a sound from above. She moved quickly and managed to dodge a piece of broken ceiling that crashed down behind her.

"Are you okay?" Rogue called over their comlink.

"The ceiling is getting weaker." Pagan started as a gush of water suddenly pounded the burning vehicle, and she berated herself for being so jumpy. "The fire crews are in here." She watched them trying to tackle the blaze. For a moment she flashed back to another burning car, but Rogue's voice in her ear brought her back to the present.

"Looks like some people managed to escape by going through to the hotel stairs. I think they realized something was wrong before the car hit the building. I really don't think this was just some random act against the perils of gambling."

Pagan set off to find Rogue. She tracked her to a doorway marked Executive Suite situated at the very back of the ground floor. Rogue beckoned her closer.

She aimed her flashlight through the door at what Rogue could see. The office room had been trashed. The desk drawers had been tossed, their contents littering the floor. Photos had been ripped from the walls and the glass smashed to pieces.

"This room is too far back from the blast. The noise in here must have alerted the revelers to something not being right. This definitely happened before the car exploded." Rogue pushed the door open a little further. "As, I think, did this."

A huge Big Six Wheel, the Wheel of Fortune, stood in the room, clicking around and around courtesy of a motor attached to it. An ornate brass roulette rake speared through the body of a man, pinning him to the wheel. As he spun around, dice fell to the ground.

Rogue stepped closer.

"There are dice shoved in his mouth." She leaned nearer and touched his throat. "I think he was choked on them." She spared Pagan a look over her shoulder. "Somebody sure was a bad loser."

"Any idea who he is?"

Rogue looked around the room and scooped up a smashed picture frame. She held it up against the man's head. "I think it's Louis Miller, the owner of this casino." Rogue turned the machine off, and the wheel clicked softly to a halt. "And it's safe to say his luck has just run out."

Pagan could hear Rogue talking to Melina over the comlink, but she was distracted by something out on the casino's main floor. For a moment she was certain she could see someone sitting in the front of the burning car. Pagan didn't hesitate; she scrambled over the rubble and debris to check. As she got closer she realized she had been mistaken and it had just been the reflection of a firefighter trying to dowse the front of the car. She took a deep shaky breath and closed her eyes for a second.

The sound of cracking caught her attention, and she looked up to see a large piece of ceiling break away right above the firefighter. She yelled at him, but he was too involved in trying to put the fire out. Pagan leapt forward, knocking him out of the way. She sent him sprawling to the floor, his hose flying from his grasp. The falling debris smashed into her right shoulder and knocked her across the room, where she landed with a sickening thud against a row of slot machines. One spewed out coins at the force of the blow. Pagan remained deathly still for a moment, in so much pain she feared she'd pass out. She could hear Melina screaming in her ear and Rogue yelling from across the casino.

"I'm okay, a little bruised and banged up, but I'm fine." Pagan tried to smile as Rogue skidded to a halt beside her.

Rogue carefully ran her hand over Pagan's neck and shoulder. "Well, you didn't ruin your jacket, so that's one good thing."

Pagan gasped as pain rolled through her shoulder. She looked around her at the coins still spilling from the machines. "I hit the jackpot without spending a dime, how lucky is that?"

Rogue carefully helped her to her feet and looked around for the firefighter Pagan had saved. He was getting back to his feet a little shakily, but he tipped his hat to them in gratitude. Other firefighters were already trying to get back out of the window with a few survivors in tow. "Let's follow their example and get out of here. We've seen enough for one night."

The casino parking lot was a mass of activity. Fire engines clustered together, their hoses spraying every corner of the building. Ambulances were transporting the injured to nearby hospitals. Pagan saw Casper and Earl standing to one side. She and Rogue hastened over to them.

Casper quickly signed, his hands almost a blur as he asked how Pagan was. Pagan tried to assure him she was fine, but the pain was making her so nauseous she couldn't speak. Weakly, she ripped her breathing mask from her face and sucked in clean air.

"Do you need help getting back?" Earl asked.

Rogue shook her head. "We have a ride coming to get us." She tapped at her ear so the men knew Melina was coming for them. She looked back at the casino. "The Council will have plenty to talk about tomorrow."

"We need to do some talking of our own, see what we can dig up." Earl clasped Rogue's free arm. "I wish we were parting with a happier ending."

"I'm fine. I just got the wind knocked out of me," said Pagan.

Rogue sighed. "Young Sentinels, they seem to think they are invincible."

"I just have to dodge ceilings when they fall. I learned that lesson well tonight."

Both men bid their farewells, then ran across the parking lot to wire ride their way back up to the opposite tower.

Pagan watched them go. "Guess I won't be doing that tonight."

Rogue carefully maneuvered her across the parking lot and into the darkness cast by a neighboring tower block. Once they were hidden in shadows and out of sight of prying eyes, Rogue removed Pagan's mask.

Pagan watched her, silently wondering what Rogue was looking for and fearful for what she might find. She felt gentle fingers touch over her face. "My head wasn't hit, Rogue," Pagan assured her, realizing Rogue's shaking fingers were looking for a blood trail. "The ceiling just smacked into my shoulder and sent me head over heels." Rogue seemed to look inward, the look she got when Melina was talking to her in her earpiece alone.

"She's okay," Rogue assured Melina. "But we need to get her shoulder checked out by our friend at the hospital." Rogue cocked her head as she listened to the voice in her earpiece. "Mel's bringing us a change of clothes so we can go visit our Sentinel-friendly doctor at the local emergency room."

Pagan took her mask back from Rogue. "Let's walk a little closer to where Mel is picking us up so she can see for herself that I'm all right. I can almost hear her chewing your ears off." She put her mask in place and then looked around the edge of the tower they were leaning against. Behind them the casino was in ruins. The once bright lights now served only to spotlight the damage caused by the explosion and fire. Through the smoke and flames engulfing the building were the remnants of the casino's signatory large dice, shattered to pieces. The neon lights had been cracked, knocking out some of the letters in the casino name. Pagan read the message left to blink mournfully into the night.

Do Die.

She felt that message had been heard by all of Chastilian that night.

CHAPTER SEVEN

Pagan awoke slowly in her bed. Her head felt heavy, her whole body lethargic and leaden from the drugs she'd been pumped with the night before. She lifted her head slightly as she spied her bedroom door opening and saw Melina's head pop around it.

Melina's face brightened when she saw Pagan was awake. "Rest easy. Rogue is taking over your duties for the day. After last night, I think Ammassari will be more than excited to have Rogue herself fitting his security cameras around the lot." She sat on the bed so Pagan could read her lips more easily since her aids were out. Tenderly, Melina ran a hand through Pagan's hair, just like she had when Pagan was a child.

"My shoulder feels terrible. I feel like the whole casino came down on me."

Melina grimaced. "You were lucky you only got clipped by it. And that firefighter was very lucky you were there to save him."

"At least there was someone I could help. We couldn't do anything for the ones who were already gone." Pagan closed her eyes. "I never want to see that many dead again, Mel."

"I was watching you last night. I saw through Rogue's lens what you did. You were amazing."

"How? I nearly got my fool head smacked off by falling debris."

"Your reaction speeds are phenomenal. And you react to sounds like no one else I've ever seen. That firefighter wouldn't be here if it wasn't for you."

"I saw something," Pagan mumbled, hating to have to admit it out loud.

"When?"

"I thought I saw someone in the car while it was on fire. All I could think of was Mom and Dad and what happened to them, and I just ran to the car like I did when I was small. You'd think I'd have learned from that mistake too."

Melina cupped Pagan's chin and lifted her head slightly so she could see her. "It's a very natural reaction. You're a Sentinel; your first instincts are to go help whoever needs you. I might have been more worried had you *not* reacted. You have feelings, Pagan. It's what makes you human and alive." She smiled softly at her. "I want you to sleep a little more and then come down for something to eat. Rogue says you're to stay in bed all day. No wandering down to the office and messing with the computers. I'm looking after the office today."

"Did the police get the remote wielder?" Pagan asked, her mind still buzzing with all she'd witnessed the previous night.

"No, he escaped in one of the other cars. Sergeant Eddie Cauley, the chief's son, was on the scene. Like father, like son. He kept the Sighteds aware of all that was happening. They did get one of the drivers. He was too busy watching the show to notice that the police were gathering around him. Maybe they'll get some answers from him." Melina shrugged. "But I wouldn't bet on it."

Pagan snuggled back down to make the most of her sleep-in. "Maybe if I sleep a bit more my shoulder will feel better. If I'm a really good patient, do I get pancakes for breakfast?"

"You can have whatever you want." Melina rose from the bed and tugged the sheets closer to Pagan's chin. She took a step away, hesitated, then returned to kneel beside Pagan's bed.

Pagan stared at her, wondering what was on her sister's mind.

"My greatest fear was that, somehow, someday, you'd be hurt in a fight. Last night I watched that fear come true without a punch being thrown. Yet as I watched you save that man, I was so proud of you. That's not to say I wasn't hysterical, which I will freely admit to being. You're my baby sister, after all. But you are a true Sentinel, just like Rogue said you'd be. I know Mom and Dad would be so proud of you. You are worthy of carrying their Sentinel mantle."

Pagan blinked at the rush of tears that threatened to spill from her eyes. Melina smiled at her.

"We'll see you later. Rest now. You had a busy night."

Sleepily, Pagan thought that Melina had an alarming penchant for understatement.

❖

At the Ammassari Dealership, Rogue got out of the van and took in the large number of prestige cars and rows full of vehicles for sale. She spied Ammassari with customers and purposefully didn't attract his attention. Instead, she headed toward the main office and strode down the corridor with one intention in mind: to see the face that bore the freckles that had Pagan so enraptured.

"Hey, Pagan O! I thought I heard the chariot that you just rode in on!"

A small red-haired woman bounded out of the office and very nearly bowled into Rogue.

Rogue looked down silently at Erith, who had stopped still and was staring up at her in confusion.

"You're not Pagan," she said in an almost accusatory tone, looking down the corridor in case Pagan was lagging behind.

Rogue remained silent for a moment as she stared Erith down. She was surprised to see that she didn't look away and instead stared right back with her own intensity. Rogue stuck out her hand.

"Rogue Ronchetti."

Erith's face lit up fractionally. "The sister's lover! Hi." She took Rogue's hand and shook it firmly. "Where's Pagan?"

Rogue was impressed by Erith's one-track mind. "She couldn't make it today." She saw the disappointment color Erith's pale face. Rogue handed her the small bag she had carried in with her. "She asked that you be given this." It was a lie, but Rogue needed an excuse to meet Erith and felt that bringing lunch would suffice.

Erith took it carefully, obviously not trusting Rogue right away. She peered into the bag and smiled. "Lunch. She didn't have to do that."

"She said you should eat." Rogue let her gaze drift down Erith's slender form. She could see why Pagan was concerned. It was hard to see exactly what weight Erith carried when her body was hidden by the oversized shirt she was wearing. Rogue could still see that she wasn't the healthiest weight for someone her age.

Erith thanked her and then leaned back against the door frame. Her sharp eyes sized Rogue up. "You made sure those guys that hurt Pagan were sorry for what they did to her, didn't you?"

Rogue marshaled her face not to give away any reaction, but she started a little from the surprise. *What does this girl know?* "Guys?"

"The ones fighting outside that restaurant the other night. Those idiots that landed the lucky punch to Pagan's jaw. She said you sorted them out for her."

Rogue took a deep breath and nodded. "Oh, those were sorted out with very little problem. They won't touch anyone again for a long time."

"Good. She doesn't deserve to be hit." Erith turned away from the door. "No one does." The last was whispered almost to herself.

Rogue heard the softly spoken words and wondered again at the waiflike woman who had drawn Pagan's attention.

"So will Pagan be back tomorrow?"

Rogue nodded. "I'm sure she will be."

"Good. Tell her to bring enough for two." She held up the bag and shook it slightly. "It's no fun eating on your own."

Rogue turned to go but was halted by a soft voice.

"Hey, Rogue?"

Rogue dutifully turned back.

"Are all Pagan's family so tall and intimidating?" Erith was once again leaning against the door to her office, staring at Rogue with a piercing emerald gaze.

Rogue shrugged. "I like to think we're just larger than life, Erith," she replied.

"God, I bet Melina has her hands full with you." Erith chuckled, then laughed more heartily when Rogue's eyebrows rose in surprise. "So you're what Pagan is going to grow up into." She looked Rogue up and down with a studious air.

"We're not connected by blood," Rogue said.

"You don't need blood between you to be influenced by someone important in your life. It's obvious she worships you. I can hear it in her voice."

"She's a remarkable person in her own right," Rogue replied. "Believe me, the adoration goes both ways."

"Good. Will you tell her hi from me?"

Rogue nodded. "Have a good day, Erith."

"I will, Rogue. Thanks for bringing me lunch."

Rogue left the office with the distinct feeling she was being laughed at. She turned back to stare at the door, but Erith was no longer lounging against it. She chuckled. *The little fiend knew I was checking her out. Good, that way she knows that if she hurts Pagan in any way she has me to deal with.*

❖

Rogue was already halfway around the car lot before Tito Ammassari caught up with her.

"These cameras aren't going up a day too soon!" He rubbed a handkerchief over his face. "Did you hear about the casino last night?"

Rogue looked down from atop her step ladder. "I heard. Random acts of violence in this city make for headline news."

"You think it was random? I think Louis Miller was targeted." Tito leaned closer to the ladder. "A big man like him, his casino made lots of money for the city. I heard he was killed before the explosion blew out his gambling floors."

"Nothing about that was mentioned on the news, Mr. Ammassari."

Tito looked around furtively. "I keep my ear to the ground. I've been in this city too many years not to have my sources. You have to watch your own back, Ronchetti, because no one will watch it for you."

Rogue considered this, then went back to attaching a camera in just the right position. "Did you know Mr. Miller?" She saw the nervous twitch that betrayed Tito's answer.

"I knew of him. I remember him from years ago. Kids on the street, you know?" He rubbed at his face again, wiping away the copious sweat that was running from his brow. "But you grow apart, grow up, then you start a business, make a family." He shrugged. "Life goes on and you move on."

"I heard he had a troubled background." Rogue fixed the last wire into its connector and flipped shut the casing.

Tito was quiet for a moment. "Years ago, Chastilian wasn't what it is now. You either ran with the crowd or you were chased by them. Some people had to do bad things before they could start doing good."

"And yet some people are just good from the start." She gestured to the car lot. "I'll fit all your cameras outside in the lot today and get you hooked up to the mainframe you wanted installed in your home. I'll install everything you need in your home this afternoon. Then tomorrow, we'll install your detectors inside the offices, and you'll be good to go."

"Safe and sound, eh?" Tito didn't look convinced.

"As safe as anyone can be in life." Rogue cast one last look up at the camera she had installed. It looked just like all the rest, except it had an extra transceiver. Just one more eye in the city for the Sighted to see with.

CHAPTER EIGHT

Sitting out a night of Sentinel duty chafed at Pagan's sense of responsibility. Her shoulder still bore the pain of the previous night's adventure, so she sat beside Melina to watch over Rogue as she stepped out into the night alone. She was less than happy about having to remain behind and watch the city through Rogue's eye-view. She rustled through some papers that were coming off the printer beside Melina. It was the direct fax line between the Sighted and the police. Her attention suddenly focused on the information she was halfheartedly reading.

"Mel, we should start checking out known associates of Louis Miller, both past and present."

Melina leaned back in her chair to see what had Pagan's attention.

"What has young Sergeant Cauley sent us?" She reached for the sheets Pagan held.

"It would seem Eddie has done a little digging into Miller's past. Miller, in his younger days, was a friend of Tito Ammassari. They were arrested together a few times for minor offenses."

Melina frowned as she read the information. "No wonder Ammassari was so frightened today. He knew the guy more than he admitted to Rogue." She read through the rest of the report quickly. "There was usually a third man with them. It wouldn't hurt to check him out." She began typing. "Richard Quaid..."

"Isn't he the one who runs the Jewelry Quarter in Chastilian? Quaid Quarter? Every piece of gold and silver, and any gemstones, go through his hands first in the Quarter."

Melina's fingers flew over the keyboard. "Rogue, can you please head back to the lighthouse and pick up your set of wheels? I need you to go check out something for me a little farther afield."

Rogue's voice sounded clear through the room. "I'll head back now. Where am I being directed to, may I ask?"

"Quaid's Quarter," Melina replied, her attention firmly on the computer as she brought up maps of the area.

"Are you hinting after an eternity ring?" Rogue's tone teased her over the airwaves.

Melina laughed. "I'll keep on hinting until I receive one from you. But I'd rather we shop together for that in the daylight. Tonight, I want you to check in on an old acquaintance of both Miller *and* Ammassari."

"Sounds intriguing. I'll be back shortly and get my motorcycle."

Pagan made a face. "Great, the one night we could take to the streets, and I'm out of commission." She moved her shoulder experimentally and winced at the dull pain.

"There'll be other nights, Pagan. I promise you."

Pagan looked at the screen showing Rogue's view of the city and yearned to be out there by her side.

❖

Once briefed at the lighthouse, Rogue fired up her motorcycle and raced through the outskirts of Chastilian, enjoying the speed of her machine and the cool night air on her face. Rogue thrilled to the feel of the bike. It was styled like a racer, fashioned with sleek lines and angling the rider to crouch low over the tank for a more aerodynamic ride. Rogue had helped design the motor that purred silently beneath her. It was the trademark of the Sentinels: silent running. She enjoyed the fact there was no noisy revving to disturb the night ride. It was just her and the motorcycle leaving behind the noise of the city.

"Been a while since you've fired up a cycle." Melina spoke softly in her ear, and Rogue smiled at the tender voice.

"Yes, it has, but it feels like second nature to be watching the road through just the beam of my headlight after being blinded by the city lights for so long."

Rogue lifted her head a little and peered into the night. The long roads out to the Quaid Quarter bordered a rare stretch of countryside. She steered through the curves. The fields were dark, the stars shone brighter in the night sky, and all was oddly quiet. Rogue grew uneasy as her journey continued. She rounded another corner and the Jewelry Quarter came into view. A series of buildings fashioned in a U shape comprised the strip mall that housed Chastilian's jewelry center.

"Mel, you need to get the fire crews out here."

There was no mistaking the flickering flames that licked through the building just ahead. Getting closer to the target, Rogue eased her motorcycle to a halt and got into a position so that Melina could see everything she did.

"Why set fire to that particular shop?" Rogue used her night vision binoculars to try to see more of what was happening. The fire had already taken hold of the main building and was traveling along its roof to the smaller adjoining shops.

"That's Quaid's own personal shop," Pagan replied over Rogue's comlink. "I've got a map here on the Internet of what is sold in each facility. That was where he started. It's the keystone of his business."

"Again with the personal attack." Rogue quickly turned her attention to a figure that stalked away from the burning building. "Mel, can you get a fix on that guy using my mask cam?"

"He's got something obscuring his face. I can't get a clear view of him."

"I'll get in closer," Rogue said and began to quickly make her way across the field to the back of the warehouse. "Damn it, where's he gone now?" She raced up to the back of one of the end shops and peered around the corner cautiously. She swiftly drew her head back so she wasn't seen. "There are more men here than I thought." She watched as one man, tall and slender, seemed to direct the others as they ran to and from the other shops. "I think we have a ringleader, but there is no way I'm going in alone against that many. I count at least nine, maybe ten men with him." She backed away from the wall. "Do we have time to get other Sentinels to my position?"

"I've put out a call to them," Melina said.

Rogue edged her way along the buildings, conscious of the fact that the fire was dancing from one rooftop to another with amazing speed. She peered into a window to see if any of the buildings were occupied. She edged along until she came to the one that Pagan had told her was Quaid's shop. She stretched up to look inside and found herself peering into a back room filled with boxes, and a table and chairs. Seated at the table was a man, his arms tied to the back of his chair, tape placed across his mouth. On the floor by his feet were countless blocks stacked up one on top of the other. A bird molded crudely out of a white material was sitting on the table before him. Detonators were stuck into the bird's base. The man saw Rogue and he began to struggle, his eyes wild and plainly terrified.

"Rogue, get out of there *now!*" Melina screamed.

Rogue ran as fast and as far away from the building as she could.

"Just keep running. That amount of C4 will blow the place sky high in a matter of—" She was cut off by the explosion that ripped through the shop and blew slate and debris high into the air with a deafening boom.

Rogue threw herself to the ground, covering her head as pieces of the building flew past. She felt the air around her shudder with the force of the explosion and grunted as something hit her squarely on the back. She kept her head down until debris stopped landing around her.

"I'm okay," she said over the comlink. She sat up and looked back at the buildings. They were now all engulfed in flame.

"There was someone in there." Pagan couldn't keep the tremor from her voice. "How many more were tied in place by this gang?"

"This crime lord obviously has no care for innocents," Melina said. "Rogue, can you see the gang? Are they still there?"

Rogue got out her binoculars and scanned the area. She bit back a curse. "They're all fine and dandy. They're in a van driving back to the site." She watched the same man she'd seen earlier alight from the van and walk toward the buildings. "He's going back again. I'm going to follow him."

Rogue set off running across the field. As soon as she reached the burning buildings, she sought cover amid the ruins. "What is he doing?" The man casually lit a match by flicking its tip with his thumb. The small flame it produced seemed inconsequential in the roar from the fire that was burning through the rest of the buildings. He flicked the match upward; as it fell to the ground, the air was suddenly rent by an enormous *whoosh*. It was the unmistakable sound of gasoline being ignited. Rogue ducked back behind the building at the rush of hot air that reached out even at her distance away. She could hear faint laughter and the sound of an engine starting. She quickly ducked from behind the building to try to see the van.

"It's too late, Rogue. He's gone. He and his henchmen have taken off."

Rogue cursed softly and watched the taillights of the van disappear down the road, leaving the burning shops behind.

"Mel, do we have access to the Earth's Eye satellite?"

"What do you need, Rogue?"

"When you have a fire burning already, you don't usually set another on the front lawn." Rogue got out her palm-sized screen and waited for Melina to send her what she had found. The Earth's Eye satellite was used by the military to zero in on points on the globe. Rogue had found a way to use that technology to her own advantage by piggybacking the signal and using it to find targets of her own. Sometimes an eye in the sky gave the best view.

"Sending you the data now."

Rogue watched the screen. The city grew larger as the satellite's eye drew closer, and then Rogue's location was visible as a bright fiery patch on the ground. As the camera drew in closer, it was possible to see individual landmarks. The buildings set alight, the surrounding land covered in smoke, and burning brightly in the middle of it all, the distinct shape of a winged bird. The ferocity of the flames made the bird appear to be flying, its wide wings lifting it up and its lengthy tail trailing behind. It was both beautiful and grotesque.

"It's a Phoenix."

Rogue heard the distress in Mel's voice. She looked up at the blazing buildings before her and then back to the screen.

"I'm coming home. Call the other Sentinels back. There's nothing more to be done here." Rogue headed for her motorcycle, her need to understand who had done this warring with her need to get back to the people she loved. The past was rising from the ashes and burning all too brightly in the symbol left burning for Chastilian to heed.

❖

An endless stream of noise sounded through the lighthouse as the scanner announced the activity of the police and fire crews on scene at Quaid's Quarter and what they were finding. The Sighted were in contact over their own secured lines. The Council had been convened, and they were discussing theories back and forth over the airwaves. Melina sat before her computer, directing it all.

Pagan heard none of them. The flaming Phoenix burned brightly on a monitor, and she was unable to take her eyes from it. She was chilled to her very core by its significance.

"Could it just be a prank?" Pagan asked Melina, finally tearing her eyes away from the symbol that was seared onto her brain. "A copycat lowlife using an old name in Chastilian's history to generate fear?"

"Maybe, if it was just the burning Phoenix we had scorching the dirt in a field. But this came after blowing up Quaid's Quarter. I think there's deliberation in both the building and the placing of the symbol right at the entrance to the Quarter." Melina leaned back in her chair. "Xander Phoenix is dead. He died within weeks of being taken into custody for killing our parents. He was found knifed in his cell. The police never could say who did it, but they believed it was a hit orchestrated by Phoenix's own gang to keep him quiet and not implicate them." Melina shrugged. "But the strange thing is the extortion our parents fought against stopped once Xander Phoenix was imprisoned. The Phoenix's gang just disappeared."

"And yet now, so many years later, he is symbolically set alight after a second night of terror." Pagan ran a hand through her hair as her mind raced with endless fears and possibilities. "I think we need to have a chat with Ammassari. Maybe he can shed some light on this newly risen Phoenix and why he's targeting Tito's old friends."

"He might be too scared to tell. He's already shown his fear by equipping his home and workplace with the latest security equipment."

Pagan crossed her arms and returned her attention once more to the burning sign left at Quaid's door. "Then I'd say he knew full well this Phoenix was about to resurface from the ashes. He was preparing for a storm before we even had a hint of rain."

CHAPTER NINE

As Pagan drove to the Ammassari Dealership the next day, her head was full of thoughts of last night's fire. She blindly followed the traffic as Chastilian's residents continued with their daily lives. Not for the first time, Pagan wondered if ignorance *was* truly bliss.

Once at the dealership, Pagan parked her van and grabbed her computer case. She gathered what equipment she needed, testing out her damaged shoulder and then switching the box of supplies to her other side. She looked up briefly and saw Erith heading straight for her. She rested the box back down in the van and waited.

"Where were you yesterday?" Erith launched straight in for the attack, grabbing at Pagan's arms to hold her still.

"Sick in bed," Pagan replied. "But today I'm much better, thank you."

Erith stared at her, her gaze seeming to bore right through her.

"Really, I am," Pagan assured her quietly.

Erith dropped her hands slowly. She seemed to have found something fascinating to look at on the ground. "I missed you yesterday," she said. "And I was worried. There's so much craziness happening in the city, it's hard to feel safe anymore."

"I'm okay," Pagan repeated.

"You don't strike me as the sickly type, you being so big and all."

"I very rarely get ill," Pagan said. "Yesterday was a fluke. But I'm here today, large as life and twice as ugly." Pagan hoped to get a smile out of Erith.

"No one in their right mind would ever call you ugly," she said, favoring Pagan with a look that all but stopped Pagan's breathing. "So, what was wrong with you? Twenty-four-hour flu? Hangover? Too much sun?"

"I had a touch of vertigo," Pagan replied, using an excuse Melina had concocted to cut through Erith's wild guesses.

"Vertigo? You're *that* tall and you get *vertigo*? Isn't that a fear of heights?"

"It's an imbalance in the inner ear that causes the sufferer to experience dizziness and be unable to stand," Pagan said. "In short, it's an ear infection that plays mean."

Erith snorted at her. "If I were you, I'd just tell everyone you had a hangover. Your cool status will rise through the roof."

"I wasn't aware I even had a cool status," Pagan said, picking up her box again and slamming the van door shut with her hip.

"You don't, but you keep hanging around with me long enough and we'll soon change that," Erith teased.

Pagan nodded. "I might be able to manage that. Hanging around with you, I mean. Just to look cool, you understand." She chuckled when Erith slapped her lightly in the stomach. "Hey! Still recovering here." Pagan pretended to be hurt by the blow.

"You're a big girl. You can take it."

"I could take *you*," Pagan said and then felt her face flame as she registered the innuendo as it slammed belatedly into her brain.

Erith stopped in her tracks and stared up at Pagan with a raised eyebrow. Pagan cursed the fact her own face had to be turning fifty shades of embarrassment.

Erith opened her mouth to say something but then closed it again. She crooked her finger to summon Pagan to lean down so she could whisper something to her.

"One day, I'll remind you of that statement, Ms. Osborne, when we're not in the middle of the car lot with expectant buyers looking for four wheels that scream 'babe magnet.'" She patted Pagan's cheek and then swaggered away, leaving Pagan dumbfounded in the middle of the lot.

Pagan blinked and swallowed hard at the rise of arousal that caused her stomach muscles to tighten. *I don't think she meant* take *in the fighting sense of the word*. Pagan shivered as her active imagination filled her mind with other interpretations of the word. She felt dizzy and shook her head to clear her suddenly fuzzy brain. "Damn vertigo," she muttered, and forced her feet to move so she could catch up with Erith.

❖

Later that night, Pagan sat on the edge of an apartment building high above the city. There was a handy little niche where she could perch and watch the city go about its nightly routine. It had been a curiously quiet night. Rogue surmised that was because of the absolute chaos the fires had caused the previous night. The fires had been contained, and the loss to business calculated. The loss of life was also being counted. Miraculously, survivors had been found in the blast-damaged casino. Its owner, Louis Miller, however, had been a trophy kill, put on display, awaiting an audience to find him. The Jewelry Quarter bombing had yielded a body count of just one: Richard Quaid. He was the second owner of Chastilian's more wealthy enterprises ceremoniously killed at his seat of power.

Pagan curled into the wall pressed solidly against her spine. She looked at the windows opposite her in a more run-down apartment building. She sat motionless, her eyes darting back and forth, her ears tuned in to her surroundings. The aids offered her hearing but never the real, true sounds. Pagan had forgotten what rain really sounded like, but she could hear it as it fell. She blinked as the first droplets hit her face. Rain that had only been warned of earlier that evening now began to fall in earnest. She turned her head to stop the water from getting in her eyes and saw someone scurrying along the sidewalk below. Pagan got out her binoculars and trained the night vision lenses on the figure.

"Pagan, don't stay out in the rain too long." Melina's voice sounded in her ear.

"Yeah, you're big enough. You don't need the extra watering." Rogue's voice also came through her comlink. Pagan could see her atop a building across from her. They were keeping a separate vigil tonight.

"Ha ha, very funny," Pagan grumbled halfheartedly. Her attention was drawn away from Rogue's chuckling, drawn to the man she was watching hasten into the building and disappear from her sight. She frowned as she tried to place what was so familiar about him.

"Mel, did your police contact ever get a fix on the guy who was at the casino manning the remote control?" She trained her binoculars at the windows to see if she could see a light come on to show which apartment he entered.

"No, they never did get any leads on him. Why?"

Pagan lowered the binoculars and stared at the apartment. "Because I think I just saw him enter the building across from me." She turned her head fractionally, listening beyond the city, and caught the sounds that teased at her senses. She heard raised voices, angry and threatening. Carefully, Pagan slipped from her position and slid down the wall to land on another ledge to better hear which direction the row was coming from. She waited and listened, then took her wire gun and shot a wire across from her building to the other. She felt the bite pull on the gun as it hit its target.

"Where are you going, Pagan?" Rogue's soft voice rumbled in her ear.

"There's a disturbance across the way. I hear a loud voice and much anger. I want to see if it's more than just harsh words." Pagan jumped the gap between the two buildings and rode the wire to land just under the window where an argument could be heard. She flinched at the angry sounds. The instigator was a man with a guttural voice. He was bellowing at a woman, her voice barely registering in Pagan's ears as the man yelled over her, stopping her from answering.

"Dad, calm down!"

Pagan's heart jumped in recognition of a third voice. *Erith?* Pagan flipped a switch on her gun to disengage the wire from both secured ends while she quickly scrambled onto the fire escape beside her. She managed to maneuver close to a window, but there was no one to see. Instead she saw what seemed to be Erith's bedroom. Pagan was amused that for someone who favored such dark clothing, Erith's bedroom décor leaned a great deal more to the feminine. She grinned as the belligerent face of a female pop singer stared at her from one wall. A door slammed suddenly and Pagan felt the vibrations through her fingertips. She drew back slightly as she watched Erith enter the room and shut the door behind her. Erith then dragged a heavy chest of drawers across the floor. Pagan watched the door bow as Erith pushed all her weight against the chest of drawers, as if her added strength could hold back the force behind the door.

"You'd better stay in there, girl, if you know what's good for you!" the man warned angrily, and Pagan saw Erith flinch at the tone. Erith stayed braced at the door for a good ten minutes before she finally relaxed. Pagan listened for his return, but from what she could hear from another room, he had found far easier prey.

"Pagan," Rogue rumbled, "you can't investigate every domestic. That's not what Sentinels are here for."

"Rogue, I know the woman inside," Pagan whispered, her eyes never leaving Erith's face as she too listened to the sounds coming from the room next door.

"All the wiser for you to retreat, then," Rogue said simply.

"I will," Pagan replied, but she stayed where she was a little longer, staring at Erith, who had shifted to sit on the floor, wrapping her arms about her knees for obvious comfort.

"We can't save the world, Pagan," Melina said softly over the comlink. Pagan knew Melina could see all that Pagan was viewing back on a monitor in the lighthouse. "Domestics are the police's domain. They are better equipped to deal with them."

"I know," Pagan said, understanding but still unable to leave Erith. She started as Erith stood up suddenly and walked toward the window. "Shit!"

Erith opened the window and stepped out to stand on the small fire escape. She lifted her head to let the rain hit her face, oblivious to the fact that Pagan was underneath her, dangling precariously from the fire escape rail. Pagan held her breath and tried not to alert Erith to her presence, her fingers clutching mere inches from where Erith stood.

Erith, her eyes closed, hung her head over the railing and let the rain pour onto her hair, bleeding into the vibrant color, darkening it, soaking her skin. She looked up again into the night, the bright stars hidden by the clouds crowding into the sky.

"If I have a guardian angel, I sure hope you're watching over me right now."

Erith's voice floated down to Pagan's ears, making her heart clench at the sorrowful tone. With a heartfelt sigh loud enough for Pagan to hear, Erith retreated back inside her room and closed the window, leaving Pagan alone in the rain.

❖

Early the next morning, brushing her tiredness aside, Pagan drove through the traffic with a little less care and more speed than usual. Once at the dealership, she parked the van at a haphazard angle and swiftly vaulted up the steps toward the offices. The sound of arguing, very obviously one-sided, radiated from behind the closed office door. Pagan checked over her shoulder. No one else had heard the raised voice inside the office. She reminded herself to have a word with Ammassari about safety for the employees that went beyond cameras and alarms. As she neared Erith's office, Pagan could make out Erith trying to placate an angry man. Pagan hastened her steps, opened the door to the office, and then stepped inside. Erith jumped at the sudden intrusion, and Pagan was pleased to see the man also jumped guiltily at her entrance.

"Erith, is there a problem here?" Pagan would not let a disgruntled customer take out his fury on Erith. She moved to position herself between the stockily built man and a visibly cowering Erith.

"No problem. He was just leaving," she said as she slipped around Pagan and took the man's arm to direct him out. He pulled his arm back sharply and caught Erith's arm roughly in his hand.

Pagan applied pressure to the man's wrist to force him to let Erith go. He hissed in pain, letting her go, and cradled his hand.

"You bitch!" he fumed.

"Who is this man, Erith?" Pagan asked as she pulled Erith behind her to shield her. She got a closer look at the man, and something about him gave her pause.

"He's my father." Erith sighed and leaned back to rest against the desk.

Pagan stared down from her superior height at the man before her. "In my family, men treat their women with more respect." She leaned forward menacingly. "Don't let me find you here again threatening your daughter. Otherwise, I might be forced to send my family after you, and you might not like how real men treat bullies."

He glared at Pagan, his eyes narrowing as he looked her up and down. "Poor excuse for a woman," he spat contemptuously at her.

"More man than you'll ever dream of being," Pagan replied calmly, her whole body poised in case he decided to express any further anger with his fists.

"Leave, Dad. Just go." Erith's voice was strained and oddly toneless.

"I'll deal with you later," he said and turned to leave, only to be brought up sharply by Pagan's hand on his collar. She lifted him off his feet a little and, for a moment, real fear ignited in his eyes.

"And I'll deal with *you* later if I find you have harmed her in any way." Pagan watched him swallow as he tried to budge from her grasp but couldn't. She let him go with a flick of her wrist, causing him to stumble when his feet touched the ground again. He scrambled to get out of the office. She then turned to Erith, who wouldn't meet her eyes.

Erith sighed and tried to make light of the situation. "Not exactly how I envisioned you meeting my family. I had imagined a little less of the violence and more handshakes and hellos."

Pagan looked down the now empty corridor that Baylor had run down. "He doesn't strike me as a 'hello' kind of guy." She noticed how Erith sought protection from her familiar position behind the desk. Pagan searched to find any marks on Erith's pale skin. She let out a small sigh when none were visible.

"No, I guess not." Erith began to sort through her paperwork. "So, what brings you here? I thought everything was installed and up and running?"

Pagan raised an eyebrow at her brusque manner and, before answering her, sat down uninvited. "I'm just tying up loose ends." Pagan had no legitimate reason for being there. She was in Erith's office solely because she had not managed to rid herself of the disquiet that had settled in her chest from what she had witnessed just a few hours previous. *How long have you lived this kind of life, endlessly terrorized by the one person who is supposed to protect you?*

"You're staring at me."

Erith's quiet words broke through Pagan's thoughts.

"I'm just watching you. I'm in awe of your obvious smarts and business brain to clear through all that work on your desk."

"I'm not *that* smart, Pagan. I do the paperwork for a car lot. It isn't exactly rocket science."

"You're smarter than you like people to think, Ms. Baylor," Pagan answered back. "There's no shame in that. Beauty and smarts, they are a heady combination."

Erith shifted in her chair, her face warming under Pagan's scrutiny. She was quiet for a long time then looked up at Pagan. "Beauty?"

Pagan nodded. "That's a given," she said simply. "Why hide how clever you really are, Erith?"

Erith looked around the office furtively. She leaned forward to whisper, "Because sometimes it's best to keep secrets hidden so they can't be destroyed by careless hands."

Pagan looked at her with a silent understanding.

Erith smiled finally. "I'm going to get back to my work now. Time and car sales wait for no woman."

"Okay," Pagan said easily and was silent for barely a second. "Do you have any brothers or sisters?"

"Whoa! There's a question right out of left field!" she said, visibly surprised. "No, no siblings at all. Just little ol' me in the Baylor clan. And I have been reliably informed that one of me is one too many."

"Who told you something as cruel as that?"

"My dad. He and I don't exactly see eye to eye, as you got to witness firsthand."

"What about your mom? Do you get along with her?"

Erith shrugged. "She has a martyr complex she finds kind of hard to shake off." She stared at the table and began picking at a piece ingrained in the wood. "I need this job. I need to be able to prove my smarts to the great wide world, earn some money, and get the hell out from under their feet."

"I'm still in the family home too. I work for my sister and her partner, as you well know. I've grown up in the family business, so it was only natural I would become a part of it. Though sometimes I can't help but wonder what I *could* do if I didn't have their backing and I was left to fend for myself in the world."

Erith rubbed at her forehead as if gathering a headache under her fingertips. "Not everyone gets the lucky breaks with family, Pagan." Erith swiftly gathered up her paperwork and headed to the filing cabinet. "I envy you, Pagan. You have a charmed existence. You're loved by your sister, defended by her partner. You're living in a lesbian utopia. I hope you appreciate it."

"I do," Pagan said. "Erith, what—?" She stopped as her cell phone rang. She checked the screen and saw Rogue's number. "Damn it!"

Erith shrugged. "Go do your duty, Pagan. It pays never to ignore the call of family." She shut the cabinet drawer with a resounding clang.

Pagan hesitated and only moved when Erith made shooing motions for her to get out of the office. Once out, Pagan rubbed at her forehead, frowning. "What the hell's a lesbian utopia when it's at home? I'll ask Rogue. She's sure to know." She left to have a swift word with Tito Ammassari about keeping an eye on who entered the offices without his knowledge. Once in the van, she returned Rogue's call.

"Before you ask where I am, can you please run a check on the name Baylor? I think I've just met our remote-control-car guy face to angry face."

❖

Joe Baylor's crime sheets were curiously devoid of anything but petty thieving when he was a young adult. Then he had just disappeared from sight. Pagan crowded close to Melina, reading over her shoulder on the computer screen.

"It looks like he got in trouble early on and then just vanished from the radar. I'm guessing he got smarter and never got caught again," Melina said. She pointed to something on the screen. "But he does seem to travel around a lot. Look at all the places he's lived in."

"Erith said she never got the chance to settle in school long before she was whisked off to another."

"Erith's father is obviously part of this new Phoenix's gang." Melina shot Pagan a considering look. "Tread warily, Pagan."

Pagan bit back a sigh and instead stared at the monitor. "Just because her father is involved doesn't necessarily mean she has to be." She felt her sister's hand on her sleeve and lifted her head to meet caring eyes. "I'll be watchful, I promise. I followed in my parents' footsteps to keep watch over Chastilian. Erith's just a part of that."

"It seems to me that your feelings for her are more than just concern for who her father is."

Pagan didn't reply. All she knew was she was inexplicably drawn to Erith. As a Sentinel, it was her duty to protect her. As a woman, Pagan found she had the same overwhelming need to keep Erith safe.

❖

Later that night while the Sentinels were on watch, the light from Erith's window drew Pagan toward it stronger than a siren's call.

"Where are you heading, Pagan, as if I didn't know?" Rogue asked via the comlink.

"I just need to put my mind at rest that she's okay. Today was not the nicest of starts," Pagan said. "And I think I annoyed her with my questions too."

Rogue sighed. "Young love," she said in an astute tone, causing Pagan to suddenly halt before she got onto the fire escape. She looked back to where Rogue was waiting. In the concealing shadows of night, Rogue was just another black silhouette amid the dark.

"I have never mentioned the L-word, Rogue."

"My apologies," Rogue said, feigning a bored air.

Pagan narrowed her eyes at her, all too aware that Rogue couldn't see her from this distance. She continued her silent stalking to sneak a look into Erith's room. She found no sign of Erith's presence in the empty bedroom. She didn't know if that brought her any kind of comfort.

"Call it a night, Sentinels," Melina announced in their ears. "Nothing is happening, so you might as well return home."

Pagan looked again through the window. "Where is she? It's four a.m. She should be in bed."

"As should you," Rogue said.

Pagan nodded and reluctantly moved away.

It wasn't until both she and Rogue were on ground level that she saw the woman she had been looking for. Pagan ducked back against the alleyway between the buildings and observed from the cover of darkness. Erith rode past quickly on her bicycle, her legs pumping to keep up speed. She skidded to a halt beneath her building and dismounted. Erith shouldered the bicycle and began to walk up the fire escape. Pagan watched as Erith got to the ledge outside her room and then carefully eased her bedroom window open. The bicycle was pushed through the open frame and then Erith climbed in after it. Pagan waited for just a moment longer until the muted light from the window was distinguished. She heard Melina in her ear.

"Can *you* come home now that you know *she's* home?"

"On my way," Pagan replied. She jogged down the street to catch up with an already moving Rogue. She glanced back only once to make sure the light didn't come back on and to assure herself that Erith was indeed home.

"Pagan, have we mentioned before that personal feelings cannot enter a Sentinel's field of operations?" Melina asked with a detectable smile in her voice.

"I'm merely putting my own mind at rest that tonight the occupant of that room is safe and sound."

"Nothing personal at all, eh?" Rogue's voice came from before her.

"Purely professional," Pagan said.

Rogue grunted. "I can't help but hear that damn L-word in that tone. What say you, Sighted?"

"I would have to concur. My monitors are picking up some curious readings coming from the young Sentinel. I fear her hormones are in an uproar."

Pagan puffed at them both. "If I ever find out what a lesbian utopia is, you two are so not invited!"

CHAPTER TEN

There was a part of Pagan that didn't want to see Erith that morning. She was curious as to what would keep her out so late into the night. She knew that her own timekeeping was a little odd, but she had the Sentinel duty as an excuse for traversing the city at night. She wondered what had kept Erith away from home, or what had happened to negate the need to get away. Her own theories were too frightening to contemplate.

She found Erith at her desk in mid yawn. Erith quickly put her hand over her mouth to hide her tiredness.

"Good morning, Pagan. Excuse me for nearly swallowing you. I overslept and I'm playing catch-up this morning." She waved a hand in the direction of the chair by the desk. Pagan ignored it and instead crouched at Erith's side.

"How are you feeling today? You seemed a little out of sorts yesterday." Pagan decided to broach the subject head-on and deal with any fallout she might encounter from Erith.

"Must have been a time-of-the-month thing," Erith said lightly. "Just let it go, Pagan O. Everything's okay."

Pagan gave Erith a face that she had learned well from Melina. She was heartened to see Erith shift uncomfortably.

"So, what made you oversleep?" Pagan asked.

Erith shrugged, shuffled her papers loudly, and set them down in a tray. "Rough night. I get them sometimes."

Pagan knew she wasn't going to get anything further from her. She stood and heard Erith's soft chuckle. Pagan frowned.

"While you were crouching, I forgot just how tall you are," Erith said.

"Does it bother you *that* much?"

Erith shook her head and put a hand on Pagan's arm. "I like it. It's kind of cool."

"Cool?" Pagan smiled. "How so?"

"It's like being protected when I'm with you."

"I *would* protect you, Erith."

"You know what? I think you would. *If* I needed protection, which I don't."

Pagan nodded as if in agreement. "Of course not. Something tells me you'd be pretty darn tenacious on your own without needing help from me."

Erith puffed out her chest. "You'd better believe it."

"Care to join me for an early lunch?" Pagan asked, unsure if Erith would accept her invitation. "I'm on my way to another job and just happened to be in the neighborhood."

"I'd love to."

Pagan gestured for Erith to precede her as they left the office to go enjoy the midmorning sunshine outside. Erith stopped suddenly, causing Pagan to walk right into her. Erith grabbed at Pagan's arms to steady her.

"I wondered if I would see you again." She looked up at Pagan shyly. "After all, the car lot is now alarmed to the hilt with your high-tech equipment. We're just short of being body scanned before we step inside to work."

"I was worried I'd made you mad after yesterday," Pagan said.

Erith shook her head. "No, no, you didn't. I just get… Don't worry about us, okay? You and I are fine. We're better than fine." Erith hugged Pagan to her. "We're becoming the best of friends. Nothing can change that. Right?"

Pagan held Erith close and relished the feel of her in her arms. "Nothing can change that." Pagan wished her heart would calm down. She feared Erith would hear its thundering.

Erith pulled back out of Pagan's hold. Pagan swallowed hard under the steady eyes sweeping over her.

"You aren't *that* tall after all," Erith mused. "You're a huggable height, and I get to lay my head on interesting places!" With a cheeky grin directed at Pagan's chest, she grabbed for Pagan's hand and led the way.

Pagan felt as if her feet weren't even touching the ground. *Full body contact with Erith and I lived to tell the tale*, she thought giddily. She dazedly followed Erith, wishing she could tell her how she felt and ask for another hug. *All in the name of science, of course.* To test the theory that her heart didn't really miss a beat when she felt Erith pressed close to her, that her blood didn't really race at lightning speed and make her feel light-headed. To prove that Pagan had never felt anything as sweet as being held by such small arms that hid so much strength. But Pagan kept silent and just followed Erith's lead outside to find a spot to eat, pretending that her whole being was not crying out for one more touch. Pagan had had too much practice in not hearing things. The urges of her body were just something else to turn a deaf ear to for now.

The rough seating area outside the office was oddly quiet as Erith accepted the sandwich Pagan offered her. As Erith's baggy sleeve slipped up her arm, Pagan saw a series of red marks on her exposed flesh. Erith hastily pulled her sleeve back down. "I fell off my bike," she explained quickly. "It's no biggie. It happens sometimes when I ride to work. Traffic's a bitch."

Pagan shook her head angrily, resisting the urge to grab Erith's arm and look more closely at the bruising. "They are bruises shaped like fingers, Erith. Unless you're telling me someone grabbed you off your bike, I would have to say you're lying."

Erith's eyes widened at Pagan's blunt words, and then narrowed defensively. "Gee, Pagan, I never figured you for the investigative type. Just leave it, okay? It doesn't concern you."

"It does if it hurts you."

"Why, Pagan? Why should you be so bothered about a scrappy little thing like me?"

Pagan studied Erith's posture, heard her belligerent tone, and saw the defensiveness that blanketed it all. She recognized the stance of someone who had been beaten down and yet still managed to stand and wait courageously for the next blow to land. Someone who didn't recognize her own worth or see that she could be valued by another.

"Why?" she asked with a small smile. "Because you're my friend and I happen to care about you."

Erith sat motionless, staring at Pagan. "I haven't had many friends who cared."

"You've got one now."

Erith sighed and seemed to reach a decision in her head. Shielding herself from any other prying eyes, she rolled up her sleeve, showing Pagan the full extent of the damage. "My dad got a little drunk last night. He doesn't know his own strength sometimes." She pulled her sleeve down to hide the bruising once more.

"Does he get drunk a lot?" Pagan asked, her eyes fixed on the area where Erith was hurt. The marks there burned onto her brain and fueled her anger.

"About as many days as there are in a week."

"Does he hurt *you* a lot?" Pagan steeled herself for the answer.

Erith chewed at her bottom lip a little, gnawing away at the soft flesh. "Not as much as he does my mother. But once she's down, I'm the next target." Erith rubbed a hand over her face. "Just another sparkling entry in my journal of existence," she said flippantly. "It's okay, Pagan. I've lasted this long, a little longer won't kill me."

Pagan didn't hear the near silent "I hope" that Erith whispered. Instead Pagan read it on her lips and saw it etched in her eyes. Then Erith changed the subject, and Pagan graciously let her lead the conversation away from hurtful things.

When lunch was over and Pagan couldn't drag out her time with Erith any longer, she reached for her wallet and drew out a card. She took a pen from her pocket, wrote her number on the back of the card, then slid it over to Erith.

"This is my business card. I've put my personal number on the back. If you need me, any time, day or night, you call me." Pagan tapped on the card to emphasize her words. "*Any* time."

Erith picked the card up and looked it over. She ran her fingers lightly over the embossing. "Thank you. I'll keep that in mind."

"I have to go." Pagan was loath to leave but had other duties to perform. Without thinking, she tucked a loose strand of Erith's hair behind her ear. "Take care, okay?" She froze as Erith captured her hand and pressed it to her cheek. The warmth and softness of Erith's skin burned through Pagan's palm.

"I will. *Careful* is my middle name." Erith slowly let go of Pagan's hand.

Pagan stared at her briefly before she had to tear herself away. The responsibilities of her job paled in comparison to the fire that lit up Erith's eyes at Pagan's touch.

CHAPTER ELEVEN

Pagan fastened up her jacket and shifted around to make the bulky covering fit more comfortably. She picked up her mask and paused in mid task. Beside her, Rogue finished tying up her boots.

"What's bothering you, Pagan?" Rogue asked, her soft inquiry drawing Melina's attention away from her station at the mass of computer screens.

Pagan opened her mouth to answer, then hesitated. She turned to look back at Melina who was waiting also, then down at Rogue's expectant face.

"You can tell us anything," Melina said.

Pagan looked down at the mask in her hands and made her decision on whether she could keep silent or not. "Erith had marks on her arm today."

"What kind of marks?" Melina asked.

"Bruises, handprints." Pagan held up a hand and mimicked a tight grip. "They looked like grab marks. She's got really pale skin so the marks stood out on her arm."

"What did she say about them?" Rogue asked.

Pagan rolled her eyes. "At first she said she'd fallen off her bike, but I called her on that excuse and told her she was lying." Pagan blew out a small puff of breath. "Then she told me her dad did it. That when he isn't taking out his frustrations on her mother, he turns them on her."

"The aftermath, perhaps, of what you saw that night through her window," Rogue said.

Pagan nodded. "I don't think this time she got away quick enough.

I can only imagine how much it must hurt. The bruises looked so angry. He must have gripped her really tight to leave evidence behind of it."

"Do you feel she is in danger?" Rogue asked.

"All I know is she is being hurt and she doesn't deserve to be." Pagan fastened her mask in place.

"No one deserves it, Pagan," Melina said. "I think you should check in on her tonight. Like you weren't going to check in on her building before you came home anyway."

"There's just something about her," Pagan said in a whisper.

"We'd already reached that conclusion," Rogue replied.

"I don't like her being hurt. No one deserves that, especially her."

"Then we'll have to make sure she isn't anymore," Melina said. "There is the little problem of her father being a part of our city's newest crime gang. But we'll deal with that when it raises its ugly head a little higher. For now, we'll concentrate on dealing with Erith alone."

Rogue nudged Pagan from her thoughts. "You really are worried about this woman, aren't you?"

Pagan nodded. "I saw the fear in her face as she tried to hold her father back from her bedroom door that night. I saw the same fear again today as she tried to shrug off his abuse as a drunken occurrence. I have seen him face-to-face and witnessed his hold on her through fear and anger. What kind of Sentinel would I be to ignore such an obvious cry for help?"

"She might not want your help," Rogue said.

"Then she can turn down the Sentinel if the Sentinel is called in. I won't take that personally, but as her friend I will be there for her."

Rogue patted Pagan's arm and looked over at Melina. "How did we ever raise such a noble Sentinel?"

"I don't honestly know, given that she had your influence," Melina replied saucily and laughed at Rogue's affronted look.

"You and I will talk later," Rogue said with a growl as she leaned down to kiss Melina's smiling lips soundly. She pushed a chuckling Pagan toward the elevator doors. "You're supposed to be noble. Stop giggling."

"Hey! Sentinels do not giggle," Pagan said as the elevator doors slid shut.

❖

Chastilian's towers were framed against a backdrop of stars. The moon hung heavy in the sky, lighting the rooftops in a brilliant silver hue. A police car stood idling in an alleyway, its lights on low, casting more shadows than shedding light into the darkness. Rogue stood in one of the shadows waiting for Sergeant Eddie Cauley to make his move. When he finally got out of his car, Rogue stepped forward and greeted him.

"Good evening to you, Sergeant. What brings you out at such an unsociable hour?"

Cauley held up a handful of files. "I told your Sighted I had come across some old files documenting the reign of terror perpetrated by one Xander Phoenix. It looks like someone is killing off his old gang members."

"So there is a connection between the last two deaths?" Rogue was pleased to have the Sighted's findings validated by the police's investigation.

"Miller and Quaid both ran in Phoenix's gang. Bear in mind, though, he was just beginning, but he started with such an explosion of power that his crimes seemed to come out of nowhere fast. He escalated from extortion to murder in the blink of an eye, and thankfully, because of the Sentinels, he was caught before he could continue." Cauley gave Rogue a considering look. "My father knew one of the Sentinels back then. He would never tell me his name but refers to him as 'that great man.'"

Rogue knew her father would be pleased to be thought of so highly by the chief of police who still ran the department and gave his support to the Sentinels of this generation. "Names aren't important as long as we fight against the same darkness that threatens Chastilian."

Cauley nodded. "Still, I'd love to meet the woman behind the voice of the Sighted I speak to." He grinned a little sheepishly. "She sounds beautiful."

Rogue stood a little taller, knowing it was Melina he spoke of so highly. "I'm sure your wife and various offspring would be agreeable to you meeting with some other woman on the strength of her voice."

Cauley let out a surprised bark of laughter. "How do you know about my family? Ah, the Sighteds, of course. So it's true. They really do have eyes and ears everywhere."

"Rest assured, the Sighted who has captivated your ears has a partner who worships the very ground she walks on."

Cauley's eyes narrowed a fraction and then he smiled. "I'm glad to hear that." He handed over the files. "These are copies I made for you. Also"—he opened one file and withdrew a photograph—"I had this copied too."

Rogue held the photograph up to a strip of pale light in the alley. She searched the faces of the men captured entering a restaurant. She recognized it immediately. "This is the Last Port in the Storm restaurant."

Cauley nodded. "We think this was taken by Mr. Osborne, the only proof we have of the gang threatening his business. Sadly, he died at their hands, as did his wife. But this photo shows five gang members and one Xander Phoenix."

"It's hard to make out the faces of the rest of the gang, but I recognize Miller and Quaid from their mug shots."

"Do we need to reinforce our firewalls at the station?"

Rogue merely smiled at him. "We'd just circumvent them again like usual." She tapped at one partially hidden face. "Who is this guy?"

Cauley leaned closer to look. "We have no idea. The trouble is, we know that Phoenix had more accomplices. He had to because he had some with him the night he killed the Osbornes, yet there were others setting fire to the restaurant."

"So why is this new guy going after the gang?" Rogue rubbed at her chin as she looked at the photograph. "Unless…"

"What?"

"Unless the ones being targeted are proof of the rumor that Phoenix was targeted in custody by his own men."

Cauley grinned. "That would make perfect sense! So now we need to identify these men so we can stop them from being next on the list."

"If these are the ones we are looking for. As you pointed out, not all the gang is here. And so far, we have had two deaths of very high-ranking people in the city. From gang roots to big trees with mighty roots. Miller and Quaid had huge business connections in Chastilian. They made good."

"But they started from badness."

"And the rottenness finally caught up with them."

❖

Pagan leaned against a wall close to Rogue and Sergeant Cauley. She could hear every word they were saying and desperately wanted to look at the photograph Rogue held. She started a little when Melina's voice sounded in her ear over the comlink.

"Pagan, I need you to come back home."

Pagan was instantly alert. "What's wrong?"

"We have a break-in in progress. It's Erith, and she's in the lighthouse."

"Repeat, Sighted?"

"You heard me. Get back here immediately. I'll fill Rogue in after. I think you might want to deal with this alone."

Pagan set off at a run.

"Is the lighthouse secure?" she asked as she took a shortcut through an adjacent alleyway and cut across the main road.

"I had everything secure anyway, but the minute the alarms triggered, I performed the double lockdown. She can't get any farther in the lighthouse. Although it appears she hasn't gotten any farther than to switch a computer on. She seems to be waiting for something else, because I know our computers don't take that long to load."

"Give me five minutes and I'll be there."

"I don't think this is a social call, Pagan."

"I don't think it is either, but I need to know why she's there and what she intends to do. And I need to do it before Rogue finds out, because she'll kill her and then very likely me too!"

"Rogue's still discussing theories with the sergeant. They'll be at it for ages yet."

"I'm near the lighthouse. I'll go through the back entrance." Pagan could feel the dread clawing at her guts as she got nearer. "Thanks, Melina."

"For what?"

"For calling me alone."

"She's your friend."

"Some friend that breaks into your home." Pagan disappeared behind the buildings that were adjacent to the lighthouse and entered the Security building. Once inside, she paused to take a breath and calm her racing heart. The base of the lighthouse had two entrances, the front door that housed the small office and a second entrance that doubled as a fire escape and led into the main building itself. Pagan opened that one carefully and stepped inside. She was hidden by the shelves of files and equipment that were housed at the rear of the room. Pagan hesitated a moment, knowing who she was going to find in the office. She steeled herself and moved a little closer to get a better view. It *was* Erith. Disappointment wrenched the air from her lungs, and she sagged against the doorjamb. She watched as Erith sat before the computer screen, seemingly mesmerized by the animated screensaver of a lighthouse. She wasn't even watching it, she was just *still*. Pagan couldn't help but wonder what Erith was thinking. She decided to find out and pushed herself away from the door.

"Do you have anything particular in mind, or are you just browsing?"

Erith let out a piercing scream that she hastily stifled behind her hands. She shot back from the desk on her chair and stared toward the door as if trying desperately to see who stood there. "What the fu— Who the hell are you?" Erith demanded. "What the hell are you doing in here?"

"Shouldn't I be asking that question?" Pagan asked.

"I…erm, I…" Erith slowly reached out to pick up her flashlight from the desk.

"You have no need for a weapon against me, Ms. Baylor. I can assure you of that."

Erith's eyes widened. "How do you know my name?"

"You're known to us."

"Us? There are more of you here?"

"No, just me and a thousand eyes. Did you really think you could just walk into a highly respected security office and not set off alarms?"

Erith sighed. "I thought it was strange that I wasn't greeted by the wailing of a million sirens. I thought I'd gotten lucky and that the owners were so sure that they were safe they hadn't alarmed their own place."

"No one is truly safe, Ms. Baylor. And the owners of this business are not stupid."

"Who are you?"

"Call me the *Night Watchman*, Ms. Baylor. You have no business being here." Pagan leaned back against the wall, staying in the shadow. "Care to tell me why you are?"

Erith tilted the flashlight up and caught Pagan in its beam. "How many night watchmen wear masks?" she asked, running the light down Pagan's body. "Who are you?"

"I'm someone who watches the city while it slumbers. And you are not sleeping." Pagan took a step closer. "What's on that computer that's so important that you cannot rest?"

Erith looked back at the screen. "I'm trying to tell myself that what I'm supposed to be doing is necessary." She gestured to the screen with a wave of her hand. "But I'm failing miserably. I never even got as far as trying to find the password to let me in. I just don't want to do it anymore." She leaned back in the chair and stared at Pagan. "Do you ever feel you are being pulled in two directions at once? One way is the good and proper path and the other…" Erith once again toyed with the torch that lit up her face and unwittingly revealed the exhaustion etched on her fine features. "The other is the one you have to tread if you don't want to trigger the consequences."

"What consequences will you face?"

"The same ones I've dealt with all of my life. If I don't do what is required of me, someone gets hurt."

"Is that someone you?"

"If it were just me, I could handle it. I'm stronger than I look."

"I have no doubt of that," Pagan murmured. "So make a stand. Don't do what is expected of you. Let everyone face their own fate."

"People could die."

"And you'd be to blame?"

"I'm always to blame." Erith took a business card from her jacket pocket. "I've let them down again, but even worse, I've let *her* down. She gave me this card, trusted me with it and with her. And I used it to get this address and broke right into her business. She has shown me nothing but kindness, and this is how I repay her." Erith put the card away. "What kind of friend am I?"

"But you didn't do what you came for."

"No, I didn't, and I will pay for that dearly. I've already had to sell my soul and risk my job. I stayed late one night and left the place unlocked so that someone could come in and take something. Turned out to be my boss's car."

"Take it away for what?"

Erith shrugged. "I wasn't privy to that piece of information. Just warned I needed to do it or else. So I did as I was told, like a good daughter should." Erith clamped her mouth shut as if realizing what she had just admitted.

"What does he need from here?"

Erith switched the computer screen off abruptly, plunging them into near darkness. Only the light shining from the moon outside lit the small office. "It doesn't matter."

"It matters to me, and it obviously mattered to you, otherwise you wouldn't be in here trying to steal whatever it was that was so necessary."

"This company did the security system at the car dealership I work for. They also did his private home. I was sent to get the security codes for both, to copy the layouts and find out how to disable them."

"Any idea why?"

"My father doesn't fill me in on the details. He just uses threats and then follows through on them."

"Why didn't you at least try to access the computer? The screensaver is nice and all, but you needed more information than that could give."

"Honestly? I'm frightened what this knowledge could be used for. Mr. Ammassari has been nothing but kind to me. And I've seen the news. There are nasty, despicable things happening in Chastilian, and I'm terrified my father is mixed up in it somehow. I won't trade my life for Tito's. Whatever my father is caught up in, they're going to have to do it without my help anymore. I won't be a part of the violence."

"Do you think your father is a part of the Phoenix's gang?"

Erith looked confused. "Phoenix?" She shook her head. "I haven't heard of anyone connected to my dad with that name."

"What's your father's trade?"

"He used to work in demolition," Erith said. "As for what he's doing now, he keeps it very quiet. But he's out a lot, so the apartment knows a little peace. I'm thankful for small mercies." She took a shaky breath. "Are you going to turn me in now?"

"Let me just walk you home. You have no more business here tonight." Pagan escorted Erith out of the office.

"You're not going to arrest me?"

"I'm not a police officer. Besides, you couldn't have gotten any information from that computer anyway. It's got more encryptions than the pyramids have hieroglyphics."

"Do the Ronchettis employ you to watch over their business?"

"I was in the neighborhood. It's my duty to seek out those who are where they don't belong."

"I don't think I belong anywhere. And I really don't want to go back home, but it seems I have nowhere else to go."

"Don't you have any friends here in Chastilian?"

"I have one friend," Erith said finally.

"Do you want to go to them?"

"No, just take me home. She doesn't deserve the baggage I bring along with me."

"She might think otherwise."

"Not tonight. Just let me go home." Erith started down the pavement and halted suddenly. "What are you going to do about my father? Are you going to inform him his daughter gave him away to the Sentinels?"

"No. He can remain ignorant in his bliss for now. But I need you to be careful around him, for your own sake."

"I have my bicycle here. I don't need an escort all the way back home, as scintillating as your company has been this evening." Erith seemed reluctant to go. Her gaze ran over Pagan's uniform. "Are you *really* a Sentinel?"

Pagan folded her arms. "What do *you* think?"

"I think the tales we are told as kids are nothing compared to the reality of seeing one in the flesh. Do you really live to protect the city?"

"As best we can."

"You know that there's something really evil brewing here, don't you? Here in Chastilian? My father seems to be involved, and he keeps trying to drag me in too. Can you stop him without him being hurt?"

"We can try. Go home now, Erith. You're safe tonight."

Erith let out a breathy laugh. "Sure I am, on the streets. It's behind closed doors where Sentinels don't step that the real danger lies." With that said, she mounted her bicycle and pedaled away from the lighthouse.

Pagan watched her go with a sinking feeling in her chest. "You can lock everything back up now," she said for Melina's ears.

"Rogue's nearly finished. You might as well come back in for the night."

Pagan watched Erith as she disappeared from her view. "She's in more trouble than I realized."

"We'll check closer into her family, see what the connection is she was talking of. I don't think she's any more involved except for what her father keeps pulling her into. But she needs to be warned. She's mixing with the wrong people and could get dragged deeper into their violence."

Pagan stared into the distance, not seeing anything but the red rage that was rapidly filling her sight. "Then her guardian angel needs to get her ass in gear, because they're starting to let their charge stand too close to the Phoenix's flames."

Pagan began to run in the opposite direction. She channeled all her fury, her disbelief, and her helplessness at Erith's predicament into pounding her feet on the pavement. Her mind was whirling with accusations and anger at Erith's stupidity for getting involved in something that could only end badly. Pagan followed the Sentinel way of life, but she also understood not everyone saw the world as she did. It was like a knife edge ripping into her flesh to realize that she had fallen in love with someone who apparently had started to follow the darker path in life. Pagan skidded to a halt so abruptly that she caught her shoulder on the edge of a building and spun herself around. For a long moment she stood doubled over, gasping for air, feeling the dull pain starting up in her still-damaged flesh. The night air burned her lungs as she sucked it in, and she tried to steady her frantic heartbeat.

Fallen in love. Pagan lowered her head and closed her eyes against the truth. She gingerly straightened and pushed away from the wall.

She looked up at the stars that had been her constant companions for so many years while she was out on patrol.

I've fallen for a bad girl. I finally make a connection with someone, and she's working for the other side! She shook her head at the stars. *Is this part of my destiny? To fight against evil, to avenge my parents' deaths, and to stupidly fall for the one redhead who happens to be unwittingly helping my archnemesis, Phoenix?*

"Pagan, are you all right?" Melina's voice came softly over the comlink.

Pagan stood up straighter and gave the stars one last curious look. "I'm fine, Sighted. Just marveling at the universe and its crazy plan for us all."

"Come home, stargazer."

Pagan jogged back toward the lighthouse whose beam called her home. But all the way there, she looked back over her shoulder at the indiscernible tugging that drew her heart in another direction.

❖

"Sighted, you've been awfully quiet in my ear this hour." Rogue spoke softly over the comlink. She was watching the police car finally drive away and was surprised to notice that Pagan was no longer in position.

"I called Pagan back to the lighthouse. We caught a Red Fox raiding the chicken coop."

"Say again?"

"We had a visitor in the lighthouse office."

Rogue began to head home. "And you let them in why?" She knew all too well that the lighthouse was fitted with enough security to scare away anyone daring to even lay a finger on the doorknob after hours.

"I was intrigued as to why she was daring to break and enter a place that has to be alarmed."

"This Red Fox of yours, do I know her?"

"It's Erith Baylor."

"I'll kill her!" Rogue fumed, her anger putting an extra speed to her step.

"Which is why I called Pagan away to deal with her. It would appear our fair Fox isn't pulling the strings but having hers pulled instead."

"A certain father figure in the background, perhaps?"

"I'll put out a more intense search on him. I don't think he's just a bully to his family. I think something bigger might be involved where he is concerned. And I found something out tonight. Seems Baylor knows his way around explosives. He's a demolitions expert."

"He's a worthy member to have on your team if you want mayhem and destruction to be your signature." Rogue clutched the files tightly in her hands. "I have information too. I have a picture of Phoenix's gang taken in your father's restaurant, and you won't believe whose face I recognize. None other than our friendly neighborhood car dealer, Tito Ammassari."

"No wonder he wanted security," Melina said.

"I think he's preparing for a visit from a new friend with an old name."

CHAPTER TWELVE

T he next morning, Pagan called the Ammassari Dealership and
    was told that Erith had called in sick. Pagan hung up.

"Who you calling?"

"Erith never came to work today."

"She was out late last night trying to hack into our computers.
Maybe she was too tired to go in today," Rogue replied, her irritation
more than apparent.

Pagan tried to ignore Rogue's simmering anger. "She's been
out much later than that and still come into work. I'm just worried
something happened when she got home."

"You need to keep your mind fixed on those sales slips and off the
sneak thief."

"*Rogue!*" Pagan was incensed by Rogue's remark.

"What are you going to do? Drive over there only to turn up
on her doorstep and question why she isn't at work? You're going to
look pretty damn foolish if she's off with a stomach bug or something
equally contagious. Keep your mind on the job at hand, Pagan. We have
a business to run."

"I'm just worried about her. It took a great amount of nerve for her
not to attempt access to what she'd been sent to retrieve last night."

"If she is in danger we'll race in, batons blazing, okay? I don't
want to see her hurt any more than you do." Rogue paused a moment,
then qualified, "Even if I am mad as hell at her at the moment."

"Thank you, Rogue."

Pagan had learned all too painfully that a Sentinel needed to
keep her identity hidden. Falling for a woman who might ultimately

betray her because of her own loyalty to family only added to Pagan's dilemma. Erith was linked, however unwittingly, with the Phoenix, which could carry dire consequences where the Sentinels were concerned. Pagan let out a deep sigh, torn between her loyalty to her family and the love she felt for Erith. As a Sentinel she was sworn to protect, but how could she protect someone who might ultimately bring all her secrets to light?

❖

Rogue shut the door behind her carefully and looked over at Melina, who was seated behind her desk. "Erith didn't turn up for work today."

"I had a feeling Pagan would have to check in on her. Did you stop her from charging over there?"

"Barely."

"I did a little investigating of my own. One of the Sentinels who lives nearby very kindly answered my call to check them out. She went masquerading as a door-to-door evangelist and was thankful she wasn't invited in, but she saw Erith and said she looked okay, subdued but okay. She also said she heard Erith call out to her mother and heard a voice answer back. Joe Baylor, however, is nowhere in the vicinity. It looks like he's out for the day already."

"He's probably got other business to attend to. But he'll be back." Rogue pulled Melina into her arms and nuzzled into her neck. "What are we getting ourselves mixed up in?"

"Something that obviously is already dragging Pagan in, heart first." Melina tightened her hold on Rogue's arms. "You saw this woman for yourself, what did you think?"

"On first glance I didn't see her emblazoned with the mark of the Phoenix, if that's what you want me to say. I saw a woman who really needs to eat something because she is so slender. I'm guessing she doesn't get to look after herself much. She's obviously as smart as a whip to have managed to survive in such a terrible situation for so long. All I got from her that day was her disappointment that Pagan wasn't the one visiting the car lot."

"If this is the one for Pagan we're going to be kept on our toes."

"She waits all this time to find a woman and then picks one that is trouble personified."

"But bad girls are more fun." Melina kissed along Rogue's jawline and grinned when Rogue pulled away to stare at her. "They are! They are larger than life, amazing to understand, and have that sense of danger that is such a huge turn-on."

"*I* am not a bad girl."

"No, *you* are very good at everything." Melina tugged her head down to kiss her.

"You're trying to distract me," Rogue grumbled, but let Melina kiss her way around her face until she could take it no longer and directed Melina's lips back to her own. She let Melina's tongue enter her mouth and twist lazily with hers. She took advantage of Melina's distraction and kissed her back with tender ferocity. Rogue felt her melt into her arms and let Rogue take what she wanted. When they finally broke apart, Melina looked both dazed and aroused.

"How long before Pagan finishes what she is doing?" Melina's voice was husky with longing.

Rogue ran her hands through Melina's long hair and marveled, not for the first time, at her beauty. She was eternally grateful to know where Melina's loyalties lay and was secure in the knowledge that when she needed someone, Melina was the one for her. "She'll be long enough for you to see how bad I really can be." Rogue led Melina out of her office and up the stairs to their bedroom. The lighthouse with its damnable secrets and Erith Baylor with her mysterious involvement could all be put on hold while Rogue gave her full attention to the one thing that really mattered in her life.

❖

Pagan had never known so few hours to go so very slowly. She had seen to her duties in the Security office with more than her usual determination, anxious not to have Rogue berate her for not being able to keep her mind on the job at hand. But the time for Pagan to don her Sentinel suit was a long time coming, and it chafed her to remain away from Erith's door. The whereabouts of Erith's father were still unknown. The Sentinels had been warned about him. The ever-watchful eyes of the city were seeking him out, waiting for him to come home.

Pagan impatiently watched the clock's slow hand tick away every second of the daylight and draw the night ever closer.

"What makes you so certain something will happen tonight?" Rogue asked as she finished her nightly routine of closing up the shop.

"What makes you think there won't be trouble?" Pagan stood at the window with her arms folded, watching the waning sun sink a little lower in the sky. "She didn't get what she'd been sent to collect. There are consequences, she said. And we know that the one he hurts to keep Erith in line is her mother."

"Which would go a long way to explain why she's never just up and left."

"Family has a huge hold on you when you love someone." Pagan shoved her hands in her pockets to stifle the need to punch something hard. "If you know how to use that particular tool against someone, it can be devastating."

"You need to be focused. Calmness and a level head will serve you better than anger and the need for revenge."

"Sometimes I feel a rage so deep inside me that it wants to burst to the surface and make my head explode." Pagan couldn't bring herself to look at Rogue. She feared she'd see nothing but disappointment there. She was surprised when a hand tipped her chin up and Rogue fixed her with a look of understanding.

"It's good to recognize the power that rage holds inside you; it's even better to temper it and use it wisely. In some ways you are very much like your sister, so noble and bright following the path destiny has laid out for you, for all it has taken from you."

"And in other ways you are the spitting image of Rogue." Melina entered the room and reached out to hold a hand from each of them. "So determined to save the world single-handed. Sentinels are not ones who fight alone. They call upon their fellow Sentinels to assist them. They rely on the Sighted to guide them. And they have the backing of the families that love them and support them in all they endeavor to do to keep this city safe." Melina turned to Pagan. "We know what you want to do. You want to go out tonight and check that Erith is okay."

"I have to," Pagan said.

"And if we tell you that what you are electing to do is both foolhardy and stupid, then what?" Melina asked.

Pagan felt her anger bristle but tried to temper it. "Then I'd hear your words and ask you to understand mine. I need to go to her. I think she's in grave danger and I need to help her."

"We can't save everyone," Rogue said.

"But I need to save *her*."

"Should you be needed to aid someone who has come to mean much to you, then you need to do so wisely. Who you are cannot be jeopardized for the sake of one in trouble. If you are recognized, then we are all in danger. Never compromise your family," Melina said.

"I understand."

Melina shifted her attention to Rogue. "You know this city like the back of your hand. It's your territory. But tonight, this will be Pagan's call, as it has been from the start. So I'm going to request that you remain here until we are certain that Erith is safe and Pagan can once again put the rest of the city first."

"She's to receive no backup from me?"

"This is going to be Pagan's mission. If she is intent on going against our wishes in this matter, then she needs to go it completely alone." Melina cocked her head at Pagan. "Think you can handle it?"

Pagan was astounded by Melina's directive. She didn't expect them to leave her without backup. Only then did Pagan realize what it cost her sister to let her go. "I have been taught by the best," she said.

Rogue snorted. "Flattery will get you nowhere."

"I speak the truth." Pagan looked over her shoulder as the sun dipped lower. "I've held back all day. Let me go out now. Let me put my mind at rest that she's safe."

Melina released her hand. "Go suit up and prepare for the night."

"I won't let you down. I promise. But she might need me, and I have to heed that call tonight."

❖

Pagan ran from the room.

"What are you doing, sweetness?" Rogue asked Melina.

"If she truly believes she has to save this woman, then she has to do it herself. She's old enough to be her own Sentinel and she needs to prove it to herself. Some day, this city will be hers alone to watch over."

"So soon to put me out to pasture, are you?"

Melina chuckled at her. "No, but when you're too old to race across the rooftops I'd like you here in my arms in one piece for me to cherish while our Pagan keeps us safe in the night."

"Time to let go of the reins, eh?"

"Time for us both to let our girl grow up and meet her own destiny head-on as the woman she is now."

Rogue hugged Melina to her. "Tonight should be quite a night, then."

"You can do this, Rogue. You took her as your own, you gave her some semblance of hearing back, and you've helped me bring her up to be such a wonderful adult. Now let her be her own Sentinel, big and brave enough to make her own mistakes."

"And if she needs my help tonight?"

"Then let her ask for it."

"I can do that."

"I have every faith in you." Melina's praise was accompanied by a wry smile.

Rogue blew out a breath. "God, who knew kids could be so hard?"

Melina just chuckled at her. "Like you didn't enjoy every minute watching her grow. Maybe we should have had some of our own for you to adore." She turned and sauntered from the shop floor. "We still have time. I could ask any number of cousins who are willing to aid us." The door closed softly behind her, and suddenly Rogue found that Pagan being out on her own that night was the least of her worries.

❖

Just as Pagan left the lighthouse, another Sighted confirmed her worst fear; Baylor was on his way home. She sped across the city, leaping from rooftop to fire escape, all the while focusing on the apartment building she knew was just a little farther ahead. She listened to the satisfying snick of the wire shooting across one wide divide and felt the pull as the grapple reached its target. Pagan launched herself once more into thin air and slid down the wire to land with her feet firmly planted on rusted steel bars. With silent stealth, she situated herself on the fire escape outside Erith's room. It had been a race across the city to see who got to the building first.

Joe Baylor won.

Pagan could hear the awful sounds coming from inside the apartment. A sudden crack in the glass in the window next to Erith's caught Pagan's attention. It spiraled out like a huge spider's web.

"I'm going in," Pagan said.

"Be careful," Melina said over the comlink.

Pagan eased up the window in Erith's room and slid inside. She could hear Erith's voice, the tone wavering, her words shaking with obvious fear.

"Come on, Dad, calm down," she was pleading, her voice thick with tears.

Pagan cautiously peered around the door frame. She first saw the prone body of a woman on the floor, half in and half out of the hallway, her face bloody and bruised. She could only hear Erith, but what she heard chilled her to her core.

"I have done everything you have asked from me. I have tried to be the dutiful daughter you seem to think I am incapable of being. But this is wrong, Dad. Can't you see that? I can't keep doing the things that you want. Sooner or later, I'm going to get caught doing your dirty work."

"You deserve to be, you little coward. All I asked was for the codes, and you couldn't even do that for me. You are pathetic, just like your mother."

Pagan heard him smash something, and Erith's scream signified it had obviously hit a little too close for comfort.

"I should have pushed her harder this morning when she told me you weren't here with what I'd asked for. Her excuses were lame, even for her." His laughter was cruel. "It's just a damned shame these windows are built so strong. You could have come home to find your mother waiting on the pavement for you."

Pagan wondered just where Erith had spent the night once she'd supposedly returned home from the lighthouse. The lights in the room suddenly went out with swift pops, plunging the room into darkness.

Pagan sent a silent thank-you to Melina, who she knew was responsible for that feat. Melina had called it her favorite party trick to overload the circuits and blow out all the lights.

Pagan carefully opened the door a little further and then stepped in. She saw Erith's eyes widen as she witnessed her enter as if from nowhere. Pagan headed straight for Joe Baylor and grabbed his arm to disable him. He roared with surprise and rage and then with pain when Pagan applied enough pressure to make him drop the knife he'd been brandishing at Erith.

"Who the hell are you? Get the hell out of my house!" he screamed, trying to punch Pagan with his free hand.

Pagan ducked easily as she kicked him in the back of his knees so he collapsed. She swiftly cuffed his hands behind his back with her plastic binders and secured his legs as well. Then she picked the knife up and attached it to her belt.

"What the hell are you doing here, you freak?" Baylor spat out. "Who do you think you are, coming into my home, stealing my knife, all dressed up like some clown?"

Pagan grabbed a handful of his hair and smacked his head into the carpet. "Shut up," she said. She looked at Erith, who was stock-still in the middle of the room. Pagan looked closer, and even in the near dark she could see an angry-looking bruise already starting to form on Erith's face.

"Are you okay?" Pagan asked, her fear for Erith coloring her voice and pitching it at a deeper tone.

Erith nodded dumbly, obviously shocked by the turn of events. Gathering her wits, she rushed over to her mother, who was gingerly fingering her bloodied face.

"She needs a hospital," Pagan said and was startled by the pitiful keening sound that came from the woman's mouth.

"Noooooooo," Mrs. Baylor wailed, sounding like an animal in distress.

Pagan looked at Erith, who just shook her head. "If she goes to the hospital, they'll ask how this happened, and she won't ever tell them."

"Smart woman," Baylor hissed.

Pagan bounced his head off the floor again for good measure. She had the satisfaction of hearing his nose break.

"How about you?" Pagan said to Erith.

Erith touched her cheek and gingerly worked her jaw. "I'm sick and tired of this," she said.

"Shut up, girl, or I'll cut you another lip!" her father warned.

Pagan got up from where she'd been kneeling beside him. She ignored his protests as she laid her boot on his head and kept him chewing the carpet to shut him up.

"If you want to leave, I can help you." Pagan held his head down as she felt him writhe beneath her. "Both of you."

Erith looked at her mother. She shook her head. "Mom, please," Erith said. "This can't keep happening. You're running out of bones to break."

"My place is with your father," her mother said weakly.

Pagan felt Erith's pain as she stared at her mother in utter disbelief.

"Even now, after what he did to you *this* time, after what he was going to do to *me*?"

"For better or for worse," her mother replied, eyeing Baylor fearfully. Even with him bound and pinned to the floor, the woman's absolute terror of him was palpable.

Pagan caught the faint sound of approaching sirens. "The police are already on their way."

Mrs. Baylor began to wail, and Baylor began to struggle again under Pagan's boot.

"They won't keep him long. Mom won't say anything against him."

"What about you?"

Erith looked at her father tied up on the floor, his face smashed into the carpet under Pagan's boot. Erith shook her head sadly. "It's more than my life's worth." She sighed. "He'd just take it out on Mom yet again."

Pagan held her hand out to Erith. "If you want to leave, I can take you somewhere safe."

Erith looked at her mother, who pushed her toward the Sentinel with a weak hand. "Go, I'll be okay. You need to go. It's way past time you left us."

"Run, girl," Baylor muttered.

Erith ignored him, her attention firmly fixed on her battered mother. "I can't keep living like this, Mom. I thought this move would stop it, but it's just gotten worse."

"You can come back later. He'll be better again, like he always is. For now, just go," her mother said.

"How do you know you can trust this clown, Erith?" Her father struggled to turn over to fix angry eyes on her.

Erith knelt down and kissed her mother's forehead, then carefully picked her way over broken furniture to where Pagan stood. Pagan tried not to look away too quickly and hoped the shadows hid her identity.

"Eyes don't lie, Daddy," Erith said simply. She crouched down beside him. "Please try to get help this time."

His features softened fractionally and he nodded. "Get out of here."

Pagan took her foot off Baylor's head and he flipped over to look at her. "Hurt her and I'll be down on you like a ton of bricks."

"I'll leave the hurting to you, *sir*. It seems you're quite the expert at it."

Baylor sneered. "This Phoenix will rid Chastilian of you Sentinels. He'll blow you all away. I'll be sure to dance a merry jig on your grave especially, *sir*!"

Pagan turned to Erith. "Gather what you need now."

"I'll be ready for you next time," Baylor said.

Pagan stared at him while Erith rushed past her to get things from her room. She leaned closer to him. "You won't get the chance to even see me if there is a next time." She had the satisfaction of seeing him swallow hard. She straightened back up and cast an eye at Erith's mother, who was watching her fearfully. "Lady, I suggest that you find a way to inject the strength you have just shown for your daughter into your own backbone." With that Pagan left them alone.

Erith held up her backpack for approval when Pagan entered her bedroom.

"Is that all you need?" Pagan asked.

"I was getting ready to run away. I was already prepared." Erith looked at her opened window. "Is that how you got in here?"

Pagan heard the distant footsteps of the police heading down the hallway. "Later. We need to go now." She led Erith out onto the fire escape. She let Erith shoulder her backpack, then stopped her from heading down the stairs. "We need to go another way. The police are gathered below."

"But you're one of the good guys, aren't you?"

"Yes, but that doesn't mean I cavort with the police at every given moment." Pagan held out her arm. "Trust me, please. I'm here to keep you safe."

"My very own guardian angel, eh?" Erith said shakily as she stepped into Pagan's hold. Pagan fastened a connecting hook from her utility belt to Erith's body.

"Something like that," Pagan said and helped Erith up onto the fire escape railing. "Hold on tight!"

Erith's startled scream was lost amid the high-rise towers. Just another sound among millions in the noisy city where screams were commonplace and ignored by tired ears.

Pagan shot out her wire to the next building, and they glided across the gap between the towers. She held Erith close, protecting her from the landing as they careened toward the wall. Pagan stopped mere inches away from the brickwork, then she slowly let the wire lower them to the ground, changing its settings to facilitate the move, marveling once more at the technology in the palm of her hand.

Erith watched her with open fascination. "Where does all that wire go? Is it all in that gun casing?"

"Pretty much." Pagan focused on getting them to the ground in one piece. Having another body on the wire was affecting the swing, plus having Erith's body against her own was affecting her concentration.

"That's an ingenious design." Erith's eyes were trained on the wire above them. She then looked down. "Geez! That's a very long drop!" Her hold around Pagan tightened. "You're not going to suddenly let go, are you?"

"Never," Pagan replied solemnly. She looked down to find Erith's bright eyes looking intently into hers. Pagan looked away first. "We need to get you to a safe place."

"I'd settle for a bed somewhere where Dad can't come in and drag me out to watch him beat the living daylights out of Mom again."

"Why doesn't your mom just leave him?"

"Because he'd kill her."

"And what he's doing now is okay because he hasn't killed her yet?"

"For some people, fear and pain are the only ways they know they are alive," Erith said as she crowded in closer to Pagan's side. "My mom died inside years ago, I think."

"You were very brave to leave tonight."

"Your timely arrival gave me the strength to do it. I felt I could really leave this time. And I just can't take it anymore. I've stayed with my parents longer than any child should. I hoped that my being there would help my mom, but instead I just got more and more tangled in the violence, both in the house and out, it would seem."

"Will he come after you?"

"No, he knows I'll go back sooner or later because of Mom," Erith said glumly. "And to see him. He is my dad, after all."

Pagan nodded, respecting Erith's feelings though not entirely understanding her loyalty.

"Familial loyalty is a curious beast, Pagan," Melina said softly, her voice finally returning to Pagan's ears. "Take your charge somewhere safe. You know where is available. Then come home. The other Sentinels are watching over Chastilian tonight. If they need your help they'll call."

"How safe is the place you're going to take me to?" Erith asked.

Pagan couldn't help but wonder if that was what Erith had really been about to ask. She had seen something else written on her face.

"Very safe." Pagan made a spur-of-the-moment decision. She eased them carefully to the pavement, and with a press of a button, gathered up the wire with barely a sound. She was gratified to note that Erith didn't shift very far away from her even when she unfastened the hook.

"My dad recognized you as a Sentinel," Erith said, her eyes running over Pagan's protective leather.

Under the intense scrutiny she was receiving, Pagan wondered if she needed to strike a heroic pose as proof to her Sentinel status. She tried not to smile as that thought tickled some crazy part of her tired brain. "Must be all the leather that gives me away."

"I didn't think they existed until last night. I thought they were just a fairy tale that the people of Chastilian lulled their kids to sleep with. 'Go to sleep, sweetie, the Sentinels will watch over you.'"

Pagan smiled at the thought. "That's cute. I've never heard of us being compared to baby sitters."

"Not wearing those masks and suits, no." Her eyes drifted up Pagan's body. "My mom used to tell me the stories about the Sentinels that she'd heard watched over Chastilian, and that when things got bad, they would come and save people." She chewed on her bottom lip. "Not so much a fairy tale now, are you? You did exactly what she said they do. You came in and saved *me*. Twice now. You're the same one from last night, aren't you? My own private Sentinel." Erith shook her head as if clearing it of the stories. "So, what are baby Sentinels told as tales to make them fall asleep?"

Pagan grinned. "Probably stories about red-haired baby girls that need baby Sentinels to rescue them."

Erith punched at Pagan's arm in laughter and shook her hand as it landed solidly. "Ow! What is it with me hitting people who are made out of stone?"

"Hit many, do you?" Pagan asked.

"Just the one, she's as solid as a rock as well." Erith stuffed her hands into her pockets. "But soft too, I'm learning."

"Soft is no bad thing."

"No, it's wonderful," Erith replied. "So tell me where my new home is before the excitement kills me and I don't get enough sleep before work tomorrow."

"It's somewhere you'll feel safe and hopefully will come to look upon as home," Pagan replied, changing directions from her intended route. She heard Melina in her ear question her course, but she very slyly turned the volume down and tuned her out.

"Pagan, if you are considering what we think you're doing!" Rogue's voice sounded in her head. "Turn your feet around right this second, Pagan Osborne!"

"You'll be safe there, I promise. They're nice people. You'll like them," Pagan said over the muted sounds of disbelief she could just make out in her aids. She had never been more conflicted as to where her loyalties lay. Erith represented all that was dangerous to bring into the heart of a Sentinel home. The risk of exposure alone was enough to make Pagan question her motives. She looked down at the woman beside her and took a far greater leap into the unknown than she ever did when jumping from Chastilian's towers. This time she had no wire to guide her flight. Pagan took the riskiest leap of all, one of faith for Erith.

CHAPTER THIRTEEN

The Ronchetti Security lighthouse beam shone into the night sky and drew Pagan and Erith toward it. Erith was still as close as she could be to Pagan without knocking her over. Pagan briefly wondered if Erith had noticed the same recognizable height difference that was so obvious to her. She was curious at Erith's instinctive trust for the masked figure that had broken in and taken her from her home.

Erith gasped as they rounded the corner. "Tell me you're not taking me there!" She quickly spun around and started back the way they had come.

Pagan easily caught hold of her arm and halted her flight. "Whoa, wait a minute."

Erith pointed at the lighthouse almost in accusation. "You know I can't go there!" She crowded in close to Pagan to harshly whisper, "You caught me in there just last night!"

"You need a safe place. Where's safer than with the local security specialists?"

Erith stared at her incredulously. "You're crazy!"

"Maybe so, but I guarantee you'll receive a better welcome there than you would if I took you back home." She watched as Erith conceded that point. She nudged Erith forward again.

Erith was favoring the lighthouse with an exacting eye. "Look at how the light doesn't truly beam out at a concentrated strength. I wonder what filter they used for that trick."

Pagan looked down at her with unmasked surprise. Erith grinned back up at her.

"What? Don't I look like someone who would know that kind of thing? You'd be surprised what I know."

"I try to not judge anyone by their appearance," Pagan said sweeping a hand down at herself with a deprecating gesture. Erith just chuckled at her.

Pagan guided Erith across the road to place her at the front door to the shop.

"This isn't what I expected when you mentioned a safe house." Erith cupped her hands upon the windowpane and peered inside the darkened shop.

"It's going to be perfect for you," Pagan said and began to back away.

"Hey!" Erith grabbed Pagan to pull her back. "You can't just leave me on the doorstep like some unwanted kitten."

"Ring the bell," she said softly and slipped away into the darkness, leaving Erith on her doorstep.

"Pagan Osborne, you and I are going to have some serious words about your idea of safe houses," Melina said in Pagan's ear when she finally turned back up the volume on her comlink.

"Her father is involved with this Phoenix. And she's been forced to do some of his dirty work. Would any place be truly safe for her with that knowledge?" Pagan asked.

"You're going to have to be quick to pull this off," Rogue grumbled through Pagan's comlink.

"Quick is my middle name," Pagan muttered as she rushed through the underground garage to get into the lighthouse. She was shaking with nerves as the elevator whisked its way up into the lighthouse tower.

"No, I believe *trouble* will be your middle name from now on."

Pagan winced at the anger in Rogue's voice as she stepped from the elevator. Pagan then heard the doorbell chimes ring through the building. She burst into the tower to be confronted by Rogue and Melina, both with their arms folded and harsh looks on their faces.

"Well, don't just stand there. Go let her in!" Pagan said as she hastily tried to divest herself of her outer layers. Neither Melina nor Rogue moved. They just watched her stonily. Pagan nearly toppled over trying to get her boots off. "Please!" she said. "She needs to be safe, and for now I feel that she's best cared for by us."

Melina looked at Rogue uncertainly. Rogue's face remained stony.

"Don't look at me like that. She's *your* sister," Rogue said and turned abruptly. "Come on, Mel. Let's go greet our unexpected *guest*."

Melina dutifully followed after her. She gave Pagan a look before she closed the door. "You'd better hurry and come get your friend settled."

Pagan nodded and hastily hung up her leathers and her mask. She ran into her bedroom, grabbed a pair of sweatpants, and jumped into them. She looked around her room carefully, making sure there was nothing visible to reveal her secrets. Once she was satisfied, she clattered out of the room and down the stairs toward the shop. She paused at the bottom to catch her breath. She sneaked a look around the door frame and could see Erith standing nervously at the door. She was twisting the straps to her backpack under the curious stares of Rogue and Melina.

"Sorry if I woke you guys up," Erith began with a faltering voice. "I think this might have been a huge mistake."

"Who are you?" Melina asked. "And what are you doing here at this time of night?"

"I'm Erith Baylor," she replied, and then rolled her eyes expressively. "And you wouldn't believe me if I tried to explain why I'm here. I think this is someone's cruel idea of a joke." She looked at them both. "I was told this was a safe place for me to be by some person in a mask…" Erith's voice faltered as she saw Pagan coming through the back door. "Pagan!" The relief in Erith's voice was painfully obvious, and Rogue and Melina stepped aside as Erith rushed past them. Pagan's arms immediately wrapped about her to hold her close.

"Are you okay?" Pagan asked.

"I take it you know this woman, Pagan?" Melina asked, playing her role well.

"This is my friend Erith from the Ammassari car lot, *remember?*"

"Take her upstairs." Rogue sighed and began to once more lock up the shop.

Pagan led a still-clinging Erith into their living quarters.

"I'm sorry to have bothered everyone," Erith mumbled as she looked between Pagan and the others. Her brow furrowed as she took in their clothing. "Weren't any of you in bed yet?" she asked, noticing the lack of nightwear.

"The security office never sleeps," Rogue said bluntly.

Pagan helped Erith take off her backpack and then settled her on the sofa. She knelt before her, very aware that Erith was shaking slightly.

"You're going to think I'm crazy." Erith rubbed a hand over her forehead. "I'm beginning to think I am. You would not believe the night I've had so far." She looked around at everything and everybody. Her eyes fell back on Pagan. "Do you know how distinctive that lighthouse of yours is?"

"I'm so used to it I tend to forget," Pagan said.

"It's beautiful." Erith raised hopeful eyes to meet Pagan's. "Is it really a port in the storm to ones who need it?"

"You know you're very welcome here, if you need a place to stay."

"I was brought here," Erith said. "They said I'd be safe here."

"Really?" Melina asked, easing down beside Erith on the sofa armed with a bowl of warm water and a few medical supplies. She began to clean up Erith's face as if she did it for every visitor who dropped by in the dead of night. "Who brought you here?"

"A Sentinel."

Melina's eyebrows rose. "You met a Sentinel?"

Erith nodded. "He said...no, wait...you know, I don't think he was a he after all." She sat motionless while Melina wiped away blood from her forehead "There was something..." Erith paused. "You know the feeling you get when you think you know someone but you don't?" Melina nodded. "I got that feeling with the Sentinel. I knew I could trust him, her, whatever."

"So they brought you here why, exactly?"

Pagan gave Melina a long stare that she studiously ignored.

"My dad was beating on me and my mom. The Sentinel came in and stopped him before he could go any further. Then the Sentinel asked if I wanted to leave."

"So you left your parents?" Melina continued her questioning, palpitating Erith's cheek to check that no bones had been broken.

"I couldn't take it anymore," Erith whispered, her horror at the evening, and countless others just like it, evident in her face. "He'd gotten a knife this time. He doesn't usually have to resort to weapons. His fists and feet are lethal enough."

Melina nodded slowly, eyeing the furious mark on Erith's face. "The Sentinel must have known you needed to be with someone you would be comfortable with. A friend would especially fit that role." She looked at Pagan, who was hanging on her every word. "I'm Melina, Pagan's sister. I'm pleased to meet you, Erith." Melina laid aside her bowl and held out her hand.

Erith shook it solemnly. "Thank you for your kindness. I will try to repay you somehow, someday."

"I don't need anything from you except a promise that if you need anything, you will come to us and ask."

Erith cast nervous eyes over at a silent Rogue. "We meet again, Rogue."

Rogue nodded just once. Erith turned back to Pagan and leaned forward to whisper, "I'd still want her on my side of a brawl too."

Pagan choked back a chuckle and even Melina bit back a smile. Rogue just stared at them, her arms folded, obviously still fuming.

"We have a spare room for guests," Pagan said. "You need to sleep. We both have work in just a few hours."

Erith yawned and then belatedly held her hand up to her mouth. "Sorry. Who'd have thought flying through the city would make me so sleepy?"

"You flew?" Pagan asked, reaching for Erith's backpack. She held out a hand to help Erith up off the sofa.

"Yeah, the Sentinel flew me right out of my bedroom window." Erith mimicked the movements with a series of grandiose hand gestures.

"Yeah, right," Pagan snorted.

"Did too!" Erith punched at Pagan's arm and then frowned. She shook her head as if to clear it. "This has been a weird night."

"Let's get you settled," Pagan said as she ushered her up the stairs.

"Pagan, I still need to talk to you," Rogue said.

"Tomorrow, I promise. We'll talk and I'll do whatever you need me to do." She left Erith halfway up the stairs and backtracked to kiss Melina good night. "Thank you," she whispered. Melina nodded at her. Pagan looked at Rogue, who just stared at her and then raised a finger and tapped on her cheek. Pagan smiled slightly and dutifully kissed her cheek.

"I am going to beat you so hard in training tomorrow you won't have any thoughts left in your damn fool head," Rogue whispered sweetly.

"Thank you, I look forward to that," Pagan said with a smile, but she swallowed hard as she tried not to let the fear show on her face.

"You have a nice family," Erith said when Pagan rejoined her. "Do you always kiss them good night?"

"Sometimes, if it's been a rough kind of day," Pagan said. "I'd hate not to let them know that I love them."

"I kissed my mom good-bye tonight, but not my dad."

Pagan remained silent, waiting for Erith to continue.

"Does that mean I love him any less?"

"No, maybe it just means you knew your mom needed it more."

"You haven't asked me anything about what happened tonight, do you know that? Your sister did, but you haven't."

Pagan directed her into the guest bedroom.

"This is lovely," Erith said, running her fingers softly over the bed cover. "Why haven't you asked?"

"Because I figure in time, if you want me to know, you'll tell me. And if you don't want to tell me, that's okay too. I just want you to know you're safe here."

"The Sentinel brought me to you, didn't she?"

"So you think it's a *she* now?" Pagan teased.

Erith sat down on the bed and began to undo her boots. "Let me put it another way. The gender-nonspecific Sentinel, who swooped into my home, rescued me from my tyrannical father, and then flew me around Chastilian suspended only by a wire…brought me to *you*."

"Did you tell this Sentinel about me?"

"No," Erith replied. Her eyes suddenly grew very large. "Do you think they can read minds?"

"I haven't heard of that particular specialty among the whole flying and fighting things. Your innermost thoughts are probably safe."

Erith relaxed a little. She dangled her feet above the floor like a little child. "So, you live in a lighthouse?" Erith's grin was contagious.

"How cool is that?" Pagan grinned back.

"Very cool. It must make for one hell of a night-light."

"You can never lose your way home, that's for sure."

"That's a good thing to know." Erith stared at her feet. "Do you think Melina and Rogue are mad at me for being here?"

"No. They recognize you need to be here. The Sentinel must have brought you here for a very good reason."

"I think it was *you*," Erith said softly.

"*What*?"

"I think the Sentinel brought me here *because* of you," Erith explained further.

Pagan let out a soft, slow breath. "I see." She felt her heart rate go back to something resembling a normal beat. "We must have friends in high places who know about us."

"I guess so." Erith finished her words with a large yawn.

"You need to sleep. The kitchen is to the right of the stairs we just came up. I'll see you down there at seven thirty in the morning. I'll take you into work."

"I'm going to sleep all through the typing I have to do tomorrow," Erith mumbled as she began to divest herself of her jacket.

"You could do it blindfolded, I bet." Pagan made to leave the room but was halted by a hand tugging on her waistband.

Erith stood, and standing on her tiptoes, placed a soft kiss on Pagan's cheek.

"What was that for?" Pagan asked huskily, relishing the fleeting feel of Erith's lips on her skin.

"Thank you for letting me stay here."

"You are very welcome. I'll see you in the morning...*later* this morning." She closed the door behind her and for a moment just stayed outside the door, listening to the sounds of Erith moving around inside. She touched her cheek where Erith's lips had rested, deciding that whatever punishment Rogue was going to mete out to her, that gentle kiss had made it all worth while. Everything that Pagan had done that night, both masked and unmasked, had been worth it for that one simple kiss of gratitude.

❖

Pagan paused at the doorway to the kitchen and watched as Erith diligently listened to Melina's instructions. She grinned at the sight of

Erith, in her black baggy clothing adorned with flames, being taught how to make the perfect Last Port in the Storm breakfast omelet, something Melina had learned from her mother when the restaurant had been in its prime.

Melina towered over Erith as she supervised her whisking. "Of course, you realize, if you reveal the ingredients to this omelet, I will be forced to make sure you disappear from the face of the earth." The threat was somewhat belied by the smile on her face.

"I promise not to tell a soul on point of torture," Erith vowed and poured the frothy mixture into a waiting pan.

"How do you feel this morning?" Melina asked, reaching out to push back a bright red lock of hair so she could better see Erith's face. The marks stood out angrily on Erith's pale skin.

"Surreal," Erith replied. "I mean, I'm taken from my home in the middle of a domestic dispute, rescued by somebody in a very funky leather suit and mask. I'm brought here, which just happens to be my friend's home." She shrugged. "And I'm being shown how to make omelets, which is a first for me as I was brought up on a diet of cereal and doughnuts. Suffice to say, I'm feeling anything but ordinary."

Melina handed Erith a spatula to flip the omelet over. Pagan watched as Erith did so with much care and attention to Melina's instructions. She finally sauntered into the kitchen, lured in by the tantalizing aroma of breakfast. Erith's smile lit up the room when she saw her.

"Good morning, Pagan."

"Good morning. What are you making that smells so divine?" Pagan sniffed appreciatively at the air and moved closer to peer over Erith's shoulder.

"Omelets," Erith said, watching the concoction sizzling in the pan. "My first, using your sister's ingredients."

"Oho, you can't ever leave now," Pagan said. She raised her gaze to her sister. "Did you make her swear the blood oath?"

Melina shook her head. "I was saving the blood thing until *after* breakfast. That way, I get to clean up everything at once."

Pagan and Melina shared a wicked look as Erith's head bobbed between them as she tried to gauge their seriousness. Erith shook her head at their obvious teasing.

"Oh, this is just perfect. I get left on the doorstep of Bobo the

Clown's Home for Wayward Jokers." She turned back to her omelet and dismissed their laughter.

"Hey, you pair." Rogue's voice sounded over Pagan and Melina's amusement. "No teasing the hired help." She joined everyone to stand over Erith. "Nice touch," she said as Erith flipped the fluffy omelet onto a plate.

"I'm very talented with my hands," Erith said and then blushed a shade as deep red as her hair.

Rogue patted a mortified Erith on her shoulder. "My, my, aren't you the answer to many a maiden's prayer."

Erith's face burned even brighter.

"Erith, I think you should eat your omelet, considering all the hard work you've put into it." Melina pushed her toward the table and handed her the plate.

Erith sat down but placed the plate before Pagan. "I'd like you to try it," she said.

Pagan looked at her before picking up her fork. "Are you sure?"

Erith nodded. "I believe you should share a first with a friend."

Rogue apparently choked on a swallow of juice, and Melina rushed to her side to pound on her back.

Pagan cut a piece from the omelet and held it out for Erith to taste. Erith did so, then Pagan cut a piece for herself and chewed the soft eggs.

"How is it?" Erith asked.

"Wonderful," Pagan replied, ignoring Rogue's coughing. She handed Erith a fork and gestured for them both to eat Erith's first homemade breakfast.

"Think your sister will let me pay room and board while I'm here?" Erith asked quietly. "I'd like to pay my way."

"We'll see," Pagan replied, and unobtrusively made sure Erith had plenty to eat.

Rogue finally joined the breakfast table while Melina continued preparing everyone's breakfast.

"It's nice to have breakfast without a bottle of whiskey taking center place at the table," Erith said. She took a mouthful of omelet, then asked, "Do you think my mom's all right?"

Melina turned from the stove. "I'll find out for you, if you'd like. I have friends I can ask."

"Please, if it's no bother."

"Leave it to me, then."

Once breakfast was over, Pagan and Erith both disappeared to finish getting ready for work. Pagan found Erith waiting for her at the bottom of the stairs.

Melina held out lunch in separate bags.

"Thank you," Erith mumbled, then shyly hugged Melina. "Thank you for all the other lunches too that I think were more your hand than Pagan's here."

"You're very welcome, Erith." She drew back but didn't release Erith from her gentle hold. "You're safe here. Don't think otherwise. I know it's all a bit confusing for you, but it will be okay. We'll sort things out day by day, all right?"

"Can I ask something?"

"Go ahead."

Erith seemed to almost change her mind under Melina's silent scrutiny but then forged on. "Do you know the Sentinels, or does the fact that I was just dropped on your doorstep out of the blue by one of the city's biggest mysteries not faze you in the least? I mean, last night, I came in here battered and bloodied, and you just cleaned me up like it happened every night of the week."

Melina considered her answer for a long moment. "You're more than aware that some things are best kept silent?"

Erith nodded.

"Then know that you were safe with the Sentinel who brought you here, and you're safe with us now."

"So, you're on the good guys' side? You and Rogue?"

Melina nodded, then asked, "Why didn't you include Pagan?"

"I've known Pagan was a good guy from the minute I laid eyes on her. It's a given where Pagan Osborne is concerned."

"A natural hero, eh?"

"Heroine," Erith corrected.

"Well, this Pagan, who doesn't feel very heroic this morning because she has three places that need wiring for alarms ASAP, thinks we should get going."

Melina gave Erith a small hug and then released her. "You two take care today. Erith, don't worry about your mother. I'll see what I can find out for you. And, Pagan?" Melina caught her gaze. "Rogue will see you when you return."

Pagan swallowed hard, the icy feeling of dread making her whole body go cold.

"Do you and Rogue have something important to do today?" Erith asked.

"I think she wants to show me something that I haven't had to deal with before. The security business is a constant learning ground." Pagan shuddered at what she feared Rogue was going to do. She had disobeyed the cardinal rule of the Sentinels: *Don't bring your work home with you.* Pagan hastened her steps toward the van to take Erith to work. She realized that she was running in her haste to get away from the shop, and Erith was having trouble keeping up. "Sorry." Pagan immediately tempered her pace and tried to steer her mind away from what lay ahead. "Melina told me that you show great talent in the culinary department."

"I actually made an edible omelet on my first attempt." Erith grinned. "So, do you think she'll let me put in some of my wages while I'm with you so I'm not sponging off you?"

"We don't see it like that, Erith."

"I need to feel like I can contribute," Erith said, brooking no argument. "After all, I have no idea how long I'm with you all for. The Sentinel never gave me a time schedule and, to be honest, I'm at a loss as to what I can do next."

"Just take it one day at a time and we'll see what happens. You've still got your job at the car lot. And I have my rounds to perform. You'll be plenty occupied. I know I never seem to have a minute to myself."

"We'll be able to see each other, though, won't we? Between me working at the car lot and you working here?"

"We all have things we need to do to keep the business running. Sometimes, that might mean I won't be around all the time because of what needs to be done. Security, for some strange reason, isn't always a nine-to-five experience. But believe me, you'll see plenty of me."

"Is that another of those things not to question?"

"See, you're thinking like family already." Pagan grinned.

"Pagan?"

"Hmm?"

"Have you ever seen a Sentinel?"

"Why do you ask?"

"There's a part of me that doesn't believe what happened last night."

"That's understandable. Maybe, when it's time for you to believe, you will."

"Who made you a wise old sage this morning?" Erith grumbled softly and nudged an elbow into Pagan's ribs.

"I don't know. Must have been something I ate."

"Next time I'm putting an extra something in your omelet."

"Then I will share my omelets with you. If we go, we go together."

"Sounds like a deal to me," Erith said quietly.

Pagan smiled down at her. "Then we're sorted. Now come on, Ms. Bikeless, let's put some speed into your feet. Not all of us can swing through the air like the Sentinels can."

"I'd throw up my breakfast." Erith hurried her steps at Pagan's side.

"And that would be a criminal waste of good eggs!" Pagan said as she led their way. "So, we're agreed: no flying this morning, just walking to the van, very fast. We don't want you to be late."

"That would mean some explaining, and I really don't want everyone to know the full details. My face is already telling tales before me."

"We'll give Ammassari an abridged version. Your secret is safe with me, Erith."

"Somehow, Pagan, I had no doubt of that whatsoever."

Chapter Fourteen

"Reiterate once more why bringing her here, into our home, could jeopardize all that we stand for?" Rogue asked as she aimed a particularly nasty looking blade at Pagan's legs.

Pagan jumped high above the blow and deflected it with a staff gripped tightly in her hands. "I have left us wide open to being found out. 'Sentinels cannot hide among outsiders when the outsiders are among us,'" she quoted.

"And she thinks you are where right now?" Rogue aimed a lethal swing at Pagan's arm, which she deflected and managed to knock Rogue back a step with the force of her reaction. Rogue, for all her ire, looked impressed with the return blow. She didn't let it show for too long; she had a lesson to teach.

"She thinks I'm busy fitting new alarms at the local produce market." Pagan tried to sweep Rogue's feet out from under her.

Rogue dodged the move and flipped backward away from Pagan's attack. She landed on her feet and swung her weapon with great speed and agility, handling the blade menacingly. "And you'll explain the bruises later how?" She lunged for Pagan with a series of devastating combinations.

Pagan backed up under Rogue's onslaught. She only just managed to deflect the blows that were raining upon her. With her staff, Pagan batted away at the blade, and the sound of tempered wood hitting metal rang through the room.

"I'll try not to acquire bruises." Pagan winced as the blade hit her arm with its broad side. "Or else I'll wear long sleeves for the rest of the week." She grimaced at the pain but had no time to check her wound as she continued to dodge Rogue's nonstop barrage of blows.

"And if she comes to your room at night to talk with you and finds that you are not in your bed?" Rogue continued while trying to cut through Pagan's defenses. "When instead of being asleep like normal folk, you are in fact out in the city fighting crime?"

"I'll tell her I inherited the Osbornes' weak bladder control!" Pagan flicked out swiftly with the tip of her staff to smack Rogue's wrist. The blow caused Rogue to mishandle the blade for a moment. In that split second Pagan tried to disarm her, but Rogue merely flicked the blade skyward and caught it in her other hand. Pagan groaned.

"It's not fair that you can use both hands with equal expertise," she grumbled.

"Your sister has never had any complaints!" Rogue said and struck out once more at Pagan, putting her back on the defensive. "Watch your feet," she said as she lurched forward, ever the trainer teaching her pupil.

"Sometimes I feel like a lumbering oaf," Pagan replied, her eyes never straying from Rogue's weapon and just managing to deflect its blows. The vibrations shook through Pagan's body like miniature earthquakes. One blow hit her so hard she swore she could hear her teeth rattle inside her head.

"Your heart sometimes leads you into unwise endeavors, but you're no oaf. Foolish, stupid, misguided, and muleheaded, but no oaf."

"I tower over Erith like a behemoth."

"Everyone knee high to a toadstool does, I'd imagine," Rogue said, making Pagan release a bark of laughter, which Rogue instantly berated. "Don't lose your concentration. Feelings don't enter into fighting. And what else don't we do?" Rogue was not going to let the subject drop or her blows falter. She backed Pagan toward the wall under the repetitive attacks. Blow after blow weakened Pagan's strength and her resolve.

"We don't bring our work home with us."

"Who blatantly ignored that rule?"

"I did."

"And what are you going to do about it?"

"I don't know," she replied honestly in a small voice. "I didn't think beyond getting her away from her family and into the safety of ours."

"But she's not family," Rogue replied equally softly and flicked her blade up under Pagan's staff. The motion sent the staff into the air out of Pagan's grasp. Rogue caught the wood and swung it under her arm, blade brandished in one hand, the staff against her body in a defensive stance.

Pagan admitted defeat gracefully. She dropped to the floor panting.

"She could learn more here than she needs to know," Rogue said coming to stand over Pagan.

"What do I do to make it right?"

"Find out how much she can be trusted. Then decide how best to serve your family with honor."

"Yes, Rogue." Pagan dropped her head with shame and watched as sweat dripped from her hair and landed on her pants.

"We'll speak no more of this."

Pagan mentally sighed in relief. "Erith doesn't know what to do next. I have to admit, I'm uncertain too."

Rogue fixed her with a steely eye. "Her mother is still in the hospital, and her father is still with the police while they wait for her to press charges."

"Her mother won't do that."

"Then the cycle begins again, and Erith shouldn't have to return to that kind of environment." Rogue shook her head. "You should have just taken her to one of the proper safe houses, Pagan."

"I know," Pagan said. "But I just wanted her with us." *With me,* she admitted to herself.

"You thought with your heart. It's not the wisest of organs." Rogue waved her hand to signal the end of the conversation. "You're done meditating on the error of your ways. Go wash up and then go sort out what we need for our next job."

"Have we got any idea of what Phoenix has planned for tonight?" Pagan asked as she wiped her face with a towel.

"Nothing concrete yet. One good thing at least came out of you storming that apartment to rescue your maiden in distress. We now have a name to link with this Phoenix, and we can check into Baylor's past and seek out his latest associates. Your bladder will, in all likelihood, be keeping you up all night, young Pagan." Rogue shook her head at her. "Weak bladder control, some excuse."

"Let's hope I never have to use it."

"Indeed."

❖

Melina was reading something from a file when Rogue entered the lighthouse after her workout and conscientiously tried not to slam the door behind her as she fumed.

Melina seemed to eye her carefully before she spoke. "Rogue, please vent some of that anger before you blow something. Is Pagan now fully aware of the danger she has placed us in?"

"I fear this Erith calls to something other than Pagan's sense of duty." Rogue gritted her words out between tightly clenched teeth.

"It's taken her long enough. There was a time you worried she'd never find someone to give her heart to."

"*Now* is not the time! We have this Phoenix character starting to cause trouble in the city, and *now* she decides is the time to find herself someone to get close to? She can't afford the distraction."

"It had to happen sooner or later. You couldn't hold on to your hope of her not dating until she was over forty." Melina put down the file and edged her chair closer to Rogue. "What's really bothering you, Rogue?"

"We don't know this woman. She's no more than a girl. Pagan meets her, and suddenly she's having to rescue her from the home of a man who just happens to be affiliated with the one stirring up trouble in Chastilian. Am I the only one who is thinking this is more than a strange quirk of fate?"

"I think you're the only one seeing a twisted connection where the rest of us see merely coincidence." Melina brushed a hand across Rogue's cheek. "I don't think there's some nefarious plan here. I think it is merely what it is. Erith needed to be rescued and Pagan came to her aid."

"Can it really be that simple?" Rogue dropped to her knees, and wound her arms around Melina's waist, drawing her close. "Nothing is ever that simple for us."

"We Sighted are supposed to see deeper into whatever evidence we are given. I can't honestly see some hidden agenda in their meeting.

I think it was simply meant to be. And if something comes of it, then you have to accept that. This might be the someone Pagan will love."

"She hasn't got time to fall in love with the local city burglar! She has other things that need to occupy her time and energy."

"And they will, I can assure you. But I don't think the heart pays attention when it has something set in its sights. You were meant to take a role on the esteemed Council and follow in your father's footsteps. Instead, you watch over Chastilian from a lighthouse and run a security firm because your heart led you to me." She cupped Rogue's cheek. "And I, for one, am very grateful it did." Melina gazed at Rogue lovingly, then her face altered just enough for Rogue to catch it.

"What?"

"I've been doing some research. Years ago, the original Phoenix terrorized Chastilian, demanding protection money, setting fire to businesses that didn't play his game. Then my parents were killed, he was captured, and his gang just disappeared from the public eye. The Sentinels never knew where he came from or who he was, and they were never able to keep track of his gang either. We didn't have names for their faces, and we didn't possess half the technology then that we do now." Melina looked about her lighthouse and all its computers. "But now we have an abundance of technology that we can use to our advantage. I have been searching for anything I can find out about the first Phoenix and why this new man has taken on his mantle."

"A copycat, maybe?"

"How about a chip off the old block?" Melina picked up the file and handed it to Rogue. "Xander Phoenix had no ties to Chastilian. It was merely a means to an end in his racketeering. But I've found, through housing records and birth certificates freely available on the Internet, that he had family elsewhere, including a *son*. Zachary Phoenix, aged twenty-three. He's exactly the same age as Pagan."

"So the son is taking revenge for his father's murder by killing the old gang members? I'd be the first to shake his hand if it wasn't for the fact he's taking innocent lives along with those thugs."

"The Sighted will be advised about this piece of the puzzle, and the Sentinels will all be briefed. I just wanted to tell you first that I think I've found our Phoenix and the reason why he's here. I don't think it's all for revenge on his father's gang. I think he's also calling us out. The symbol left at the Quarter announced him, but only his gang and we know exactly who the Phoenix was and what he did." Melina lifted Rogue's chin from where she was still poring over the written information. "We need to tell Pagan now."

"Do you think she's aware what this will mean?"

"That we now have the *son* of the man who killed our parents terrorizing the city? I think she'll understand perfectly what that means for us."

"Phoenix's heir."

"Pagan's going to want retribution."

"She's going to have to stand in line. If he chooses to continue in his rampage across Chastilian, I am going to take him down myself. I'm just eternally thankful there were survivors the night his father struck. My own reason for living is right here in my arms."

Melina soothed Rogue's hair from her face. "The Phoenix heir will soon find that the Osborne legacy is still very much alive and able to stand in his way."

"You don't mess with the Osbornes." Rogue kissed Melina's nose.

"Not this time, because now we are a part of a force to be reckoned with."

❖

The night was unseasonably cool. Pagan's breath clung to the air as she regulated her breathing to keep herself as silent as possible. She was crouched on a window ledge sticking out over an alleyway and was listening in on the chatter of two men below as they jostled each other in play fighting, acting like overgrown children while they waited for something. Pagan was waiting with them, intrigued as to what they were doing out so late and in such a deserted area. Their comments soon caught more than Pagan's idle curiosity.

"So Baylor's old woman wouldn't turn him in, eh?" one voice growled with a chuckle.

"No, and she never will if she knows what's good for her, he told me." The other voice was distinctly younger.

"What about the daughter? I heard Baylor's got an unruly bitch."

"He said she's run away, just up and left. He said he was better off without her, said she can do what the hell she likes and he could care less. Then he said she's old enough to go find herself some poor beggar to screw and get stuck with kids of her own."

Melina's voice was gentle in Pagan's ear. "Looks like you've stumbled upon someone linked to Baylor. Strange there was no mention of the fact she was taken from her home by a Sentinel. That's very interesting. He could have added that to Phoenix's list of things to hold against us."

Phoenix. Just the mention of the man's name made Pagan's blood run cold. Her head still spun with the details that Melina had laid out for her before she set out for the night. She marveled at how calm her sister had been as she delivered the news that the man behind their parents' deaths had left behind a son. One who was now following in his father's footsteps and terrorizing Chastilian in his own right. Pagan could feel the anger once more rise to the surface, and her hold tightened on the wall as if she could somehow vent that fury through crushing bricks and mortar. In just a few words, Pagan's world had once again turned upside down. *He* was taking revenge in his father's name. Pagan, like the good Sentinel she had been brought up to be, had told Melina and Rogue she wanted justice served. Now, in the darkness of the night, watching two of Phoenix's men go about their schemes, talking about Erith like she was trash, Pagan knew only one thing.

She wanted this Phoenix as dead as the first.

Trying to push such thoughts aside for the sake of the watch, Pagan again looked down on the two men. She watched their every move. They frequently checked the end of the alley, obviously waiting for something. In the sparse light she could barely make them out in their black clothing. The flames on their bandanas, however, were a giveaway in the darkness. Pagan wondered if that was a sign they wore, like gang colors, to set them apart. The younger man sported blond hair cut close to his head. The older man was dark skinned and thicker set. Both fidgeted and made way too much noise as they waited impatiently.

"How come Baylor's joined us down here? He's kind of old to be a member of Phoenix's team."

"Word has it he had connections with the gang years ago when the old Phoenix was here. When he got killed, the gang scattered and Baylor went into hiding too, for a while. As soon as the call went out that the new Phoenix had arisen, only Baylor came back to serve." The younger man sounded impressed with the knowledge he'd garnered.

"Those are some credentials. I'd better treat him with more respect than just thinking of him as a stupid wife beater."

Both men laughed, then hastily hushed each other as their amusement sounded loud in the night air.

"Intriguing," Melina muttered over the comlink. "This Phoenix tried to recruit his father's cronies as well as new staff. I wonder if the son has had more luck finding the exact ones who betrayed his father than we're having."

"So what time is the shipment due again?" the younger man asked.

"The same as it's been every time you ask me, dumbass! Midnight." The older man rubbed his hands together gleefully. "I hear it's a major cache this time, sent with love and kisses from an old friend of the Phoenix family. I heard they broke into a military compound for these gems."

Pagan's eyebrows lifted behind her face mask. She heard Melina gasp.

"What the hell have they gotten hold of?" Melina grumbled. "Great, now among all the other things I'm checking into, I need to have eyes on the military bases too. I'll get Uncle Frank to call around. He's ex-military, he has connections there. Pagan, you're going to have to slip in closer when they move so that we can see what gifts are being exchanged here. Rogue, hold your position until the vehicle comes. You're more exposed on that side of the alley."

"So Phoenix is upping the stakes even more?" Rogue whispered through the comlink. "Any hopes this is a rocket we can strap the bastard to and launch him into space?"

Pagan tried not to laugh out loud and instead held her pose as still as a statue, molded to the brickwork as if she were a living part of it. Her gaze never left the two men below her.

At precisely twelve o'clock a truck rumbled into the alleyway and the two men ambled in its direction, flagging it down. Pagan followed from above, edging along the window ledges, using them like stepping stones until she could climb down the side of the wall to get a better view. She clung precariously to a ledge where a crack left a secure hand hold in the wall. She made sure she could see the license plate so that Melina could run it through their databases. Pagan once more marveled at the amount of hidden technology she had concealed on her that let the Sighted back at the lighthouse truly see. The mask was just one vital part that allowed the Sighted to see what the Sentinels saw. The city's closed circuit TV cameras were another way the Sighteds watched over Chastilian, but Pagan was disappointed that not every corner employed them. This area of the city was blind to what was taking place below.

The man who drove the truck jumped down from the cab and swaggered around to join the two men eagerly waiting for him.

"Greetings, boys." He casually flipped open the doors at the back of the truck, revealing its contents. "Think your Phoenix will be pleased with this offering?"

Pagan leaned out carefully to look into the truck bed. Her eyes widened at what she saw. Five handheld missile launchers, complete with boxes of ammunition, lay in the truck.

"I'd say he'll be overjoyed!" The older man clapped his hand across the back of his companion and they all laughed as money exchanged hands. "Oh, the fun he could have with these babies! Who needs bullets when you can *bomb*?"

"Seize and capture, Sentinels!" Melina said sharply.

Pagan and Rogue dropped down from their positions. Pagan landed on top of the blond thug and managed to knock him out with a few swift punches. She rolled away from the boot that the driver aimed at her rib cage. He tried to turn and run, but Pagan dove and grabbed at his legs, tackling him.

Rogue brought the older man to the ground with a few well-aimed punches and had him tied up in moments. Pagan crawled up the struggling truck driver's body to drag his arms behind his back and tie plastic cords to his wrists.

"That was easy enough," Rogue said, moving around the truck and punching the truck driver in the nose as he started spouting obscenities. "Watch your mouth. There might be ladies present."

They made sure the men were all securely immobilized and then left them propped up together to await collection by the police.

"Directions, Sighted?" Rogue asked as she looked in the truck at the weapons.

"Take it to Akramon. He will know how to take care of it. He has the facilities," Melina replied. "I'll contact him so he's aware of you coming bearing gifts." Melina was silent for a moment and then said, "It appears the truck has a tracking device attached to it. Its GPS signal is flashing on one of my screens. Looks like whoever supplied the weapons likes to keep an eye on his men. It also means we can backtrack the signal and find its source. You might want to disable the device, though, for this evening, I've got all I need from it here."

Pagan reached into the vehicle. She found the GPS attached to the steering wheel column. "Got it." She brought the small metal bug back to Rogue. Rogue smiled at her.

"I know exactly where this will be best served," she said and headed toward the truck driver, who was still spewing profanities at her. She grabbed his already broken nose, forcing his mouth open so he could breathe. As he gasped for air, she shoved the small tracker in his mouth and clamped his jaw shut. He gagged, tried to scream, and then swallowed it.

Rogue patted him on the head harshly. "Be thankful I didn't have any soap with me," she said as he lay panting and retching. "Hey! Stop it! We don't want you bringing that bug back up. We want you tracked all the way to the jail cells."

They heard police sirens. "I'll drive," Rogue said as Pagan went to scramble into the truck.

"I know, I know," Pagan grumbled and moved around to the passenger side.

"Akramon is waiting for you," Melina said. "Safe journey. Be mindful of what you carry in the back."

Pagan sat back to enjoy the ride, her eyes blurring at the endless lights that decorated the city as they drove through Chastilian and on to Akramon's warehouse to the awaiting Sentinel there. "I think Phoenix has just upped the ante. Missiles do more than set a place alight," she said.

"Let's hope that this was the only shipment that was delivered tonight."

Pagan spared Rogue a sideways glance. "Something tells me we wouldn't be that lucky." She saw the grim line of Rogue's lips and knew that she had been thinking the exact same thing.

❖

Akramon drove them back as close to the lighthouse as possible without arousing suspicion in the quiet hours of the morning. The windows were blackened to hide the masked occupants inside.

Pagan heard Melina come back online in her comlink. "Pagan," she said, "We have a small problem."

"What's wrong, Mel?" Pagan asked, her heart instantly beating faster.

"It would appear that a certain *Fox* has left the den."

"Damn it!" Rogue growled from the front passenger seat.

"Do you have a fix on where she is?" Pagan just wanted confirmation of her worst fear.

"She's gone back home," Melina replied.

Pagan sighed in resignation. "Her dad isn't out of jail yet, is he?"

"No, but it's late, and she's out in the city on her own."

"Something tells me that's nothing new for this particular fox," Rogue muttered.

Pagan looked out into the city. "Let me out here, please. I'll escort our runaway home myself."

"Sure you don't want backup in case she proves to be a handful?" Rogue settled herself more comfortably in her seat, apparently not having any intension of following Pagan at all.

"I think I can handle her myself." She pointed to a street sign. "I'll get out here. There's a lot of good cover that I can hide in until I reach her building."

The car drew to a halt and Pagan got out swiftly. "Thanks for the ride, Akramon. I hope the next time we meet it will be in better circumstances."

"Take care, little one," he replied with a smile. "You'll have to bring this girl to meet the family, let us welcome her into the fold, seeing as she is so sweet on you."

Pagan paused in closing the door. She shot a suspicious look at Rogue. "Have you been talking about me?"

Rogue pointed a finger to her chest. "Me? Never. Not a single word has passed my lips about you and your hot little redhead."

Pagan took a deep breath and let it out slowly. "I should have left you in Akramon's warehouse."

"Her place isn't with me," Akramon said. "She belongs with your sister and you. Destiny, dear Pagan, has a way of bringing people to you so they can take their place either at your side or against you."

Rogue touched Pagan's hand. "Go find her and bring her back safely. Then we'll all get together and set some ground rules on what is acceptable nighttime activity. We have enough in this city to contend with without having to monitor her movements as well."

"Maybe she's sleepwalking?" Pagan offered weakly.

"Then go guide her home. We'll be sure to wake her carefully when she returns."

Pagan closed the door and watched as the dark car disappeared like a shadow along the road.

"She's still at the apartment. The tracer I put on her jacket is showing she's stationary at the moment."

"You bugged Erith?"

"No, I *traced* her. Seems like it was worth it, wouldn't you agree?"

Pagan took off in the direction that would lead her to Erith, the one route that she felt she was fated to choose.

❖

Pagan leaned lazily against the wall, watching as Erith carefully eased herself out of her bedroom window and slowly pulled the frame down to latch it again. Pagan knew the instant Erith realized she wasn't on the fire escape alone. She swiftly stifled any sound from her scream. "Shh," she whispered. "You'll wake up the entire city!"

Erith ripped Pagan's hand away from her mouth. "What are you doing here?" She began down the fire escape.

Pagan followed after her. "Shouldn't that be my question? What are you doing out so late?"

"I had to get to something," Erith continued down the steps.

"Did you let anyone know that you were leaving?"

"No, I just snuck out," Erith said. "I'm a big girl now. I don't have curfew."

"How did you get past the alarms?" Pagan asked.

Erith hesitated a little in her flight. "I disabled them," she said softly. "But I reactivated them when I left so everything's back up and running again."

"What the…? She's right!" Melina exclaimed over the comlink. "I need to have a serious talk with that young lady. She all but slipped out from under us without leaving a trace."

"How did you do that?"

Erith dug in her pocket and pulled out a small box that fit perfectly in the palm of her hand. It looked like a simple calculator.

"And that does what exactly?" Pagan asked.

"It blocks the signals to alarms to give me enough time to get in or out."

"Did you design this?" Pagan reached for it and turned it over in her hands.

Erith nodded and took it back. She stuffed it in her jacket and headed down the stairs again.

"So, you're what? A mild-mannered secretary by day and some kind of electronics whiz kid by night?"

Erith laughed. "I have highly honed burglar skills. It's not exactly the same thing."

"I think you sell yourself short. That's not just to break in or out. It's too sophisticated for that."

"And there's more to you than a mask and flying prowess." She stepped back a pace and Pagan immediately stepped into shadow. "Elusive, though."

"Sentinels aren't exactly supposed to make idle chitchat," Pagan replied.

"Yet *you* do."

"Yes, *you* do!" Melina grumbled in Pagan's ear.

"Let's just get you back home."

"Home?"

"Your safe home. Which, obviously, isn't safe enough if you can break in and out of it."

"How do you know so much about its alarm system? First the shop, then the home," Erith asked.

"I'm a Sentinel, I know all," Pagan said. "Besides, what would be the point of me taking you somewhere safe if I didn't know how safe it was?"

Erith nodded, conceding the point.

"Are you okay there?"

Erith nodded again. "They're great. It's a fantastic place to live, and I'm with my best friend. What more could I wish for?"

"Your bike, obviously," Pagan said pointing to the contraption that Erith was wheeling along.

"I wanted something that was mine. I only have my clothes. Nothing else there is mine. And I can't keep having someone drive me to work every morning. I won't be a burden to these people."

"You could have gone home during the day for it."

"Dad might have been there. I couldn't risk it."

"Would he hurt you without your mother being there?"

"It's not so much that, I'm used to that. He'd want me to go back there to look after Mom when she comes out of the hospital. But I can't get caught up in that again. And I know he's tangled up in something much worse than he ever was where we lived before. I'm frightened he's a part of everything terrible that I see on the news." Erith looked at Pagan. "I don't know exactly what he does. My dad has many talents." She patted the pocket where her gadget was hidden. "Some I inherited and some I learned from him directly. I'm guessing this Phoenix is just the latest in a long line of hoodlums my dad has hooked up with. He seems to attach himself to badness with alarming regularity."

"He's with a major crime lord."

Erith's eyes widened as she heard her worst fears confirmed. "What has my dad gotten himself into?"

"Your father is part of the worst criminal gang in Chastilian."

"He hates the Sentinels, doesn't he? My dad said something about this Phoenix wanting to wipe you all out. Then take the city back and run it into the ground."

"He can try," Pagan said with a shrug, then added dryly, "And he is trying, regularly."

"How can you live with that?"

"How did you live with your father battering you and your mother on a regular basis?"

Erith halted in her steps, pulling the bike to a stop. "Because I had to until I had the power to change things."

"Ditto."

"Do you like being a Sentinel?" Erith tried to catch Pagan's eyes again. Pagan evaded her.

"I was born for it."

"Are there many *female* Sentinels?" Erith asked.

"Why do you ask?"

"I just wondered." Erith grinned at her, seemingly enjoying their banter. "I am, however, beginning to think you are the only one who tours these streets. Seems to me the only objective you have is to catch me doing something illegal."

"That does seem to be a regular occurrence. You might want to temper the urge more."

The lighthouse made its majestic appearance as they rounded a tower block, and they stepped onto the street to cross over into the quiet road.

"You can find your own way from here, I take it?" Pagan asked. She noticed a small light in the front window. "Looks like you have someone waiting up for you."

Erith swallowed audibly. "I hope it's Pagan."

"Is this Pagan over six feet tall and wears a very stern face?"

"No, I'd hazard a guess that would be Rogue." Erith sighed. "I am *so* in trouble." She looked up at Pagan. "They won't kick me out, will they?"

"Explain yourself to them," Pagan said. "And then make sure you don't betray their trust again." Pagan stayed behind while Erith slowly made her way to the lighthouse. "Go on. I have work to do other than to walk you home."

"You be careful out there, please?" Erith called softly to her.

"I will." Pagan slipped into the darkness and masked herself from Erith's sight. "Sighted, one Red Fox has once again seen the light."

"We want that device. Rogue is all but drooling over its schematics."

"Ask her for it. She's so afraid of Rogue's reaction that I think she might hand over anything. Even that precious bike of hers."

"Come on home, Sentinel," Melina said. "You've earned your rest tonight."

Pagan smiled as the light from the lighthouse drew her home, albeit on a different path than the one Erith had taken straight to the front door. It seemed Pagan's destiny was to be one who would choose the different path.

CHAPTER FIFTEEN

Erith and Rogue sat at the kitchen table in silence when Pagan entered the kitchen the next morning. Rogue knew Pagan had made the most of it being a Saturday and had enjoyed a workout on her own. Now she was scavenging for a drink in the refrigerator and had not heard the soft gasp that erupted from Erith. Rogue couldn't help but grin at the captivated look on Erith's face. The fact that Pagan was wearing only gray shorts and a matching T-shirt had caused Erith's mouth to drop open. Rogue reached over and shut Erith's mouth with a sharp click of her teeth. Erith looked at first startled, then embarrassed at being caught, but her eyes drifted back to Pagan once more. Rogue nonchalantly picked up a piece of toast crust and flicked it at Pagan's shoulder.

Pagan reacted to the feel of something hitting her and turned around. She questioned Rogue's method of calling her to attention with a lift of an eyebrow and then saw Erith also in the room.

"Hi. Forgive me. I didn't see you there. I was just getting some juice."

That's okay, Rogue signed. *You just missed Erith's tongue rolling out onto the floor at the sight of you, all muscles and naked flesh bathed in the light shining from the fridge.*

Pagan blushed and looked down at herself self-consciously.

Erith stared at Rogue. "How did you know she couldn't hear you?"

"Because she would have reacted to your gasp of appreciation and the sound of the copious drool dripping from your jaw," Rogue replied.

She watched Pagan scrutinize Erith's face as it suddenly flared with color.

"Is something wrong?" Pagan asked, looking between the two women.

"Go shower," Rogue both signed and spoke aloud for Erith's sake. "Before Erith expires on the spot."

Pagan looked back at Erith. Erith shrugged at her unashamedly, blatantly enjoying the view.

"Look at you." She gestured at Pagan, who immediately looked down at herself, wondering what was amiss. "You never looked like that when you came to fit the alarm system. You're all muscles and stuff!"

Rogue watched Pagan's reaction. It was obvious she wasn't sure how to react to Erith's interest. "I'll go shower," Pagan mumbled and took a step to get out of the kitchen as quickly as she could.

Rogue nudged Erith. "Go to her before she thinks you're just teasing her."

Erith was out of her seat in a split second and just as quickly in front of Pagan, stopping her flight. She purposely took a hold of Pagan's face and made her look down at her.

"You're gorgeous," Erith said seriously.

"I was working out." Pagan touched her ears sheepishly. "My aids are upstairs."

"You're still gorgeous, and you need to teach me sign language," Erith told her, very carefully enunciating each word.

"I will," Pagan said looking over her shoulder at Rogue. She hastily turned her attention back to what Erith was saying.

"That way I will know exactly what it is Rogue is saying to you behind my back."

Pagan laughed. "How did you know?" she asked as Rogue very quickly lowered her hands from where she had been busily signing *love birds* at Pagan.

"I watched your eyes. You focus very keenly on someone when they are talking to you, be it actual speech or sign language. It's amazing what eyes can reveal about a person. Go shower. Cover up that body before I do something that will scandalize Rogue," Erith said with a wicked grin.

"She's pretty unshockable," Pagan replied.

"Don't you believe it," Rogue said, watching them interact and realizing why this woman was so important to Pagan. There was a connection between them that was almost tangible.

"Do you want to do something today?" Pagan asked Erith shyly.

"Yes." Erith's reply was unhesitant.

"Great, then I'll go make myself more presentable." Pagan placed her empty glass on the countertop and reached for an apple. "Then you can tell me why you were out all night while the rest of us slept on unawares and you're still alive to tell the tale!"

"Who told you?"

"I may be deaf, but the walls have ears," Pagan said and chuckled when Erith spun around to give Rogue a look that could kill.

Rogue rocked back on her chair and just watched them. It looked like Pagan had found herself a suitable sidekick after all.

❖

Pagan stood in line for their movie tickets while Erith perused the candy counter. Erith carefully picked out their choices and then managed to cleanly juggle both popcorn and beverages as she made her way back.

"Is your popcorn okay?" Erith asked with amusement as Pagan began immediately digging in as they made their way to their screening room.

"I love this stuff," Pagan said around a mouthful. "You can't see a film without the customary kernel of popcorn stuck in a tooth somewhere." She led the way down the aisle. "Is this all right for you?"

Erith nodded. "I haven't been to the movies in ages," she said. "Thank you for inviting me."

"No, thank you for letting me bring you along on what has been my weekly diet of action since this film came out."

"You've seen it that many times?"

"It's my favorite film. I can't see it enough."

"What is it about it that keeps bringing you back?"

"The curious mix of religion and modern technology blended into the storyline, coupled with the philosophy of world faiths linked to a cyber intelligence where machinery rules over mankind. Add to that, special effects that are truly mind blowing, and all that wrapped up in a love story that transcends gender."

"And the fact that the leading lady looks very butch in her shiny black leather has nothing at all to do with it." Erith leaned forward conspiratorially. "I saw the poster outside."

"That might be the *major* factor in my repeated viewings, if the truth be known."

They settled down to watch the trailers before the movie. Pagan fiddled with her aids to take in the sounds in the best quality she could.

"Are those things fitted with high-definition surround sound?" Erith asked.

"No. They need to be turned down so I don't lose any more hearing from the sound system they employ here," she teased. When she was settled, Pagan was surprised to find a small hand seeking out her own.

"Is this okay?" Erith asked. "I'm getting the feeling we've been heading toward this. Slowly, mind you, but surely."

Pagan grinned. "It's more than okay."

Pagan marveled at the strength in such a tiny hand. It was so pale against her own much darker skin, something she could see even in the darkness of the movie theater. She squeezed Erith's hand and enjoyed the feeling of fingers twining around her own. *Yes, we have been heading toward this.* She was grateful that Erith had taken the first step to get them closer. Pagan thought back to earlier that morning. Erith had stood close enough that Pagan had smelled the soft fragrance of her skin. It had teased at her senses and made her want to burrow in closer to the source. Desire and need burned deep in her chest. They were unfamiliar sensations, but Pagan welcomed them. She shifted in her seat so she could relax and enjoy her film in the company of the woman holding her hand. She just hoped that she could keep her attention on the screen.

❖

There was a glorious pink tinge to the afternoon sky when they finally surfaced from the movie. A large crowd was waiting to get inside for the later showings, and outside the theater, weary shoppers battled through the weekend crush. Pagan kept a firm grip on Erith's hand as she led them out through the masses.

"Where'd all these people come from?"

"It's Saturday. They amass from all corners of Chastilian to shop." Pagan looked over her shoulder to share a grin with Erith. Suddenly, the air was knocked out of her as a man was roughly pushed into her chest, and she spun around from the force of the blow. Pagan's grip on Erith's hand tightened so as not to lose her.

Seven men, their faces hidden by familiar bandanas, were forcing their way through the crowds, pushing people aside like blockers on a football field. Pagan quickly pulled Erith toward her, picking her up against her chest, and swiftly moved through the crowd to a small alleyway between buildings. She shielded Erith, arms tight around her as the men barreled past, sending people flying as they went. She watched as they rampaged through the unsuspecting throng of people, knocking over men and women alike with no regard. Pagan heard the yells as the men brutally snatched purses and wallets from the shoppers, then ran off, their mission complete and their voices loud and clear over the crowd.

"Where are your precious Sentinels now, Chastilian? The Phoenix will soon take care of your city without their interference!"

Pagan watched them go, trying to memorize any distinguishing features and the direction in which they were headed. She was startled by their words and the blatant public threat. When she felt it was safe to move, she peered down at Erith, who was safely nestled against her chest.

"Are you all right?" Pagan asked.

Erith pulled Pagan's face down and kissed her.

Pagan was at first startled by the touch of lips pressed against hers, then she melted into Erith's mouth as she drew Pagan closer still. Pagan shuddered as a soft, moist tongue touched at her lips, and she opened her mouth to grant it entrance. Their tongues touched hesitantly and Pagan felt Erith groan into her mouth. She experienced the delight of the vibration accompanying the sound and could feel Erith's body shudder against her. She marveled at the sensation of their bodies touching and craved to get closer still. Pagan let her own tongue reach out boldly and the kiss deepened into something more. Pagan cupped Erith's face in her hands, amazed at the way Erith fit so perfectly into her. She ran her hands over Erith's shoulders, down to mold over her slender hips. She lifted Erith off the ground, and Erith wrapped her arms about Pagan's neck to hold on as they continued to kiss.

It was Erith who finally pulled back, gasping for air. "Wow," she gasped. "Who'd have thought Pagan Osborne was such a great kisser." She traced her finger over Pagan's lips, outlining their shape and rubbing at their combined moisture that caught on them.

"I don't think it was all me." Pagan's voice was husky.

"I have been wanting to do that since I first met you," Erith said, her gaze still fixed on Pagan's lips. "You have no idea how drawn to you I am." She leaned forward a little to lay a gentler kiss on Pagan's mouth. "My hero. You just reached out, snatched me up, and shielded me from those men. Once I felt this body of yours against me, I couldn't wait any longer. I needed to see if your lips were as soft as the rest of you is, despite all that strength you hide away." Erith ran a hand over Pagan's shoulders. "You're holding me up as if I weigh nothing at all."

"You don't, really. Besides, I wanted you a little closer so I could reach your lips better without getting a crick in my neck."

"The closer the better," Erith said, caressing the line of Pagan's jaw and then kissing her again. She pulled back slowly and gave Pagan a decidedly goofy look. "How romantic! Our first kiss, and it's in an alleyway. You certainly know how to sweep a girl off her feet."

Pagan smiled at the memory of carrying Erith through the air as they traveled the city via its rooftops.

"What are you smiling about?"

"You," Pagan said and kissed Erith's forehead sweetly. "Us. This kissing thing that's erupted between us."

"I, for one, like it." Erith pulled Pagan closer again.

Pagan hesitated and then reluctantly pulled back a little.

"What?" Erith stilled her movements, searching Pagan's face.

"This isn't exactly the right place to continue this, not with the Phoenix's gang members running riot through the streets." Pagan stuck her head around the edge of the alleyway and scanned the area swiftly. "They've gone now. We should head back home while it's safe."

"How do you know they were part of his gang?"

Pagan went still. She could almost audibly hear her brain click into gear, and only then did she give an answer. "They mentioned him in their taunts, and they were too coordinated to be a snatch-and-grab gang. I'm assuming that this Phoenix is out to cause as much mayhem as possible." She mentally slapped herself for her slip-up. *Nothing like proving you know more than she thinks, Pagan. One kiss and you're about to spill the family secrets!*

Erith nodded and then looked pointedly at Pagan until Pagan frowned at her. "What?"

"If we need to get back to the lighthouse, you might find we'll go quicker and will get less stares if you put me back on the ground."

Pagan smiled sheepishly and gently lowered her, but not before she had deliberately brushed Erith the entire length of her body in order to do so.

Erith shuddered at the contact. "Pagan Osborne, you are a wicked woman."

"Why?" Pagan asked, feeling the excitement still prickling at her skin at the touch they had shared.

"You know why, and if this is what you are like after a few kisses while still fully clothed, God help me when you're naked!"

Pagan's eyes widened and Erith touched her gently.

"What is it?"

"You'd…you'd want to be with me that way too?"

"You really don't see it, do you?" Erith tenderly stroked Pagan's cheek. "You are so handsome, inside and out. I'd be a fool not to want to make love with you, and my dad, for all his faults, did not raise an idiot. I've wanted to be with you from the moment our eyes met, Pagan. I want more than kisses and hand holding. I want the whole thing. And if, while we explore all that entails, we find that we want forever together, I am willing to explore that too."

"You're something else, Erith Baylor," Pagan sighed, her heart oddly light and her head filled with a strange feeling of giddiness.

"Yeah, well, when you work out what, be sure to let me know," Erith said with a wry twist to her lips.

Pagan covered Erith's mouth with her own and kissed her sweetly. She liked the dazed look written all over Erith's face when she withdrew. "For one thing," Pagan said finally pulling away, "you're *mine* now."

"I like the sound of that."

Pagan signed something to her before her nerve gave out. Erith frowned as she tried to work it out. "Okay, I'm getting *I* and *you*, but what's this?" She crossed her fists over her breasts.

Pagan repeated the signing again and explained each one, saying each word shyly. "I. Love. You."

Erith's face instantly crumpled into tears. She hastily repeated the gesture back at Pagan. "I love you too."

"Tonight we'll start a crash course in sign language," Pagan said, tenderly wiping away the tears that escaped from Erith's eyes.

"I've just learned the ones I'll use the most."

Pagan planted a soft kiss on Erith's freckled nose and then peered out again from their alleyway. "It's safe for us to go now." Taking Erith's hand, Pagan led them away from the theater and the still-startled crowd. The police were starting to arrive, and the sound from the unhappy crowd was beginning to hurt Pagan's ears. She bored them a path of escape from the madness.

"I always feel safe when I'm with you, Pagan," Erith said, looking back at the people milling around looking lost and confused. "I wonder why that is?"

"Because your heart recognizes me as someone who will never do you harm."

"Maybe my heart just recognizes *you*."

❖

The lighthouse beam was unlit in the light of the early afternoon. Pagan hastened to the welcome sight of the striped lighthouse standing proudly amid the other, less adorned buildings.

"Why the rush?" Erith asked.

Pagan tried to shrug off the question and lessen her haste. "No rush, really. I have a couple of duties I'm expected to take care of, and I can't remember what time I'm due to start, so I figure the sooner I'm there the less chance I have of being late."

Before they reached the lighthouse Erith tugged at Pagan's hand, halting her. "Before we go back in…" She reached for Pagan so she could kiss her once more, long and hard.

Pagan groaned as Erith's tongue explored her mouth. Pagan couldn't help her arms from drawing Erith closer.

"Thank goodness Chastilian is a progressive city." Erith grinned as she pulled back from their embrace. "Not all cities like to have two women kissing in the street."

Pagan blushed as she looked around, expecting prying eyes to be at every window watching their passionate display.

"Are you going to tell your sister about us?" Erith asked.

Pagan was still buzzing from the kiss, so it took a while for her brain to kick back into gear so she could answer Erith's question. "Yes, as soon as I can get a moment alone with her and Rogue."

"Good, because I don't want to have to hide from them how much I love you."

"I don't want anything hidden between us either." Pagan knew that sooner rather than later, her life was going to be revealed for all it was worth.

CHAPTER SIXTEEN

Pagan and Erith wandered through the open shop door to Ronchetti Security and slipped past the people who were walking around, perusing the products. She waved at Melina, who was watching over their customers.

"I need to check with Rogue about something. I won't be long." Pagan waved Erith up the stairs to the main living area. After watching her disappear, Pagan sought Rogue out in her office where she was sorting through some paperwork.

"Hey, you." Rogue's smile was welcoming. "How did you enjoy your film this time around?"

"It was brilliant. The day it hits DVD I have to get it to save on movie tickets." Pagan closed the door behind her. "When we came out of the movie there was a gang of Phoenix's men running amok outside."

Rogue stopped what she was doing. "Before dusk? They *are* getting bold. They're not usually out from under their stones until the moon begins to rise."

"There were about seven of them stealing handbags, but with much more violence than your usual purse snatcher. They just plowed right through us all, scattering people all over the place."

"Were you or Erith hurt?"

"Not really. Erith would have gotten trampled, so I…" Pagan hesitated. "I picked her up and got her to safety."

"Literally, I take it?" Rogue laughed at Pagan's abashed nod. "And what did she have to say about your feat of strength?"

"Not a whole lot. She just kissed me."

Rogue's head shot up and then she smiled. "Well, after this morning's unabashed staring at the sight of you in your gym gear, I can't say I'm all that surprised."

"She has the softest lips, Rogue. I've never felt anything like them."

"You've kept yourself away from emotional entanglements, maybe now you'll see the reason why so many of us fall."

"She said she loves me."

Rogue's eyebrows rose. "Does she, now? And what about you? What are your feelings in this matter?"

"I told her I loved her too. I have from the moment I first saw her," Pagan said. "This is the one, Rogue. This is the woman I want to spend every day with. I can't explain why or how I know, I just do."

"Then your life is about to become very complicated, young Pagan. You've fallen for an outsider, and one inexplicably aligned with our enemy. Now you have to see if love can truly conquer everything that you believe it can."

"We've only just kissed and already I have to decide stuff?"

"Surely you knew this day would come when you found someone to share your heart with?"

"No, I never really expected anyone to see beyond my lack of hearing. It seemed such an issue as I was growing up."

"She obviously sees *you*, Pagan, for all you are. Being unable to hear doesn't make you unable to love or to be loved in return. Look at me, for instance. I was the Vigilante Council's technological wizard, the Sentinel who could create gadgets and gizmos. Give me a tool, some wires, and a fuse, and just see what I could conjure up. Then one day at a huge gathering, your parents brought in your sister because she was going to be trained as a Sighted and was old enough to be allowed into the sessions. I took one look at her and knew she was the one I wanted to spend the rest of my life with. She was barely sixteen, way too young to be thinking of romance, and in truth so was I, so I bided my time, waited, and hoped that she would see me among the sea of faces the Council presides over. She did; she caught me staring at her, and the rest is history.

"I courted her properly, and your sister helped me feel I was more than just the geek Sentinel the Council employed. Then the world turned upside down and we were thrown together even closer because of circumstances no one ever envisaged. I moved in here, learned to run a business as well as continue my Sentinel work, *and* still build my gadgets." Rogue gave Pagan a poignant look. "And I had to learn how to bring up a small child whose world had been turned upside down *and* inside out."

"You did an excellent job. I love you so much."

"I love you too. Sentinels aren't expected to fall in love. They are supposed to love only the city and defend it beyond all costs. So when a Sentinel finds love, it is sweeter than anything else they will ever experience."

"Erith seems to have a way with gadgets like you do," Pagan said.

"She has a Sentinel's way of getting in and out of places, I'll grant her that."

"Maybe I can break the whole Sentinel thing to her gradually. I don't have to tell her everything straight away. It's not like we're picking out china patterns yet."

Rogue leaned back against her desk, arms folded across her chest. "Are you happy, Pagan?"

She gave Rogue's question careful consideration. "Yes, I am. It's like a piece I was missing has just been handed to me, and I feel complete for the first time."

"That's a sweet feeling." Rogue smiled, then her head tilted up as she heard familiar footsteps. "Melina's coming."

The door opened and Melina stepped in. She looked at their faces and eyed them both warily. She shut the door quietly behind her.

"Okay, I've had this strange feeling for the last five minutes that something was happening. I should have known it was emanating from you two. The shop is closed for the day, so what's wrong?"

"Phoenix's men have been running amok in Chastilian's daylight hours," Rogue said.

"That is not a good sign."

Rogue edged closer to Melina, put an arm about her, and cuddled her close. "But on the bright side, Pagan got well and truly kissed by her little red fox."

Melina's eyes widened. "You're too young to be kissing!"

Pagan started to laugh and Rogue coughed politely.

"Sweetheart, please remember how old we were when we started kissing. Pagan here has a lot of catching up to do. Our late bloomer is about to blossom."

Melina was quiet for just a moment, then asked, "How was it?"

"I heard bells without the requirement of my aids."

Melina hugged Pagan to her. "You just enjoy every minute you have together. If this is the one for you, then I am very happy. She's a lovely girl."

"I think so too." Pagan gave Rogue a look. "She told me something of interest today on the way to the movie. Seems Tito Ammassari had a visit from the police yesterday. They wanted him to identify the people in a photograph they had."

Rogue shared a look with Melina. "How does Erith know this?"

"The police decided to question him in the office next to Erith's but kept the door open so she could hear every word. She said she's never seen Tito act so frightened. After they left, he kept flitting around checking that the alarms were all in place."

"Did she hear if he recognized the others?"

"She said all he kept saying was it wasn't him in the photo and he didn't know anyone else either. He denied all knowledge."

Melina sighed. "Damn it, it would have helped to have known the last two in the photograph. I wonder why he didn't tell the police anything when the one man in the photo is so obviously him?"

Rogue looked over at Pagan. "I think we should go visit Ammassari ourselves tonight. He's obviously running scared."

"With good reason. Two in the photo have already been killed."

Melina gave Rogue a hug, then slipped from her grasp. She patted Pagan on her cheek. "Now all we have to do is find a way to get you out of the loving arms of your new girlfriend and out into the night."

Pagan swallowed back a groan at how she was going to accomplish that without raising suspicion.

"Young love," Rogue said. "So fraught with dilemma."

Pagan ignored her and went to find Erith. She had a few hours yet to formulate an excuse for why she couldn't stay up until all hours on a weekend. She found Erith on the sofa in the living room, idly flicking through the TV channels. The smile she graced Pagan with pushed everything else from her head.

"All sorted?" Erith asked, moving over to make room for Pagan beside her.

"For now." Pagan snuggled in close, relishing the peace she felt with Erith in her arms.

❖

Much later that evening, Rogue walked into the living room where Pagan and Erith were still watching TV in a comfortable silence. Erith was snuggled into Pagan's chest as they took up most of the sofa in a lazy sprawl of limbs.

"Mel said to wish you both good night. She has a migraine and I've just gotten her settled in bed."

Erith stirred from her position. "Migraines are not nice."

"She'll be out for the night. She usually has to just sleep them off," Rogue said. She turned her attention to Pagan. "As for you and I, we have to go."

Pagan stared at her for a moment, then realized what Rogue was doing. "What's up?"

"We have an alarm screaming blue murder in the city. Might just be a faulty wire, or perhaps someone has been tampering with the connections, but we have to go investigate."

"At this late hour?" Erith asked.

"The alarm has already been going for a while. It's driving the neighbors crazy, so I said we'd go try to sort it out so that the city can sleep tonight without disturbance."

Pagan got up and stretched the kinks from her spine. She looked back down at Erith. "Sorry to cut our evening short. Goodness knows when we'll be back, so I'll probably see you in the morning for breakfast." She leaned down and gave Erith a kiss. It lasted a lot longer than she expected because once she'd started she was loath to stop. Rogue's polite cough broke them apart. Pagan stared into Erith's emerald eyes. "Good night."

Erith brushed her fingers along Pagan's jawline. "Be safe."

"I will, I promise." She padded after Rogue down the hallway and then up to the lighthouse's hidden lair. Pagan saw Melina firmly ensconced before the monitor screens. She ran a hand over Melina's hair and tugged at the ends.

"Hope your migraine gets better, sis."

"We'd have waited forever for you to get your ass in gear and leave both the room and your girl, so we expedited the matter."

"Any stirrings?" Pagan asked.

Melina pointed to a screen. "The Phoenix's men are out here, here, and here." She gestured at the locations viewed through the closed circuit camera's eye over the city. "They have been visible for the past hour. That's not their normal procedure. They're up to something, and they don't appear to care who sees them."

"None of us come out before dark," Pagan said. "Chastilian is supposed to hear rumors but never exactly know what *really* happens once night falls. That's the way it's always been, daylight holds the night terrors at bay."

"Something is going on," Melina said, and clattered away at her keyboard. "I need you and Rogue out there. The other Sentinels are already being deployed in this area. It looks like something is going to go down here tonight." She pointed to a specific screen.

Pagan leaned closer to the monitor to see. "The Ammassari Dealership. They're going after the car lot?"

Rogue finished fastening up her jacket. "It certainly looks like he's their next target. The extra camera I deployed at the lot has been showing us the goings-on at his place. The alarms must be going off, so Ammassari has to be aware of what is happening there. We're going to lend our weight there too."

Pagan hastily got changed and gathered up her equipment. She looked to Melina for her final orders.

"Your city awaits, Sentinels," she said. "Be careful and come home safe to me. To me *and* Erith."

CHAPTER SEVENTEEN

T he city lights sparkled in the darkness of the night. The stars competed to shine even brighter than their electricity-driven counterparts. The silent heavens above offered no competition for the blaring alarms that signified the disturbance Pagan could clearly see before her. Here there were no towers to look down from; Pagan and Rogue had taken to a motorcycle and ridden to the car lot. They parked in an adjacent unused yard. Pagan slipped from the back of the motorcycle and drew out her night vision binoculars to survey the scene.

"What are they doing?" Rogue asked as they watched a team of Phoenix's men congregated in a huddle at the perimeter of the Ammassari lot. The alarms were ringing out at a deafening rate. The front gates were buckled and torn, hanging from their frames in a tangled mass. "It looks like we missed the explosives blowing the gates off."

"Guess Baylor doesn't have to be here to have his handiwork put to good use," Pagan said, angry at his involvement and what it meant for Erith. "I can see about twenty men in the lot. Some have very bulky cylinders strapped to their backs." Pagan focused in more closely. "Okay, those aren't fashionable backpacks. Mel, please confirm I'm seeing multiple flamethrowers." She listened to Melina's acknowledgment. "Then I am seeing some major firepower in the lot, with great emphasis on the word *fire*. Mel. Please call in the fire crews. This is not going to end well if they have these things to play with."

"They're wearing the bandanas again," Rogue said. "Wonder if that's to protect their identities?"

Pagan watched as one man readied his flamethrower. "Or it could be to protect them from the smell of the fuel that seems to be leaking out everywhere from that nozzle. He's all but standing in a pool of it." She watched as some men ran inside the lot and through the cars on the tiered display area. She thought they were spilling something over the vehicles, but Rogue directed her attention elsewhere.

"We have company."

Pagan was heartened to see Casper and Earl heading in their direction. The two men crowded in close at Pagan and Rogue's vantage point.

Earl nodded his head back from where they'd come from. "We have Sentinels amassing. They are circling the perimeter of this lot."

Casper signed swiftly for Pagan's eyes.

"Circling the circlers, eh? Just stay far away from the flame-throwers. We don't want any crispy critters in Sentinel garb tonight."

Two cars drove past the hidden Sentinels, up to the gates of the lot, and were allowed to pass through.

"Aren't those the same cars that we saw at the casino?" Earl asked as he pulled out his own binoculars to check.

"That leaves one car still unaccounted for," Rogue said. "Ammassari's car."

Earl got a faraway look that Pagan recognized all too well as someone listening to their Sighted's reports over the comlink. "Speaking of which, Ammassari isn't at his place of residence."

"Do you think he knew this was going down and got himself and his family out of the city?"

Earl listened again before answering Rogue. "Seems his family left days ago, flew overseas to visit relatives. Only Tito was left to clear up business. He's not at home. One of the Sentinels has just gone to check out his property. They said that no one was there but the front door was wide open and the alarm was not going off. They searched the whole house. It's deserted."

Rogue's brow furrowed. "That can only mean he switched the alarms off himself. He alone had the code to do that. He's got surveillance cameras and everything at his home. He'd have to see what was happening here. Which doesn't explain why he fled and left his house unprotected." She shrugged. "As long as he's out of the way, then it's just Phoenix's men we have to contend with."

"Everyone is in position." Melina's voice came over Pagan's comlink. "Engage when ready."

Pagan put away her binoculars. She caught the rush of flame being ignited, and the flame handlers all prepared their nozzles. The streams of fire were aimed at the front row of prestige cars, igniting the gasoline that had been sprayed over them, and the vehicles exploded into flames. For a long moment, Pagan was sent spinning back to the night her parents were killed. It was all so terrifyingly familiar. She blinked hard to dispel her thoughts. The feelings from that night so long ago froze her in place. She was jostled by Earl nudging past her, and the spell was mercifully broken.

Casper drew her attention. Pagan smiled at him distractedly.

"Nothing like watching a car go up in flames to make you wish you'd stayed in tonight." His eyes lowered and he patted her arm in understanding. He flexed his arm at her and pointed to her own sizable bulk. Pagan got his meaning loud and clear.

"Yes, I'm a big girl now." She scanned the area and saw the Sentinels closing in. "And it's time to fight fire with fire."

❖

Pagan had long since learned that there were certain times when strategies and tactics had no place in a Sentinel's plan of action. Especially when facing off against men armed with evil intent and flamethrowers. The acrid smell of fuel choked the air, and Pagan gagged on the odor.

"Take them out," Rogue said, gesturing for them to split up and tackle a man each. Other Sentinels arrived, strengthening the numbers.

Casper signed swiftly. Pagan nodded and shared his jubilation. "Yes, the gang's all here. It's a shame it's not under better circumstances." She ducked a fist that was aimed at her head as she ran past one of Phoenix's men. "Like one with less fighting and maybe a barbeque the only thing with a flame." She detached her escrima sticks and rounded on the man who had tried to hit her. She struck at him, raining crippling blows to his hands, and heard the satisfying sound of bones breaking. As he screamed in pain and cradled his hands to his chest, Pagan cold-cocked him with her elbow and laid him out. She ran toward the flame- thrower standing in the center of the car lot.

The cars were all alight on their podiums, the sleek lines of the chassis and every chrome wheel trim warped and ruined in the intense heat. The flamethrowers spewed out their rain of fire, and it ate away at everything in sight.

Pagan brought her escrima stick down with force on the wrist of the flame handler. He yelled in pain, the nozzle dipping dangerously from his grasp. The flame continued to pour from the tip, igniting the spilled fuel at his feet. He went up in flames instantly. Pagan froze as she watched the fire lick up his body like a living thing. It raced up his clothes and burned into his flesh. Pagan could hear Melina screaming in her ear, but she couldn't see anything past the man burning before her eyes. Just like her daddy had.

Pagan could feel the heat touch her skin and came to her senses enough to jump back out of the fire at her feet. Casper came running past her and pushed the man to the ground away from the fire spreading there. Casper tugged the fuel cylinders off the man's back, then began to roll him over in the dirt to put the flames out. Casper left the man on the ground; his pitiful wails rent the air.

"I froze. I saw the flames on him and I just *froze*."

Casper shook her.

"I'm okay, I think. Why does everything have to involve fire?"

The Ammassari Dealership was ruined. Flames engulfed every car that had been on display, and fire ripped through the walls of the office building. An explosion suddenly tore apart the roof, and the inside of the dealership exploded with fireworks.

"What the hell is going on here?" Rogue exclaimed over her comlink.

Pagan looked up as the night sky glittered with every sort of firework imaginable. The air was filled with whistles and explosions as rockets flew high and dropped their multicolored sparkles down over the city.

"I am sick and tired of this Phoenix's theatrics," Rogue grumbled as she rejoined Pagan.

The flame throwers had been disabled and the Sentinels were fighting at much closer quarters. Pagan spotted the crane of a fire truck rising above the fencing. "The fire crews are here."

Rogue saw them too and gestured to a few Sentinels. "Protect the rigs. Make sure none of these idiots get close to the firemen."

A fireman readied his hose to spray down on the fire that engulfed the car lot. Pagan saw another fire truck arrive, followed closely by a police car. "We're too late. Why can't we ever stop a disaster before it's already set too far in motion?"

"No doubt the Phoenix has had this planned out to the nth degree, Sentinel. All we can do sometimes is damage control." Rogue looked around the car lot. "I think a certain Red Fox might have to look elsewhere for employment after tonight."

Pagan's shoulders slumped. "I hadn't even thought of that." She heard something odd behind her and turned to see a car ramming its way through the car lot, nearly striking them. It smashed into what was left of the main office building, crumpling its front end. The sound was sickening. Pagan turned and saw a tall, slender man standing just outside the car lot. He sketched her a salute then turned and ran.

"Son of a bitch!" Rogue pushed past Pagan and ran after him.

Pagan focused her attention on the car. She edged closer to it, afraid of what she might find, knowing Phoenix's penchant for explosives. She was horrified to see Tito Ammassari, still alive, bound and gagged in the front seat and tied to the steering wheel. Pagan rushed to help him. Ammassari's face was battered and bloody, his eyes dazed and bloodshot. Pagan tugged at the car door. It had been crushed in the crash, and she had to use all her strength to wrench it open. It creaked and buckled as she managed to pull it free of the frame. Pagan pulled out the gag wedged in Tito's mouth. He gasped for air.

"It's Phoenix. It's his bastard kid come back to haunt us all."

❖

Rogue ran out of the car lot after Phoenix.

"He's going to end up out on the main road after a sharp left turn," Melina said over the comlink.

"I'm gaining on him." Rogue cut the corner sharply and skidded to a halt. Her head whipped around, searching. "Where the hell did he go?" She jogged forward, searching the surrounding street. The main road was lined by street lamps. Their glow did nothing to reveal another pedestrian.

Rogue spun in circles, looking everywhere in each direction. She even looked up as if expecting to see him climbing the walls of the surrounding buildings.

"Sighted, any ideas where he's just vanished to?" She was furious as she realized just how close she'd come to catching him only to have him vaporize into thin air.

"There's no sign, Rogue. Wherever he went, he did so fast."

Rogue took one last look around, then headed back toward the car lot. She kicked a metal trash can at the side of the road, and the noise rattled through the silence.

"Damn him. Damn him and his father to hell and back!"

❖

Pagan tried to loosen the thick rope that tied Ammassari to the steering wheel. "You have to tell me the names of the last two men in the photo the police showed you, Tito. I need to know so we can help them."

Ammassari shook his head and seemed to drift off a little. "They're okay. I haven't heard from them in days, so I think they have left the city far behind them."

Pagan looked up at his battered face and wondered what other injuries he had. He seemed delirious. "The Phoenix is smarter than that, and you know it. What are their names? Who were the last members of the older Phoenix's gang?"

Ammassari stared at her, then his focus shifted as if he were seeing another night, so long ago. "We went out that night, looking for trouble. We were young, felt the city owed us. But we never expected Xander to expect us to kill. We'd thieve for him. We'd beat anyone up, but murder was nothing we wanted a part in. That night, we thought we were going to put the scare on a business owner who was making Xander's life a misery. We never expected there to be kids with them when we got them out of the car. Or a woman. But Xander wanted them to see he meant business, so we went along with him. None of us were comfortable with hitting the woman, so Xander came and showed us himself how he dealt with folk." He closed his eyes as if to block out the memory. "He snapped her neck. I heard it so loud in my ears.

She was screaming and then she just…stopped. Then he kicked the man in the head until he stopped moving. I didn't even know who the Osbornes were. We were just following orders." Ammassari looked at Pagan. "We all ran off after. Me and the guys went and hid out at a house we knew. Xander went and played cards all night as if nothing had happened. It was just another night for him, getting business sorted and marking his territory."

Pagan managed to free the rope and released his hands from the wheel. "*Did* you have him killed?"

Ammassari managed a small smile that broke open the dried blood on his face and caused it to trickle freely down his cheek. "That we did. We wanted nothing to do with him. The killing of the Osbornes was only going to be the start of his reign of terror. So we put out a contract on him, and some guy in the lockup got paid very handsomely for putting us all out of our misery." Ammassari turned his head slightly, revealing a nasty cut on his other cheek. "Then we all went legit. The jeweler, the gambler, the car man, the banker, and the football fan. We all turned ourselves around and made ourselves over."

"The football fan?" Pagan searched for anything else attaching him to the car. He seemed unable to move.

"Vance Deaver, owns the football stadium." Ammassari coughed and blood began to dribble from his mouth.

"And the banker? Do you mean the August Dawn bank?"

"Jackson Menard, married into the biggest banking family in Chastilian." Ammassari's breathing began to waver. He gasped and panted, and more blood oozed from his lips. He looked at Pagan for a moment and grasped her arm weakly. "Will you tell that Osborne girl, the older one, I'm sorry? I never had the guts to tell her myself. I wanted to, but just couldn't bring myself to face her. You see, I was the one holding on to her and the little one. I was so frightened that Xander would harm them too. Tell her I got the bastard for her. We got him good." He sank down in the seat. "You need to stop his son. The Sentinels got Phoenix put away and we got him stopped. You need to capture his son now. Wipe him from the face of the earth and scatter the ashes so that no Phoenix can ever rise again." His eyes rolled back and he groaned in pain.

Pagan got up quickly and smashed the back window of the car with her elbow so she could see what was holding him in place. A tire iron had been shoved through the seat and had pierced Ammassari's spine, securing him in the driver's seat for his final ride in his own stolen vehicle. She heard a crackling and saw the flames from the building climbing up the hood of the car.

"I need to get you out of here." Pagan waved over some of the others. Ammassari's words stopped her.

"It's too late." He smiled up at her. "My dying will be such a relief. I've had the burden of that night weighing so heavily on my shoulders. It will be nice to let it go." His eyes closed and his chest hitched.

Pagan leaned in closer to him. "Tito?" she whispered. "I was the other kid you saved that night." She watched as his eyes opened fractionally and his smile widened.

"I saved a Sentinel? That's got to go in my favor, right?"

"I'd say so." Pagan knelt by the side of the car and felt the stinging touch of the water hit her face as the fire engine's hose reached their side of the lot. She could tell Ammassari was fading fast, and for all he'd done that fateful night, she couldn't bring herself to hate him. She took his hand and felt him grip it. "Say hi to my parents for me when you see them."

"I'll tell them you grew up so big," Ammassari promised, then breathed his last.

Pagan bit back a sob as she watched over him and was thankful for the water that soaked her face and hid her tears. She bowed her head beside the car and let the water drench her, washing her clean of Tito's blood.

❖

Pagan and Rogue rode the lighthouse elevator in silence. Pagan felt bone tired and more than ready to get in her bed and sleep through Sunday.

"We need to get some cream on those burns of yours," Rogue said, peering at Pagan's hands. "You wanted to stay and help the fire crews, and look what happened."

"I was just trying to lend a hand. I didn't realize that I'd scorch my gloves and get burned. I'll go change into something more comfortable and come back for you to check them out."

The doors opened and Melina rushed into Rogue's waiting arms. They held each other tightly for a long moment and then Melina hugged Pagan. She kissed her forehead.

"You did a wonderful thing out there tonight."

"I gather you heard Tito's last words for you?"

"I did, and as much as I hated the thought of that man for so many years, I couldn't bring myself to hate the man who spoke to you tonight. May he find peace now."

"May we all," Rogue said. "That damned Phoenix disappeared like he got sucked into the shadows. I couldn't find him anywhere, and I was barely minutes behind him when he took off."

"I think there's much more than we realized to this boy," Melina said.

"I can't believe he was in plain sight and we didn't get him," Rogue said.

"He's an unusual leader. He actually takes part in the fighting, albeit a fleeting role tonight. But then, he did have the grand finale planned. He was obviously the one who set Tito's car in motion amid the distraction of the fireworks display," Melina said, rubbing at Rogue's neck.

Pagan smiled as she watched her sister knead Rogue's broad shoulders. Every so often Melina would reach out to touch Rogue's hair. Pagan shrugged out of her jacket, then pulled off her boots and trousers. She carefully peeled off her gloves and surveyed the damage. She pursed her lips. It didn't look *too* bad. Clad in just her underwear and T-shirt, Pagan padded off to the door in the wall. "Back in a moment," she called back, knowing full well she hadn't been heard.

She waved her hand over the secret catch that opened the door into her bedroom. The door was visible only on the inside of the lighthouse. From inside her bedroom, it was invisible to the naked eye, the lay of the wallpaper deftly hiding it from detection. Pagan entered and headed straight for the bathroom.

A voice stopped her dead in her tracks.

"Now that's something you don't get to witness every day. Let me guess, it's a walk-in closet."

CHAPTER EIGHTEEN

Pagan turned around to find Erith seated on her bed, leaning back against the headboard, dressed in her sleep attire.

"How did you get in here?" Pagan asked.

Erith held up a small penlike device. "It broke the triple locks that curiously hold the door to your room in place. No plain old key and latch for you, eh, Pagan? You're secured by locks, lights, and alarms in this place." She turned to stare at where Pagan had apparently just walked through the wall. "The door's gone. Just one more of the many mysteries this place seems to hold."

"Do you need something?" Pagan asked quietly, reaching for her sweatpants and pulling them on slowly as if afraid to startle Erith or the strangely charged mood in the room.

"I need to know what's going on. I was woken up by a series of very large explosions. I'm a light sleeper anyway, but these were fireworks that lasted for a long while. Now, unless it was someone celebrating the weekend in grand style, I'm of the mind it was something more suspicious. I thought I'd see if anyone else had heard it. I couldn't hear anything from Melina and Rogue's room and didn't want to bother the happy couple, so I came looking for you. I figured you wouldn't sleep in your hearing aids and wouldn't have heard the row that was brewing outside. I had the romantic notion we could sit hand in hand at the window and watch the display together. Imagine my surprise when the door was locked, and not just by any old means either."

"So you broke into my bedroom." Pagan was both alarmed by this thought and yet, for some strange reason, not very surprised.

Erith tossed the gadget on top of the bedsheets. "It got me where I needed to go."

"Just who are you, Erith, to break in and out of places at will?"

"I think the 'who are you' question is more mine than yours, Pagan. I can break in and out of places because I was taught at my father's knee how to evade and hide. The technology I came by through watching 'uncles' at work. Some of it fell into my hands. Men can be so careless with their toys. What I want to know is why Pagan Osborne, the shy woman who installs alarms for a living, who I find I love with all my heart, has the need for a multibolted locking system on her bedroom door."

"We're very security conscious. It's an occupational hazard," Pagan answered her, poker faced.

"Bullshit, and you know it!" Erith eyed Pagan curiously. "Why are you still dressed when it's long after four in the morning?"

"I wasn't sleeping very well—" Pagan began, but Erith held up a hand to forestall her.

Erith got up and crossed the room to where Pagan stood beside the window. The light of the dying moon cast them both in gray shadows. Pagan watched as Erith reached for her and pushed her a little out of the moon's pale glow.

"Indulge me a moment, please," Erith said and, on her tiptoes, reached up to Pagan's face. With her fingers shaped to make ovals, Erith fitted her hands over Pagan's eyes and made a mask shape that effectively covered Pagan's face.

"My own guardian angel. The one forever hiding in the shadows, by my side by night *and* day, it would seem. The one that very rarely looks me straight in the eye for fear I'll see the woman behind the mask. The same one who pitches her speech barely above a whisper, fearing that I should recognize her voice." Erith leaned back, removing her hands from Pagan's face. "Just how long have you been a Sentinel, Pagan?"

"Now why would you think that crazy idea about someone like me?"

"Because it's the only thing that would truly make sense about you."

Pagan blinked, stalling desperately as she tried to decide what to say.

"You shouldn't have brought me here, should you?" Erith asked. "My being here creates a problem when you go out to do your thing around the city. If I come looking for you and you're not here, what can you tell me? What could you possibly say that wouldn't sound fantastic or give the game away?"

"Erith…"

"And yet I've been so welcomed here, made to feel such a part of your family. Let inside, but not truly let in on what really happens here because you can't tell me. I'm a part of the ones you fight against. I'm one of the bad guys." She shook her head slightly. "You have to know I'd never betray you, or your family. You have my word on that, Pagan. I love you too much to ever give your secrets away."

Pagan stared at her and then leaned against the window ledge with a sigh. "You're right. You're not supposed to be here. I made a judgment call that I have not regretted, but I should have thought it all out first. I ended up exposing you to that which you weren't supposed to know."

"You're the Sentinel who got me away from home, aren't you? The one who took me flying through the sky, held me safe in your arms miles above the city?"

"Erith, you have to understand—"

"No, I just need you to confirm what I felt from the moment that Sentinel stepped foot into Rogue's office downstairs and found me seated before the computer deliberating whether I should do it or not. It was *you*. *You* who came into my home and rescued me. *You* who brought me to your own home. *You* who walked me safely back when I foolishly went back for my bike. The same you who is all too aware what my dad is mixed up in, what I was unwittingly brought up in, and yet still you brought the enemy's daughter into your family's home."

"Your father isn't my biggest enemy. Phoenix is. His father killed my parents. Now his son is carrying out a vendetta against his father's old gang members and the Sentinels themselves." Pagan looked out the window at the moon. "This Phoenix has to be stopped."

"By you?"

"If it is my destiny, then yes." Pagan looked back at Erith and marveled at how beautiful she looked in the pale light of the room.

"I knew it was you. I thought I was going crazy at first, but that Sentinel just seemed so much like you I trusted her right away without

even considering it. I felt in my heart it had to be you behind that mask."
Erith smiled. "You're very sexy in your leathers, do you know that?"

Pagan chuckled, relieved that the truth was finally known, yet unsure what to do next. "You have amazing skills yourself," she said, pointing to Erith's lock breaker. "Rogue is fascinated by your alarm disabler. Wait until she knows about this. And Melina will be very impressed by what you can turn your hand to."

"Is she a Sentinel too?"

"No, she's so much more than that." Pagan held out her hand. "I have to know something." She took Erith's hand in her own. "Can you still love me knowing what I am?"

"I love you, Pagan, all of you. The Sentinel is obviously a big part of you that I need to get to know, but from what I have seen, she's very much like the Pagan I know and love." Erith kissed her. "I love you, Pagan, woman and Sentinel both."

Pagan sighed against the soft lips that covered her own. "I love you too." She kissed Erith, then pulled back. "Come with me."

Erith followed her lead. "Where are we going?"

"Into the lighthouse."

"Except for Rogue's office at the base, I thought that was just a façade?"

"Oh, it's so much more than you could ever have dreamed of! Believe me, it's full of surprises." Pagan pressed at the hidden entry that led into the lighthouse. "If you care anything for me, whatever you witness here remains in your knowledge but never comes from your lips."

"On my honor," Erith said. "I may be my father's daughter, but his ideals and mine have long since parted company. I'd never do anything to betray you."

"It's not just me," Pagan said and opened the door.

Rogue and Melina looked up at the opening of the door and then past Pagan to Erith.

"I don't believe this place!" Erith gasped, twirling around slowly as she took in as much of the lighthouse's insides as she could see.

"Seeing *is* believing." Rogue pointedly looked at Pagan, then turned her attention back to Erith. "So, can you really be trusted with the knowledge of the lighthouse? Given your track record with the office below?"

Erith had the grace to look shamefaced. "I should have realized my breaking in here wouldn't have been something to slip under the radar. Not with Pagan being the one who busted me here."

Rogue gestured to the screens all displaying a point of view. "Let's just say you've caused us concerns on many occasions."

Erith nodded. "I won't let you down, any of you."

"*Again*," Rogue said.

"Ever again," Erith said.

"So, Ms. Baylor, will you share the details of your lock breaker with Rogue if I show you how we can monitor the whereabouts of people in our building, even when they should be asleep in their own beds?" Melina asked.

"No wonder you could send Pagan out after me so fast," Erith muttered, looking at the multitude of screens at Melina's work space—including one currently displaying Pagan's empty bedroom. Erith gave Melina a startled look and Melina just smiled back enigmatically at her.

"So I take it she knows everything now?" Rogue asked Pagan.

Erith stared at them all. "Oh, come on! I've spent quality time staring at her from over my desk. I know every inch of that face, that voice, and those hands."

Pagan could feel the blush slowly work up her neck and burst onto her face. She shifted surreptitiously to look at her hands, wondering what Erith found so fascinating about them. They were solid hands, with blunt short nails. She caught Rogue grinning at her and clenched her fists as if to hide them.

"She's the only person I've ever felt truly safe with, in the leather costume or out. My heart recognized the truth behind the mask long before I truly believed it myself."

Melina nodded. "You know she shouldn't have brought you here? You were supposed to go to a safe house."

"I'm guessing as much. Why *did* you bring me here, Pagan?"

"I wanted you where I would know you'd be safe," Pagan said simply. "And for me, with my family is the safest place to be."

Erith shared a smile that made Pagan's heart skip a beat. She then stepped forward and held something out for Rogue. Rogue accepted it dubiously.

"It won't bite," Erith teased. "Pagan said you'd probably be interested in what this little gizmo can do, and I owe Melina one for not ejecting me from the bedroom in the first place."

"She picked the lock to get into my room with that thing." Pagan fought down the urge to sound proud over the feat.

"You truly do live up to your call name," Rogue said, turning the pen-shaped object between her fingers, studying it from all angles.

"Call name?" Erith asked.

"We call you Red Fox over our comlinks," Melina said.

"Red Fox?"

"It wasn't my choice. Rogue picked it for you," Pagan said.

"I thought it suited you. It describes both your physical attributes and how wily you are."

"I'll take it as a compliment, then. So, what do *you* do here if Pagan is the Sentinel?"

Pagan laughed. "Erith, I am merely a fledgling Sentinel. Rogue here is Chastilian's *chief* Sentinel."

Rogue raised her eyebrows at Erith's slow and blatant appraisal.

"Did you train Pagan?"

Rogue nodded.

"Did you teach her the flying-people-through-the-air-on-a-thin-piece-of-wire trick?"

"I jumped off a building with her when she was barely six years old."

Erith looked at Melina for an ally. "What have I gotten myself into here?"

"A family that will protect you with both their love and honor," Melina replied.

"Melina is one of Chastilian's Sighted. She watches over us when we are out in the city. She sees all, knows all. She's our eyes in the darkness," Pagan said.

"You have the computers and surveillance equipment that an IT geek would sell their soul for." Erith's eyes ran over the various monitors, each with its own view of the outside world.

"On the subject of gadgets, tomorrow you and I will have a talk about just what you can make. I think we can find a better use for your talents from now on," Rogue said, still looking over the item Erith had given her.

"Does that mean I get to be a Sentinel too?"

"No. Sentinels hear their calling way before they take to the streets. But there are many facets to the Sentinel's armory. The Sighted guide them, and there are others who assist in the cause," Rogue said.

"I can assist," Erith said. She looked over at Pagan. "I might as well use my talents wisely for a change."

"Though the skill of breaking into girls' bedrooms is a talent most lesbians would kill for," Rogue said under her breath.

"We'll stick to using them for a greater good for now," Melina said with a wry chuckle.

Pagan yawned and rubbed at her eyes with her fists, then winced at her damaged hands.

"Before you fall asleep, we need to get some cream on those burns," Rogue said.

Erith's head whipped around. "You got burned?" She was immediately at Pagan's side checking her over. "Where the hell did all these bruises come from? And there's blood on your face too! Why didn't you tell me you were hurt?" She cradled Pagan's hand in hers. "I'll see to it," she said, making a face at the scorched skin. She took the cream from Rogue and reached for Pagan. "Is she done for the night now? Off duty or whatever?"

Melina nodded, clearly amused at Erith's take-charge attitude.

Erith paused for a moment before taking Pagan away. "Those fireworks were more than just exuberance, right? You guys would be the ones to know?"

"Tonight the Phoenix hit the Ammassari Dealership. The fireworks were just one part of the fire display he had to offer," Melina told her. "I'm sorry, Erith, but Tito Ammassari died tonight."

Erith's face crumpled as she received the news. "He was a nice man, a good boss." She bit at her lip and raised her eyes to Pagan. "You were right. This Phoenix has to be stopped." She paused, then asked, "My dad is still in custody, isn't he?"

"He's still with the police, yes," Melina said. "He wasn't out with the rest of the gang tonight, Erith."

"He doesn't know when he's well off." Erith shook her head and turned her attention back to Pagan, who was standing silently beside her. "I'll sort Pagan out and then get back to bed. Rogue, you and I will talk tech tomorrow."

"I'll look forward to it."

Erith led Pagan back toward the lighthouse wall. "How come the door is visible on this side of the wall but not on the other?"

"Sentinel magic," Pagan said as she triggered the secret door back to her room. She turned back to Melina and nodded toward her screens. "You can turn off the camera to my room now."

"It triggered the second Erith started working on the locks," Melina said, reaching over to press a button so the screen showed yet another angle of the city instead. "I was otherwise engaged this evening to do anything about our resident locksmith."

"Is there *nothing* you don't know about?" Erith asked before stepping through the door.

"Inside this home, no. But outside it, I could stand to know where Phoenix's hideout is," Melina replied. "It appears he can evade us at every turn."

"You'll track him down, I have no doubt of that," Erith said and pushed Pagan into her room. "Let's get you sorted and get you to bed. The hours you keep, it's a wonder you can function properly in the real world!"

The door to the lighthouse disappeared once more and Erith shook her head as the bedroom wall gave away none of its secrets. "Hidden cameras, magic doorways, Sentinels masquerading as security specialists."

"Hey, I wasn't masquerading. We really fitted all that equipment for the car lot. This business is as much mine as it is Melina and Rogue's." Pagan sat down on her bed and jumped a little when she felt Erith's small hands run across her neck.

"You need to get your T-shirt off so I can assess the damage. You've gotten a burn mark here too somehow." Erith ran a finger along Pagan's neck and tugged at the offending article. "Off!" She hastened to the bathroom and came back with a damp cloth and a towel.

Pagan swiftly removed her top and heard Erith's intake of breath at her near nakedness. She felt warm hands smooth a path across her shoulders and down her bare arms. She realized Erith was feeling the muscles under her skin.

"You seem a little distracted there, Erith. After all, it's my hands that got burned the most!" Pagan teased, sneaking a peek over her shoulder and catching Erith's absorbed attention.

"I have you in front of me in just your sports bra. Excuse me if I use that opportunity to indulge myself." Erith placed a small kiss in the nape of Pagan's neck, then pulled back reluctantly. "Pass me the cream before I forget my true purpose here."

Pagan removed the lid off the jar and dutifully handed it to Erith. Erith applied it to the angry burn on Pagan's neck. Pagan had no clue as to how it got there but was enjoying the attention she was receiving because of it.

"You get too close to something burning?" Erith asked as she traced a particularly nasty scorch mark.

"You could say that." Pagan relaxed under Erith's gentle touch. She pushed the memory of the flame handler setting himself on fire out of her mind and concentrated on the gentle soothing cream Erith's hands were applying.

Erith smoothed the salve in with quiet concentration, then kissed Pagan on the back of her head. "All done," she said huskily. She picked up the cloth and wiped carefully at the dried blood streaking Pagan's face. Then she moved to Pagan's side and reached for her hands.

"You got a little too close to something tonight," she said as she carefully washed Pagan's hands with her cloth and then smoothed in the cream.

"I've seen way too much fire in the past few days. This Phoenix takes the whole *fire bird* thing way too literally for my liking," Pagan said drowsily, the night's exertions finally catching up with her. She stretched and yawned. "I need to go to sleep. I'm so glad they chose the weekend to hit. I can sleep in tomorrow…today," she amended. She rubbed at her face tiredly and then regarded Erith. "You've had quite an enlightening night too, I'd say."

"I'm wondering if it isn't all some bizarre dream, but I look at you and it all makes perfect sense." Erith yawned. She gave Pagan a shy look. "Don't think me forward or anything, but…" She hesitated, her face flaming a little before she took the plunge. "Can I stay with you tonight?"

Pagan nodded. "Sure. I'll admit to never having had a sleepover before. Especially not at my age. You'll have to forgive me if I inadvertently take up all the bed or steal the covers." She padded into her bathroom. "I'll just get ready before I crash out on the floor and save you the worry."

After brushing her teeth and getting her pajamas on, Pagan

wandered back into her room. She found Erith already tucked under the blankets, her red hair spread out over Pagan's pillow. For a moment, Pagan's fatigue disappeared. She was arrested by the sight that lay waiting in her bed. She stared at Erith for a long moment, her eyes caught by how Erith's hair was lit by the light coming from the bathroom. She turned the light off reluctantly, bathing the room in the paler shades of light from the near-dawn sky.

"You are too beautiful for words," Pagan said as she crawled under the sheets, trying very hard not to touch Erith. Erith, it seemed, had no such compunction. She immediately snuggled into Pagan. Pagan relaxed as soon as she felt Erith's warmth permeate her flesh.

"Do you usually sleep with your aids in?" Erith asked. Pagan shook her head. "Then take them out. If I need you, I'll make sure you know about it."

Pagan nodded. She had been nervous about removing her tenuous link to the hearing world in Erith's presence. She removed the aids and placed them on her bedside table, then snuggled back down. She adjusted to the silence that descended on her. For a moment it disoriented her, but then she found her balance. She sighed, then felt a shift in the bed and opened her eyes to find Erith looking down at her.

"I can still read your lips," Pagan said. "My hearing may be lousy, but my eyesight is perfect."

Erith smiled seductively, then kissed across Pagan's cheek, along her jawline, and then lingered on Pagan's earlobe. "What are my lips saying now?" Erith made sure that Pagan could read the words before she continued to kiss along Pagan's neck.

"They are saying 'damn you for being so wrecked, Pagan Osborne.'" She chuckled.

Erith nuzzled into Pagan, her hand curling around a handful of her pajama shirt and holding on tight. "See? We can communicate perfectly." She leaned up to kiss Pagan slowly but surely, then burrowed back down to curl into Pagan's side.

For the first time, the total silence of the night held no fear for Pagan. She was anchored in Erith's arms; she could feel her breathing beside her. She moved a hand to place it over Erith's chest. Beneath her fingers she felt the strong beat of Erith's heart. It lulled Pagan to sleep with its regular rhythm. It was the most soothing sound Pagan had ever felt.

CHAPTER NINETEEN

It was some time later that Pagan awoke to find bright green eyes staring down at her.

Good morning, sweetheart, Erith signed, smiling as Pagan blinked at the sunlight streaming through the curtains.

"You've been reading up," Pagan said. She stretched her whole body like a lazy cat, then snuggled back into Erith's warmth.

"That's what the Internet is for," Erith said. "It's a mine of information at your fingertips. I was doing that last night while you were otherwise *entertained*." She held up her hands and signed very clearly. *I love you.*

Pagan smiled widely. "I love you too." She rubbed at her earlobe shyly. "I've never slept with anyone before."

Erith ran a hand over Pagan's face. "Me neither. And I didn't expect that the first time I did all I would do is actually *sleep*!"

"I was out all night. I wouldn't have wanted our first time to have me falling asleep before the fun started." She gathered up her aids. Erith halted her movements.

"Do they hurt you?"

Pagan again marveled at just how perceptive Erith was when it came to her. She thought about her answer carefully. "They don't exactly hurt as much as they take some getting used to." She put the aids in her ears, with Erith watching her closely. "I've had years to get used to what I hear when these are in, but sometimes, to be honest, I like the silence better. There's so much sound that I pick up that has to be deciphered and processed, so I know what I need to pay attention to and what I can ignore. Without them, I can be vulnerable in a huge crowd. But with them, I can hear things beyond what the other Sentinels hear."

"What kind of things?"

"Well, I heard fighting in your home way before I ended up coming in that final night. I had watched you from your window barricading the door so that your dad wouldn't get in after you."

"You were watching me for *days*?"

"I've been watching over you for a while, yes. Sentinels aren't supposed to get involved with family disputes, but I couldn't stand it any longer. So I came in, and you know the rest."

"You flew me over the city." Erith's voice was wistful.

"Sentinels have all the best toys."

"I need to spend a great deal of time in the lighthouse checking out the equipment, I reckon," Erith mused for a moment, sucking in her bottom lip in a way that Pagan found distracting. "So, you were watching over me, eh? To be honest, I never expected my guardian angel to be dressed in Sentinel garb. I was led to believe in the wings-and-halo variety, not the big boots and masked sort."

"Whether in my Sentinel uniform or out, I promise to take care of you," Pagan said solemnly.

"I believe you. Can a Sentinel in turn be looked after by a small redhead who may not have the muscle power to break up chairs, but who would move heaven and earth to make sure you're safe too?"

Pagan smiled at her. "Don't you know little red-haired girls are the strongest ones of all?" She ran a finger through Erith's soft hair.

"We are more deceptive about our powers." Erith flexed a slender arm.

"But Sentinels can see the truth behind smoke and mirrors, and I can clearly see your true strength and beauty before me."

"Are we expected down for breakfast?"

"Yes, we always have an 'after the melee' feast."

"Pity, because I would love to stay like this all day with you while we find out whose strength gives who the most stamina!"

Pagan laughed. "That may have to be something we test out on a day when Rogue is less likely to come knocking on the door." She paused and then a loud knock sounded and a light flashed in Pagan's room.

"You're amazing." Erith started at the noisy intrusion.

"Nope, I just recognize her step and know her routine, seeing as I've known her for as long as I can remember." Pagan put her hands on Erith's hips and smoothed them down over her cotton pajamas. "Time for a family breakfast with a difference."

"You're going to talk tactics all through it, aren't you?"

"And you're going to hear exactly what happened last night that caused you to leave your bed and find your way to mine."

"I can live with that. I like to be kept well informed on such important matters. It better be good to drag me away from you like this."

"There's probably pancakes."

"Sold!" Erith was off the bed in a flash.

Pagan blinked at her speed. "Great! Pancakes win over me?" she whined pathetically, enjoying the laughter she could see reflected in Erith's eyes.

"Will they have syrup?"

"Probably," Pagan said as she swung her legs out of the bed.

"Then there's no contest. Syrup is undoubtedly a winner."

"Fickle wench," Pagan grumbled and then let out a whoof of air as Erith launched herself into her unsuspecting arms.

Erith tugged on Pagan's pajama collar until she was within reach and kissed her thoroughly.

"How marvelous, you don't suffer from dreaded morning breath. This deal just gets better and better."

"*Pagan!*" Rogue shouted up the stairs.

"Your pancakes are waiting," Pagan muttered around Erith's soft lips.

"They can wait a minute. I'm tasting something far sweeter." Erith licked at Pagan's lips delicately, sending an almighty shudder through Pagan's body.

"Whoa, sugar rush," Pagan mumbled and kissed Erith back before reluctantly drawing away.

Erith took Pagan's hand. "Come on, then. Let's go gather around the table, eat our fill, and find out what happened last night."

"I know all too well what happened last night."

"Well, for most of it I was tucked in my own bed, totally oblivious.

Humor me. I want to know what this city gets up to while the rest sleep on, blissfully unaware of what *really* happens when things go boom in the night."

"If we do that, you'll never close your eyes again," Pagan said darkly.

Erith threw her a wary glance. "Why do I not think you're joking?"

"I rarely joke about matters such as these."

Erith let out a shaky breath and forged ahead. "Then I'm going to need a lot of pancakes."

❖

Pagan busied herself cleaning her uniform boots while trying not to be too obvious watching Erith and Rogue poring over electronics and tools. Erith had shown a keen interest in the circuitry that powered Pagan's aids and also formed an integral part of the Sentinel's comlinks. Rogue had explained in great detail what had been added to enhance Pagan's hearing ability. Erith had shown she was able to keep up in the technicality of the conversation. Pagan had been surprised to hear that a man such as Baylor, who used his fists to cause so much hurt, could turn them to work on delicate machinery. That skill, over his more brutal talents, had been the one mercifully realized in Erith.

Melina sat at the monitor bay and was typing in codes from her keyboard. "Pagan, how are you feeling today? Are your burns healing?"

"They're doing fine. That cream works miracles. They don't even itch now."

"I've never seen anyone heal so fast," Erith said. "The burns are almost healed over."

"We have at our disposal a wealth of experts who develop things to make our jobs easier for us," Melina said. "The ones that manufacture healing creams have long since been put to work trying to heal that which we keep on damaging."

"Do they make a fear pill to take away the fear of constantly wire-riding from tall building to tall building?"

Melina chuckled at Erith's question. "Oh, rest assured that

Sentinels are not entirely fearless. Fear is a healthy by-product of what they do. Thankfully, not all of us leap from buildings. Some of us are born to take the more sedate protector's path." She gestured at the endless screens and workings that lined the lighthouse walls.

"So, how did you get to be a Sighted?" Erith edged over to Melina's work station, her eyes on the flashing lights and endless screens.

"It's in my blood as much as Pagan was born to be a Sentinel. My calling just put me behind the computers and monitors rather than doing the physical stuff that my counterparts do."

"She was born to take our mother's mantle," Pagan said. "Mom was one of Chastilian's Sighted, and Dad was a Sentinel. Although back in their day, they didn't have half as much equipment as we utilize now. They were very different Sentinels then."

"The family business," Erith muttered, then laughed. "You said you were in the family business, and I innocently thought that meant the security part."

"I'm a part of that too. I just have two jobs, a day and a night one."

"How do you not fall asleep standing up?"

"We're not out all night generally, and we're not always called out. It's on rare occasions, like now, when the city takes on something a whole lot bigger than anyone can handle alone." Pagan flashed her a grin. "I also have good genes that let my body function on very little rest, and the blessing that is Sunday morning when I get to sleep in until dinnertime," Pagan replied, remembering the luxury of waking up with Erith wrapped in her arms. She lifted her head to catch Erith obviously remembering too. They shared a look; Erith looked away first when something on a monitor caught her attention.

"That's my dad's name." She moved closer to the screen that bore his name along with further details scrolling along.

Melina sat back and watched as Erith read the screen. "We've been keeping an eye on him so you'd know when he was going to be released."

"This is from the police station? Their reports and..." Erith looked closer at one particular screen that Melina nonchalantly leaned over to and with a press of a key on her keyboard made a certain point bigger. "You have a camera *inside* the police station watching people come and go?" She sounded both astounded and respectful.

Melina nodded.

"You really do have eyes everywhere."

"Hence her title." Rogue moved closer to read from the screen. "Your dad's being released later today. They can't hold him any longer because your mother won't press charges."

"She never does. He'll kill her one day, and she'll still think she deserved it."

Rogue put a comforting hand on Erith's shoulder and squeezed. "You're not like her. You're stronger than her. You didn't inherit the victim gene."

"I won't ever have to fear what my mom does," Erith said assuredly, casting a look at Pagan.

"You don't hurt the ones you love; you protect them with all your heart and soul."

Erith watched the small picture from the police station's hidden camera. "I don't think I want to see him just yet."

"We understand," Rogue replied. "Just because he'll be back in your apartment doesn't mean you have to go back to be with him. Your home is here with us now. This is no longer just a safe house. You have our Pagan's heart, and you've found your place in ours. You're a part of the family now."

Erith silently looked at everyone around her, apparently stunned by what she was being offered.

Rogue patted her head. "Welcome to the lesbian utopia."

"You told her about *that*?" Erith asked.

"I didn't know what it meant," Pagan said. "I figured I'd ask the brains in the family."

"I am so going to have to watch myself around you all," Erith grumbled.

"And we in turn will watch over you," Pagan said and Erith smiled at her. She knew then she'd done the right thing in bringing Erith *home*.

❖

Pagan and Erith sat cross-legged on Pagan's bed. Pagan's hands moved swiftly, tracing patterns through the air, signing a stream of words in silence. Erith watched intently and then she started her own signing, the movements not so fast, more hesitant in their execution. Pagan nodded, visually answering Erith's question.

You're very quick at picking things up, she signed.

Erith grinned. *I am if it's important to me*, she signed back. *And this is very important. I want to be able to talk to you all the time, whether you can hear me or not*. She flexed her fingers. *Although I apologize for having to spell everything out like a five-year-old! Our conversations may take some time with me still learning the correct position for an* E!

Pagan spoke aloud while still signing. "Sometimes I like not having my hearing aids in. I feel different, as if I can sense things stronger." Pagan made a face at her own words.

"Maybe you can." Erith shrugged. "What's it like, not hearing?"

Pagan chewed at her bottom lip thoughtfully, mulling the question over. *Natural*, she signed back finally.

Erith nodded and cradled Pagan's hand in her own for a moment. Then she placed it in her lap. "I look at your hands and I'm amazed by how much they can do."

Pagan moved her hand slightly in Erith's lap and began to stroke at her thigh.

"You can fight and swing from fine wires." Erith's face added wonder into the words she was saying. "Those same hands mix batter for pancakes, hold my hand during a film." She smiled shyly at Pagan. "You touch me, without any physical contact, just by telling me you love me without using your voice." She lifted Pagan's hand from her thigh and laid a kiss in the center of her palm. She then folded Pagan's fingers over to hold the kiss inside. "I love that you share this with me, showing me how to sign, sharing so much of you." She gestured to encompass all that surrounded her. "The lighthouse, the security business, your family."

Pagan signed quickly. *My heart*.

Erith nodded. "I love that most of all. I have to be honest, I love your voice."

"I don't remember what I sounded like before the accident."

"You have this marvelous clipped tone, very precise in some words, very husky and low in tone." Erith's eyes sparkled. "I love how you say my name. You don't say it quite like everyone else. You add a little accent to it that makes me shiver inside."

"*You* purse your lips very distinctly when you say my name," Pagan said. "It looks like a tiny kiss forming on your lips, kissing my name out of your mouth."

"Who would have thought lip reading could be so sexy?" Erith said.

Pagan edged forward slightly. "I can read your lips better if I get nearer," she said with all seriousness and Erith leaned forward in reaction.

"How close?" Erith asked, watching Pagan's eyes fix firmly on her lips.

"Maybe this close." Pagan leaned forward and took Erith's lips under her own. She savored the gasp she felt as she took Erith's lower lip and sucked on it. She let her tongue explore, tentatively running it along lush fullness. She tasted Erith, thrilling to her unique taste, almost as sweet as she was in spirit, as intoxicating as any wine. Erith's arms wrapped about Pagan's shoulders as Pagan deepened their kiss. Pagan shuddered as Erith's tongue tangled with her own, then moved across Pagan's slightly swollen lips. Pagan shook almost violently in Erith's arms. Erith looked up at her.

"Are you all right?" she asked softly, her lips moving to explore Pagan's heated cheeks and around to kiss at her earlobe. When Erith sucked it into her mouth, Pagan hissed at the force of arousal that flamed across her skin.

"Oh, you're sensitive there! How appropriate," Erith crowed softly and spread kisses across Pagan's brow to search out her other ear.

"You're an excellent kisser," Pagan said as she writhed under Erith's soft ministrations.

"You're marvelous to kiss." She started a path down Pagan's neck, seeking out sensitive areas, releasing Pagan's gasps and groans as she sought out responsive regions. Erith nuzzled at the V that showed off Pagan's neck but revealed nothing beyond that. "Have you ever…?" Erith's voice was shaky with arousal.

"You're the first woman I've even kissed," she said. "I just never seemed to find time between leaving school and taking to the skies."

"I've never found anyone I wanted to give myself to," Erith said. "Never found the woman I knew would be the one for me." She lifted her head to look Pagan directly in the eyes. "Until now. I want you."

"I want you too," Pagan replied, her voice so gruff it was little more than a whisper. She reached out a shaky hand to trace a line down Erith's small nose, running along her cheeks, touching the freckles that were scattered in a wild array across her skin. "I want to follow the trail these freckles take."

"I hated them," Erith said as she shifted under Pagan's touch, nudging closer under the gentle fingertips caressing her face.

"No, they're lovely. They are kisses left by the gods who found you beautiful."

"You sweet talker, you." Erith blushed.

Pagan leaned closer and ran her lips along Erith's cheek, then down her neck, nipping at the pulse point that pounded there. She nuzzled Erith's ear, then kissed her way further down, breathing in Erith's warm scent. She pushed aside the baggy neck of Erith's requisite black T-shirt. She found she could push it low over one shoulder, and her lips followed a particular trail of freckles decorating Erith's soft skin there. Erith's hands came up to spear through Pagan's hair, holding her head still in some places, pushing her past others in search of sweeter flesh. Pagan managed to nudge Erith's T-shirt lower still and followed a darker line of freckles across Erith's collarbone. The freckles disappeared into Erith's cleavage. Pagan stopped herself when she realized how far she was going.

"Maybe we should stop," she said, drawing back from the tempting flesh before her. Her eyes were drawn to the soft curves outlined more clearly through the unintentional tightening of Erith's shirt across her chest.

"I loved what you were doing," Erith said, but tugged her T-shirt back into place, once again effectively covering up her body.

"Why do you wear such baggy clothes?"

"Because it detracts the eye from me, dear Pagan," Erith said fondly. "People only see the black clothes with the lurid pictures. I am invisible inside them. I have wanted to be invisible for so long it's second nature now."

"You don't need to hide from me."

"I know I don't. Besides, I have to admit, I kind of like the baggy shorts and big boots combination. I'm butch and femme all at the same time with my long hair. It's a very fashionable look."

"I think you look great. And I like that sometimes, when you're stretching, I get to see something of what is usually concealed beneath all that black." Pagan grinned at Erith's scandalized look.

"Why, Pagan Osborne, have you been ogling me?"

"I've noticed everything about you." She sighed and rubbed at her eyes. "And as much as I would love to explore further"—she ran a finger around the collar of Erith's T-shirt—"I am due for duty in about an hour and need to get ready for that."

Erith looked over at the clock on the bedside table. "We've been signing for some time."

"Among other things," Pagan teased her. She got off the bed and out of temptation's way.

"I liked the other things too. You're going to make it very hard for me to lie in bed tonight and not dream about the fire you've started." Erith touched her lips as if still feeling the kisses Pagan had left there.

Pagan smiled at her dreamy look, feeling rather proud that she had been the one to put it there. "Melina said that you could stay up a little with her and watch what happens in the lighthouse when we're out in the city. That is, if you'd like to?"

Erith bounced off the bed and grabbed Pagan's shoulders. "I would *love* that. I promise I'll be very quiet and won't touch anything or lean on any buttons."

"She'd appreciate that." Pagan pulled Erith close to her. "You are so beautiful. I can't believe you would choose me."

"I chose you because you are the most gorgeous woman I have come across. You have that roguish smile and those gorgeous dark blue eyes, and a voice that does curious things to my insides."

"I'd bet you never realized just what you were letting yourself in for, getting involved with me."

"I was letting myself in for a world of love. Who could resist such a wonderful thing?" She paused for a moment, then raised serious eyes. "You need to promise me something."

"Anything."

Erith chuckled at Pagan's easy capitulation. "You need to promise me that you won't let your need for revenge against this Phoenix cloud those beautiful eyes of yours and lead you down a path of no return. You have me to think about now. I could be the most important thing in your life, if you want me to be. I want to be all that for you and more. But I heard the stories about the other night, and I also saw your anger at what this Phoenix is doing in his father's name. I'm not stupid. I've lived with someone constantly raging for more years than you've had that fury burning in your gut. But racing blindly after the son of the one who masterminded your parents' deaths without a care for your own life will not bring them back." She tugged at Pagan's chin. "I understand the rage, I sympathize with it, but you need to temper it before it consumes you and makes you no better than he is."

"You can't understand how it feels. I watched them die right before my eyes."

"Then honor them by being the Sentinel they wanted you to be. One that seeks justice, not claws for revenge. One that uses her might for good, not to destroy. He wrecked your world so long ago. Don't let him ruin what you have now. You are such a caring soul. It's what drew me to you in the first place. Please, Pagan, care enough about yourself that you see how much we all need you in our lives." Erith snuggled in close and held Pagan tightly to her. "I need you so much. Melina and Rogue need you too."

Pagan wrapped herself about Erith and held on tight. "I'll be more mindful."

"That's all I ask."

❖

Pagan was very conscious of the fact that Erith was watching her get into her Sentinel uniform. She fastened up the jacket and reached for her mask. Erith forestalled her putting it on.

"Even all this heavy-duty leather couldn't detract from the fact that Pagan Osborne was inside. Even with that mask hiding your face, I still knew, still recognized your spirit."

Pagan finished up her last buckle and wrapped the mask around her face, leaving only her eyes visible through the dark covering.

"Do you know you have eyes the shade of dark denim?" Erith reached up to trace the edges of the mask that rested low on Pagan's cheeks.

"Melina says I have my father's eyes." Pagan smiled as Erith's fingers trailed across her cheek and down to trace along her jaw. With some reluctance, Pagan spun Erith around and directed her out to where Melina and Rogue were waiting.

"So it's a family trait that blessed the Osbornes with such beautiful eyes?" Erith said loud enough to catch the others' attention.

Melina nodded from her seat at her computers. "Dad had such striking eyes, while Mom had a paler blue that I inherited."

"And lovelier eyes I have never seen," Rogue murmured softly, fixing her mask on and coming around to kiss Melina. Melina was smiling when Rogue released her to read something off a message screen. She grunted softly, then gave Melina a more lingering kiss. "We'd better go. The early Sentinels are being pulled back. Time for us night owls to hit the bricks."

Melina ran her hand over Rogue's heavily covered chest. "Come home safe to me."

Rogue nodded and kissed Melina's forehead. "Come on, kid. Shake a tail feather."

Pagan automatically checked her pockets again to make sure she had everything and then grinned at Erith. "Play nicely while we're away. And no touching the button that shoots the lighthouse up in the air like a rocket."

Erith's eyes grew wide. "You're kidding!" she exclaimed. "Can it really do that?" She craned her neck around, eyeing the walls, clearly trying to work out the logistics of that feat.

Pagan chuckled. "Sadly, no, but one day Rogue will devise a way. I can almost guarantee it."

Erith pouted at Pagan's teasing. "That was mean," she said, looking a little let down at the fantasy shattered.

Pagan kissed her sweetly. "Melina will look after you, and the minute you get tired, go to bed. You don't have to stay up all night. It's not obligatory."

"I won't go past what I can't endure, I promise. I'll just curl up under a table and nap if I have to."

"I'll see you later."

"Just come home safe."

"I will."

CHAPTER TWENTY

The clouds hung low in the night sky. The stars barely had a moment to shine through before the wisps of cloud covered them again. Pagan hung almost upside down over a rail, reaching out to grab at a piece of wall. She found her grasp with a practiced ease and stabilized herself, loosening her grip on the rail and stepping down onto a window ledge instead.

"Little spider, be mindful of the lights," Rogue warned as Pagan shifted to sidestep a window frame and then aimed her wire gun to traverse down the building in a controlled free fall. Pagan stopped her flight by catching hold of another window ledge, then springing off it to fly across to the building opposite on a newly shot wire. When she came to a halt she could hear Melina chuckling in her ear.

"Pagan, I was unaware that Erith knew quite so many expletives! I think the fact she could see you through Rogue's vision was quite a surprise."

"Just making my way around the city Sentinel style," Pagan replied with a grin. She looked up as Rogue joined her, then shot her wire up to carry her to the rooftop. "We're heading to the top of the city, Sighted." Pagan shot her own wire up and thrilled at the sensation that sped her through the air. She climbed over the roof edge and saw Rogue already armed with her night vision binoculars surveying the scene below. Pagan climbed up on the ledge and sat dangling her feet over the edge nonchalantly.

"Another quiet night so far," Rogue said with some distrust in her tone. "Somehow, I don't think we put that big a dent in the Phoenix's plans."

"Agreed," Melina said. "Still, the last few nights have been curiously devoid of the Phoenix's productions."

"It probably didn't help that we managed to capture a good number of his men at the car lot," Pagan said.

"True, but this Phoenix always seems one giant step ahead in his plans." Rogue put down her binoculars. "Police sources say that Vance Deaver cannot be reached. We have our own Sentinels and Sighteds searching, but he can't be found." She blew out an exasperated breath. "For all we know, he's the next victim on the Phoenix's to-do list, and he's nowhere in the city."

"At least nowhere we've been able to look," Melina added. "The football stadium is closed for extensive repairs. Sergeant Cauley is trying to get a search warrant."

"Bureaucracy. We can't afford to wait and watch, not anymore. How about Jackson Menard?"

"The latest information from our police source is his family reported him missing a day ago, so the police got them all into hiding immediately." Melina's voice was clear over the comlink. "Rogue, the Phoenix has had this planned for longer than we could possibly imagine. God bless Tito for filling in the blanks for us, otherwise we'd still be searching for who else the Phoenix wants his revenge on."

"Have we got the bank covered?" Rogue asked.

"The police checked it out the second the family gave their permission. Menard wasn't anywhere to be found there."

Pagan let her feet swing a little, tapping out a rhythm on the wall. She looked down to watch her boots and something caught her eye. "Rogue, can you look here a moment, please?" She silently directed her attention to the road below.

Rogue followed what Pagan had seen. "Well, well," she muttered. "I spy, with my little eye, something beginning with *B*." Both women trained their sights on the retreating figure of Joe Baylor scurrying down the darkened road.

"He took a while to make an appearance," Pagan said.

"But from the way he's moving, I'd say he has an appointment to keep," Rogue replied. She nudged Pagan. "What say we follow him, just to make sure he makes it to his destination without mishap?"

Pagan nodded and stood on the edge of the roof. Rogue joined her.

"West side destination," Rogue said and prepared to fire her wires.

"See you over there," Pagan replied, then spoke to Melina. "Mel, prepare your visitor. We're going flying." With her gun aimed and the wire attached, she leapt off the building and felt the chill of the overcast night pull at what little of her face was exposed to the night air. She and Rogue traversed the length of the building together, and the silent choreographed dance between the tall towers began.

Pagan and Rogue followed Baylor halfway across the city for a good half hour.

"Has this guy never heard of public transportation?" Rogue asked, keeping her voice low as they paused above him while he chose what direction to take next.

Pagan was situated higher on the building she and Rogue currently hung from. She lifted her head to check out where they were apparently headed. "Sighted, confirm what I can see in the distance, please."

"The Savernake Stadium," Melina supplied. "Home to the Chastilian Cobras, Chastilian's famed football team. Named for the founder of Chastilian, Bruce Savernake IV. Now owned by one Vance Deaver."

"Could the Phoenix really be hiding out in a football stadium?" Pagan asked.

"I'm getting the schematics now from our City Hall of Records," Melina said. "Now, that's intriguing. There are endless miles of sewers beneath this building. If you wanted to hide in plain sight but have a clear route out without ever being seen and have unlimited access to hot dogs and beer, then I would have to say this would be your safest bet. Pardon the wagering pun."

"Sewers, eh?" Rogue mused. "Is that how he can suddenly disappear from sight? Leave a sewer grill open and jump down, replace the cover and you're hidden?" She slapped at her forehead. "Damn! I never even thought to check the drainage covers. This guy is worse than a cockroach!" She watched Baylor continue on his way. "And this fool below has no idea that he is leading us straight to his boss."

"But we owe him that, because without *us* knowing *him*, you wouldn't be tailing him now to where he is headed," Melina said.

"Point conceded. Sorry, Erith, but your father is stupid. I just have to say it."

Erith's voice came over the comlink. "You don't have to spare my feelings, Rogue. Believe me. I've lived with his stupidity for years. But he's wicked smart too, so please be careful out there."

"Pagan, we'll need to go ground level soon. There's not much height around the actual stadium. God forbid people should witness the games held there for free while money can be made by selling tickets."

Pagan slipped down the building to reach the pavement once more. She soon caught up with Rogue and they silently stalked after an oblivious Baylor.

"Do you really think this is going to be the Phoenix's lair?" Pagan asked, watching as Baylor punched in some numbers to the huge gates that dwarfed the main entrance to the playing field and stadium.

"I don't think he's going in there to play a quick game of football," Rogue said as she gave Pagan a wry look. "I think he's waited long enough after his incarceration to get back into his boss's good graces. He's returning to rejoin the fold."

"I have the code, people, thank you," Melina said. "God bless the mask cameras and zoom-in mode."

The gates swung open with barely a sound and Baylor walked inside. Before the doors fully closed automatically, Pagan and Rogue had slipped inside too. They kept a safe distance behind, sticking firmly to the shadows, watching as Baylor jogged across the huge grassy expanse and disappeared through the players' tunnel.

"As much as I'm sorely tempted to follow him, we have no idea what lies in wait under this stadium." Rogue grudgingly nudged Pagan backward. "Sighted, have you seen all you need to see here?"

"Enough for now, but we need to get inside the underground facilities themselves. Phoenix could be anywhere hidden in the miles of sewer tunnels inside that place. Not to mention the fact that there are rooms and offices in the football stadium itself that he could be using as a base. We could spend forever searching. I need to try to work around that so we can pinpoint a location that could be used as a hideout. The only way we might be able to see what's going on down there is to send someone in with a tracer. With it they can provide us with important information and I'd have a better line of vision down there to plot our routes. As it stands now, I'm basically blind, which is not a good position for a Sighted. I'll keep on it. I'll get the other Sighteds to lend a hand, and we'll see if we can't dig up more information on what lies beneath that turf."

"We'll try to get back out of the stadium without setting off any alarms," Rogue said.

"That would be appreciated," Melina replied. "Come on home. Your tour is done for tonight, and we've yielded one hell of a result. Baylor has to be there for a reason, and I can think of no bigger one than to visit the Phoenix himself."

"Score one for the home team," Pagan said quietly.

❖

The lighthouse's interior was a welcoming sight when Pagan and Rogue stepped off the elevator.

"I can't believe you've found the hideout of the Phoenix!" Erith said, rushing into Pagan's arms. She made a very wry face. "Thanks, in large part, to my father. Who, obviously, wouldn't know discretion if it hit him up the side of his head."

Rogue, removing her mask, shot Erith a considering look.

"I'm okay," Erith answered her silent query. "I knew he was involved. It's not like that was any major surprise. I should have let go years ago on the whole hoping that maybe one day he'd change." She shrugged slightly. "I can't excuse him or apologize for him anymore. I've done that for too many years while he's beaten my mom and me." Erith let out a long breath. "I can't fight for the side he's chosen to be on." She touched Pagan's face, then reached around to remove her mask. "I've already chosen my corner to fight with," she told Pagan directly. "And it's by *your* side."

Pagan grasped Erith's hand and kissed her palm tenderly.

"But I can't say I'm not frightened by what my dad's gotten himself into," Erith said finally.

"I won't sugarcoat it for you, Erith," Rogue said. "He's in trouble. Phoenix is not someone you get involved with, and he's not someone you can walk away from alive either. His father was dangerous when he ran these streets so many years ago. His son kills on an even grander scale to prove his point. This isn't just a petty gang leader; this is a force to be reckoned with. This is the first concrete lead we've had on him since he started taking Chastilian apart. We need to have all eyes trained on that stadium, and search warrant or not, we need to get in there."

Pagan nodded. "I agree. The stadium is huge, though. It's going to take more than just you and me in there searching. As Mel pointed out, there's not just offices and locker rooms beneath the field. There are bound to be sewer systems that stretch for miles. We know Phoenix is not averse to getting a little dirty in his escape routes. We need to trap him in there, and that requires more power than the Sentinels possess."

Rogue considered for a moment. "Then we'll ride in under cover of the investigating police force. Two in black among the boys in blue should be able to slip in and search out the Phoenix's lair." She looked at Melina for support. "What say you, Sighted?"

"I think we need to check the stadium out as soon as possible. This might be the best lead we've had in a long time. I'll contact Eddie and ask him to move that warrant along quicker. We have two men missing, men we know are definitely linked to the original Phoenix. Our main priority now is to keep them safe."

Pagan settled on a chair and let herself relax a moment. A thought struck her. "What if there's only one man missing?"

Melina looked at her. "What do you mean?"

"Well, we have the nastiest crime lord Chastilian has seen in years taking up residence in the biggest stadium that Chastilian has to offer. It's a bold placement. If Phoenix has been there all along, then he's been ruling from a seat of power. He had to have help in taking it. The stadium may be closed for business, but that doesn't mean a villain and his henchmen can just move right on in and claim squatters' rights."

Rogue rubbed at her chin thoughtfully. "You think Vance Deaver gave him the keys and invited him in?"

"If his life hung in the balance, then yes, I'd say so. These men had Papa Phoenix killed for their own survival. I reckon they'd pretty much do anything to keep a hold on the lives they made for themselves after his demise."

"We need to inform the Council of this development." Rogue leaned forward and watched the screens. "We need the police on our side too." She pressed her lips to the top of Melina's head. "I'll leave those tasks to you. Call on Chief Cauley if you need to. Better yet, get my father to call him. I'm not above using all the big guns we have in our arsenal."

Pagan got up to see what was causing Rogue's distraction. "What's wrong?"

Rogue pointed to a monitor where the August Dawn Bank loomed center screen. "I want that building watched." She looked at Pagan. "I wish we could get someone of our own in there to check it out."

"I'm on the lookout for a new job," Erith said.

Everyone turned to look at her. Rogue spoke first.

"I don't want you anywhere near that building, Erith Baylor. You and trouble have yet to part company!"

Erith's jaw dropped comically at Rogue's admonition.

Pagan hid a chuckle behind her hand. "On that note, I think I'll get out of my uniform and go to bed." She was hanging up her jacket when Erith joined her.

"I get the distinct impression Rogue thinks I'm nothing but trouble."

Pagan looked down at her and smiled. "That's because she doesn't know you like I do."

Erith smiled and stood on tiptoe to press a kiss to Pagan's cheek. "That's very sweet."

Pagan shrugged. "She doesn't know that trouble doesn't even begin to cover it!" She laughed at Erith's outraged squeal and dodged the well-aimed hand. She caught Erith up in her arms, held her to her chest, then silenced all protests with a kiss. Erith instantly melted in her arms.

"See? Not even a hint of trouble now, are you?" Pagan's gaze lingered over the soft swell of Erith's full lips. "How about I walk you to your room so we can both get some sleep?"

"Do you really think I'm going to be able to sleep after a kiss like that?" Erith grumbled as she was lowered to the floor.

"You're going to need all the beauty sleep you can muster. Tomorrow's going to be another busy day."

❖

Pagan was fast asleep, deaf to the world and her surroundings. That did not stop her from reacting swiftly when she felt the bed dip behind her. She grabbed at whoever was hovering over her. She blinked at a startled Erith. Pagan quickly released the hold she had around Erith's throat. She shook herself more awake and hastened to sit up.

"I'm sorry," she said to a stunned Erith.

"No, I'm sorry," Erith said. "I should have known better. I should have walked around so you could see me and know I wasn't a threat. It's my own fault. I'm so sorry I woke you up from what seemed to be a very deep sleep."

"When I sleep, I sleep full out." Pagan rubbed at her eyes. She yawned and stretched. "What's wrong?"

Erith settled herself on the bed and shrugged. "I really think I need to go see my dad."

Pagan stared at her for a long, quiet moment. "I guessed as much."

"I won't betray you, you have to believe that," Erith said earnestly.

"I know you won't. I trust you, Erith, and I love you. But you need to realize your dad won't change. He sees this Phoenix character as a hero and not as the murderous thug we know him to be." Pagan tipped her head to look at Erith. "What do you want to say to him?"

"Good-bye. I need to close that door behind me. Otherwise I'm always going to wonder if maybe he *could* have changed. That if, by some wild freak of nature occurring, there might be a chance for him to stop beating on my mom."

"You don't believe that, though."

Erith shook her head. "No, I think he enjoys it too much. So I want to confront him and say good-bye without the added strength of a Sentinel taking me away. I need to prove to myself I'm strong enough to walk away from him. And if he gets taken away with the rest of the gang, I'm never going to know if I can do it. I need to see him for my own sake."

"You know I'm coming with you." She stopped Erith's argument with a raised hand. "I'll stay out of sight on the fire escape. Mel will wire you up. I'm taking no chances having you back with him, father or not."

Erith flung herself into Pagan's unsuspecting arms. She said something into Pagan's neck.

"What?" Pagan asked. "I didn't catch that."

Erith pulled back and signed her words. *I love you.*

Pagan grinned at her. "I know you do. Now let me go back to sleep. I need the rest."

Erith began to pull away, but Pagan stopped her. She ran her hand up Erith's slender arm, then up to tug at the nightshirt that she wore.

"You don't have to leave," she said shyly.

Erith immediately got under the blankets and snuggled in close to Pagan's side. She let her hand drift, exploring Pagan's muscles beneath the sleep shorts and T-shirt.

"Everything will be sorted later. One way or another, tomorrow will bring a result for us all."

CHAPTER TWENTY-ONE

Melina lifted Erith's baggy T-shirt sleeve out of the way and reached for the tracking device Rogue held out for her. She peeled it off its sticky backing and stuck it to Erith's arm.

Erith squinted at the virtually invisible patch on her arm. "You have got to share with me how you managed to come up with this device," she said to Rogue. She ran her finger over it. "This is so cool."

Rogue held up a small set of earrings. "I want you to wear a comlink too. That way, you'll know we are nearby and we can hear you, too, if you need us."

"How much trouble do you think I'm going to be in, seeing my dad?" Her face creased with anxiety. "He's still just my dad."

"We know, but he's also a known abuser who has ties to Phoenix. We're just making sure you're safe. Humor us if we're a tad overprotective." Rogue held out the pair of stud earrings, their golden color cut through with a streak of crushed green gems.

Erith held them to the light. "You a jeweler on the side, Rogue?"

Rogue shrugged. "I can turn my hand to most anything. Someone else picked out the color specifically for you." She cocked her head to a silent Pagan, who stood with her arms folded as she watched the proceedings.

"They're beautiful," Erith said.

"It's the closest I could find in Rogue's treasure trove of colors that would match your eyes," Pagan said. "I thought you'd like the streak of green. Rogue fitted them up with all the technology hidden inside." Pagan took the earrings Erith was removing from her pierced ears and watched intently as Erith fitted the new pair in and slid the rest of the comlink unobtrusively in her ear. She held back her hair to show them off.

"What do you think?" she asked.

"Beautiful." Pagan wasn't looking at the earrings. For a moment, the air smoldered between them until Rogue mercifully broke the heavy silence.

"Beautiful *and* practical. Those are my two favorite words to describe any kind of gadgets masquerading as jewelry."

Pagan carefully rested Erith's discarded earrings on a table and then turned to watch as Melina switched on a monitor.

"The earrings are your comlinks, now fully activated for us to hear you and for you to hear what is being said from the other comlinks attached to its frequency."

"Namely me as the Sighted, and Pagan and Rogue's comlinks," Melina added, fiddling with a switch and then tapping away at a keyboard to get the screen exactly how she wanted it. Melina continued once her screen was set. "The skin patch is a marvelous creation. Under the guise of supposedly stopping you craving cigarettes, it instead transmits your whereabouts to us here at the lighthouse. Wherever you go, we'll have you on our screens." Melina pointed to a screen showing a map of the city with a small pulsing triangle shape. "This, my dear Erith, is you signaling to us that you are here and stationary for the moment."

Erith stared at the screen. "I love living here. It's a techno wizard's heaven! Let's see just how sensitive this equipment is," she said and pulled Pagan down for a long, sensuous kiss.

Pagan was left panting for breath when Erith finally released her. She slowly blinked as she was released from the spell Erith had so easily put her under.

Erith looked at the screen. "Melina? The results, if you please!"

Melina chuckled. "You never moved an inch on our screen, but if we'd had Pagan monitored I'm sure she'd have shot off the map!"

"No kidding," Pagan muttered, running a fingertip over her slightly bruised lips. She looked down at Erith. "What time do you want to leave?"

"Now is as good a time as any, I guess. Let's get this over with. I say my piece, make my peace, and get out in one piece." She gave

Melina a hug. "You are the best family I could ever be a part of. Thank you for all you keep doing for me."

"We love you, Erith. And you're going to be okay. I understand why you feel you have to do this. I wish you wouldn't, but I do understand. Just remember we're with you every step of the way."

Erith pulled back slowly and eyed Rogue. Rogue held out her arms. Erith rushed into them and received a warm hug.

"You'll be fine. Pagan will be right with you, and we'll be watching over you. You know that Pagan won't let anything or anyone hurt you again."

"I know." Erith patted Rogue on the back gently. "Promise me you'll teach me how to make gadgets and gizmos like you do. I want to bring something to this family, to have a part of me travel with the ones I love to keep them safe."

"We'll start you fixing comlinks as soon as we have Phoenix and his men sorted," Rogue said. "Then you and I will put our heads together to see what else we need out there. We'll perhaps start with your handy-dandy lock pick."

Erith nodded then looked over at Pagan. "I got me a job with the family."

"The pay might not be what you expect, but the fringe benefits are excellent." Pagan held out her hand for Erith to take. "Let's get this over with so my stomach can stop rioting."

"See you two later." Erith waved to Rogue and Melina.

"We'll be right here but with you all the way," Rogue said.

❖

Pagan could not help but wonder at the prickle of apprehension as she walked hand in hand with Erith. She felt out of place dressed in casual clothing and not in her Sentinel uniform. Her free hand was clasped about a wire gun hidden in her pocket. She had the comlink and a means of escape, but without her Sentinel garb she felt exposed. She shifted uncomfortably.

"What's wrong?" Erith asked. "You're not worried because of my dad, are you?"

"There's a part of me that doesn't want you near that man, I admit.

But this feeling I have…" She shook herself as if it would shake free the feeling dogging her. "This is something else."

"What are you sensing, Pagan?" Melina asked from her comlink.

"It's nothing tangible. It's just a strange sense of disquiet that I can't seem to shake. This feels too much like a Sentinel mission carried out in daylight. It doesn't feel right." Pagan looked down at Erith. "I need you to promise me, if your dad starts anything, you come out immediately. Whether you reach closure with him or not."

"I promise. I don't want to put myself in the same old position again. I just need to do this for myself."

"I'll wait on the fire escape. If you need me I can come in through the window. You only have to say the word."

"So much for the fire escapes being secure." Erith nudged Pagan teasingly.

"If you need me, bricks and mortar won't keep me out."

Erith pulled Pagan to a halt. "I have never been loved like this in my entire life. You make me feel protected, and yet still give me the courage to deal with anything that I have to face. That's something I've never had before, someone who believes in *me*."

"You mean everything to me, Erith. Nothing and no one is going to hurt you again."

"Let me get this over with and then you and I can move on together." She stood on tiptoe and Pagan immediately leaned down so she could accept the kiss Erith had to offer.

"Be careful," Pagan said, reluctantly letting Erith's hand go.

"I will. Trust me." Erith entered the building.

Pagan looked about furtively, then leapt up onto the fire escape that ran the length of the tall building. Silently, she worked her way up the steps until she reached a familiar window. She could hear through the comlink connection Erith quietly singing under her breath to calm her nerves as she made her way to the apartment. Pagan settled on the small balcony outside Erith's old bedroom and listened to Erith's voice in her ear. She jumped when Erith knocked on the apartment door, and cursed herself for being so uncharacteristically nervous. She knew all of them were anxiously waiting for Baylor to open the door. Pagan felt some comfort in knowing that Melina and Rogue were monitoring everything that was happening. No one was alone in this.

The sound of the door opening and Baylor's voice were loud

in Pagan's ear, almost as if she were standing right beside Erith. She flinched at the noise.

"What do you want, girl?" Baylor said.

"I just need to pick up my gear and...see how you are." Erith's voice changed as she followed him back into the apartment.

"Came and got your bike already, I noticed."

"I needed it for work, and you were...elsewhere," Erith replied carefully, purposely not mentioning the word *jail*, but it hung in the room with its silent accusation.

"Guess your job went up in flames with Ammassari. Good riddance to bad rubbish, I say. They didn't do anything for you at that place. They just stuck you in an office shuffling paper. You're just like your mother. You don't have the smarts to get anywhere."

From what Erith had told Pagan, this was an old argument that had played out for years. It was a wearing-down tactic, an endless twist of the same old bloody knife. Pagan knew Joe Baylor wielded it well.

"I might just surprise you one day, Dad."

"You might at that."

Pagan couldn't help but wonder what Baylor had seen on Erith's face to change his tone, albeit slightly.

"Look at you, here now. I never figured you'd have the guts to come back again."

"How's Mom?" Erith changed the subject bluntly, expertly guiding his words away from herself.

"Coming home soon. They said she needed treatment of some sort. The doctors said she broke her face when she hit the floor this time."

"Was that before or after you beat her down?"

The growl of anger ripped through Pagan's head, and she was instantly at the window levering it open. She heard a chair scraping with some force across the floor.

"Don't you take that tone with me, girl. Remember who I am."

"I do, Dad, and that's why I'm here." Erith's voice contained just the barest hint of a quiver.

Pagan's heart broke for her. She raised the window a fraction more.

"She's smart enough to stay out of striking range, Pagan. Hold your position," Rogue's voice sounded in her ear.

"I know," Pagan whispered. "But he's like a loaded gun. I'm just waiting for him to go off." She knew that Erith couldn't hear what she was saying to those back at the lighthouse. Melina controlled the comlinks with military precision.

"Courage, Pagan," Melina said. "Believe in her. She's not as stupid as her father seems to think. She can't be. She got out."

"Acknowledged," Pagan replied and stepped away from the window, but still left it open a crack.

"Dad, I've never asked you about your work that brought us here to Chastilian. I've never asked what you are involved in. I've always done what you told me to do and got what you wanted." She paused at his derisive snort of laughter. "Except for this last time, that is. But I'm frightened for you."

There was a long silence.

"Why?"

"Because I'm worried you're involved in something darker than you realize, and I'm frightened you won't be able to get out."

"You're frightened for me, girl?" He barked out a gruff laugh. "You should be more afraid about the kind that you left here with. Word is Sentinels eat children."

Erith laughed. "Then it's a good thing I'm not a child, isn't it?"

Silence fell again. Pagan shifted nervously against the cold wall.

"You safe, Erith?" her father asked brusquely.

"Yes, Dad, I am."

"Good. Keep it that way. If you're as smart as you think you are, then you'll be best off where you are. There's something rotten in the vaults of this city; time's just ticking away on it."

"Dad, you could just go. You could go anywhere in the world. Just disappear. You've constantly moved us all my life. What's another night flight with suitcases stuffed?"

"And leave without your mother? Never. She needs me. And I like my job. It suits me."

"No kidding," Rogue said dryly in Pagan's ear. "A bully with a maniac for a boss. It's a match made in heaven."

"Dad, maybe you and Mom could start anew somewhere, start over."

"You're such a dreamer, little girl. You get that from your mother too."

Pagan heard a noise. "What was that?" she asked

"Something outside the apartment," Melina answered. There was a pounding on the front door to accompany her reply.

"As for your lack of sense in barreling right in where you shouldn't get involved," Baylor audibly sighed, "*that* you get from me. You shouldn't have come back here, Erith, not today. You're not welcome here anymore. Not since you left with that masked freak."

Pagan heard heavy footsteps heading toward the front door.

"Baylor." A high-pitched male voice sounded through the apartment. "The boss wants you in for the festivities tonight. He had to send me for you. We couldn't reach you on your phone. You forget to pay the bill or something?"

Pagan heard footsteps grind to a halt.

"Who's your girlfriend?" the man asked.

"My daughter. She was just leaving."

"No...*no*," came the reply. "She can come with us. We need new cheerleaders for the squad. The others are getting worn out."

"She's not joining the women you goons screw around with." Baylor's voice was harsh and, amazingly, held a touch of fear.

"Are you saying she's too good for the likes of us?"

"She's got smarts. She deserves better."

"Oh, I'm better, believe me."

"Get your hands off me," Erith said angrily.

Pagan heard Erith gasp in pain

"You'll make a nice addition. I know just the outfit for you too. Why hide behind the black and skulls? We'll show you blood-red soon enough. And when Phoenix hits the August Dawn Bank tonight with the full gang behind him, you'll see the whole city on fire."

"Let her go," Baylor said.

Pagan heard a recognizable click of a gun being cocked. She was instantly inside Erith's bedroom and pressed tight against the wall there.

"This is not going the way we planned," Melina moaned.

"You don't give the orders here, little man, the Phoenix does. And look who has the gun here. Shall I hold it on you, or pull the trigger on your little girl?"

"Don't hurt her," Baylor growled.

"Then she comes with us. How cool is this? She gets to watch her daddy be part of the party tonight, and then when we come back victorious, we can party on her ass all night long!"

Pagan heard Erith's intake of breath. "Don't do anything stupid," Erith said into the room, but Pagan knew exactly who she was directing the words to. "Dad, he has a gun pointed at my head. Let's just go with him, please? I don't want to get killed here. And I'd like to see where you work. You've kept it secret from me for too long. I'm a big girl now. I can handle it. It will be okay. Just do as he says and I'll be fine."

Pagan risked a swift look out from behind Erith's door and saw her being dragged out of the apartment. The door slammed shut on them.

Pagan dimly felt the pain as she banged her head against the wall in anger at her impotence.

"A bring your daughter to work day!" the young man could be heard to squeal over Erith's comlink. "How wonderful. You can show her where we work, Phoenix can show her what he does, and then I'll get my share of her later."

Already back out on the fire escape, Pagan looked down at the railing she held tightly in her hand and was not surprised to see it had bent considerably under her grip. Melina's voice sounded in her ear.

"Rogue is on her way to you in the van. You can suit up, Pagan, and follow where they lead." Melina let out a sigh that seemed to echo through the comlink. "This is it, Pagan. He's not taking any more family away from us. It's time to settle the score with the Phoenix family once and for all."

Chapter Twenty-two

There was something incongruous about the big black van that was waiting for Pagan when she raced down from the fire escape. Pagan wrenched open the back door and flung herself in.

"He's driving a sporty red sedan, license plate…" Melina's voice sounded through the van as they were linked to the lighthouse. "Oh, for goodness sake," she muttered, "license plate FE N1X."

Rogue growled from her seat. She was in her Sentinel garb, mask firmly in place. The blacked-out windows hid her identity and everything else that was stored in the vehicle. Pagan began to shed her clothing and get her own uniform on.

"What did you do to your head, Pagan?" Rogue looked back and saw Pagan's injury.

"Banged it off the wall," Pagan replied, hastily tugging on her pants and leaning to look into a mirror at the abrasion on her forehead. "It's nothing. It will heal." She pulled on her jacket. "Rogue, he has Erith."

"I know, sweetheart, and we'll get her back, I promise."

"Erith's tracer is working like a charm. The red sedan is pulling out on Crafter Street," Melina said. "There are three passengers. Baylor is driving. Erith is in the backseat with Laughing Boy."

"This wasn't how it was supposed to happen."

"Pagan, just finish getting changed. We're following right behind." Rogue pressed on through the traffic. "Mel, if we're heading to the Stadium you need to warn the police we have a hostage situation."

"I've just gotten off the line with Sergeant Cauley. He's already en route. They've gotten a tactical team on their way too. I think your father called in some huge Sentinel favors."

"Warn them to hold back until we know what is happening there. Phoenix is obviously expecting Baylor to arrive. If we jeopardize that, we risk exposing ourselves."

"I just want Erith away from these people," Pagan said angrily.

"Pagan, we'll get her back. I think she's perfectly aware of what she's doing. I think she's going to lead us right to where the Phoenix is. We won't be running in blind. She's going to have them lead us inside and straight to him," Melina said.

"We know where he is. He's in the stadium," Pagan said. She slipped on her mask and began to check through her belt for her gear.

"There's a lot of ground to cover both in and around that stadium. I need for us to know exactly where we're going before any Sentinels are deployed. I've alerted the rest of the Sentinels. If we need help they're ready to assist," Melina said.

Rogue watched the road ahead. "We're going to have quite the team going up against Phoenix's gang if we're joining with the local police force and a tactical team too."

"No arguing about territory or who has the bigger weapon," Melina said dryly.

"I just want Erith back," Pagan whispered.

"We will get her back, and Mr. Trigger Happy with her will get his ass pounded. I promise you," Rogue said. "No one messes with *my* family."

"So where is it we're going exactly?" Erith's voice suddenly sounded over the comlink.

"It will be a surprise when you get there."

"Do you have to press that gun quite so hard into my ribs, because if Dad here hits a pothole, I am not looking forward to the scar that bullet would leave." There was a small pause. "Thank you."

Pagan let out a sigh of relief knowing that Erith was reasonably safe.

"So, Dad, does Mom know *exactly* what you're involved in?" Erith asked.

"No, I figured what she didn't know wouldn't hurt her."

"No, that was all your job, wasn't it?"

"You, shut up! And you, just drive!" a whiney voiced ordered, and silence reigned inside the car for the rest of the long journey.

❖

Pagan watched helplessly as Erith was taken through the grounds to the empty stadium, and she waited for word from the Sighted. She listened to Melina over the comlink.

"Erith's like a little beacon, lighting up all the tunnels for us. I'm able to piggyback her signal, and it's blasting through their surveillance down there. I'll have a rudimentary map of where she is in moments." Melina's tone changed as she directed her next comments to Erith. "Red Fox, I know you can hear me. You are surrounded by those who love you. We can see exactly where you are and will follow you soon. You're blazing the way for everyone to enter, just as I know you planned. I'm so grateful to you. You've helped us more than you'll ever realize."

"She'll be okay, Pagan," Rogue said. "We'll get her out of there the moment the signal is given."

Pagan looked out the van window at the steadily darkening sky. Soon it would be time for them to spring into action. She could see the police cordoning off the streets surrounding the stadium. The heavily geared police tactical team were executing their own plan and moving forward toward the main gates. Pagan listened intently as Erith's comlink broadcast what was happening with her as the weaselly man received a call on his cell phone.

"Phoenix is livid! He says you've brought the police right to his door!" There was a sound of shuffling. "Why would the police be following us here? No one is supposed to know where we are. Baylor, you and your girl stay here until I know what's going on. I'll be right back." The sound of a door closing sounded loud over the communicators.

"Dad, I'm not safe here and you know it. He's barely able to keep his hands off me."

"Maybe that's what you need," Baylor said. "Make you a real woman then."

"I *am* a real woman. I just prefer not to have some sleazeball guy mess around with me."

"I can't believe I raised a—"

"Don't say it," Erith interrupted angrily. "Because as much as I'd hate myself for it, I would have to smack you right in the mouth for the bigot that you are."

Baylor was silent for a moment. "You'd hit your father?"

"I'd say it was a long time coming," Erith replied. "Where does that door lead? If the police are really coming, we're going to need to get out somehow."

Pagan listened intently while Baylor explained what went where under the ground. Pagan could hear Melina chuckle over the comlink.

"Pagan, you picked a smart one."

"The Osborne girls seemed fated to," Pagan replied. Rogue just grinned, not once taking her eyes from the electronic map she was poring over in her hands. The palm computer was blinking out coordinates and schematics for the tunnels hidden below the football stadium, courtesy of Melina.

"We have a detailed plan before us," Rogue told Pagan. "Our Sighted is now able to scan the whole area for us thanks to every step Erith took. Our Sighted is brilliant!"

"I merely use what you teach me every day, Sentinel," Melina replied. "I'm using the comlink signal to map out the stadium's underground levels. I'm supplying the tactical team and police with the same information you are receiving so no one will go in blind."

"When can we go in?" Rogue asked.

"The tactical team are entering in five minutes and counting," Melina said. "Take your positions outside the Stadium. I'm going to black out everything within a ten-mile radius, both above ground and below it. Under the cover of darkness we can sweep in and find where Phoenix has chosen to hide out, and get him."

"I have our route planned. We're going after Erith."

"Be watchful," Melina said softly. "Good hunting, Rogue. Pagan, go rescue your lady and guide her back to us."

"That's my number one priority, Mel," Pagan said.

"Lights out in two minutes, and the cameras in the stadium are under our control now, not theirs, so you'll be going in unannounced," Melina said.

Pagan and Rogue alighted from the van in the waning evening's glow. Pagan and Rogue ran to take their positions at the stadium wall.

A mass tide of bodies surged toward the Stadium. Above them, a few Sentinels were illuminated against the setting sun, standing high upon the towers, waiting. A few more came in on their motorcycles, equally silent. Rogue clutched at Pagan's arm as she checked her watch.

"Get ready."

The lights went out over Chastilian, silently plunging the city into darkness, the only light the vestiges from a swiftly disappearing sun.

Rogue nodded at Pagan as the stadium doors were slammed open by the lead tactical team. "Let the games begin!"

CHAPTER TWENTY-THREE

Pagan stayed close behind Rogue as she raced across the field behind the tactical team. She spotted Casper and Earl as they all ran toward the tunnel and into the underground lair. The four Sentinels easily blended in among the members of the elite squad that silently entered the stadium.

"Pagan, I have coordinates for you," Melina said. Pagan immediately headed off in that direction after Erith, Rogue not far behind her.

"Next left, now turn right." Melina directed their path over the comlink. "There's a door three-quarters down on the right."

Pagan flattened herself against the wall, escrima stick in hand, and reached for the door knob. She opened it quietly and heard Erith's distinct voice coming from inside. She flew into the darkened room and right into the waiting fist of Joe Baylor. The blow knocked Pagan across the room and into the wall.

A dim light came on as an emergency power booster kicked in under the stadium, and Pagan saw Baylor standing by the door, fists still raised. She quickly scanned the room and saw Erith standing some distance away. Pagan wiped at the blood that trickled from her cut lip.

"That first one was free," she said, staring at Baylor as he whipped around to face her. "But the second will cost you dearly."

"I'll gladly pay the price," Baylor said, barreling toward Pagan, who slipped easily from his reach.

Pagan called over to Erith. "Are you okay?"

"Better for seeing you," Erith said. "Dad, leave the Sentinel alone!"

Baylor grabbed up a baseball bat from a crate. "Baseball teams play here too. How fortunate is that? Ready-made weapons to smack the smug head off a Sentinel's shoulders." He swung at Pagan.

She retreated under his wild and erratic swinging. His fighting style was rough, but his anger gave him strength. "Erith, get out of here now."

Baylor halted. "You know this whelp?" He stared at Pagan. "Are you the bastard that came and took my girl away from me? You are, aren't you?" He swung again. Pagan dodged the blow, but the storeroom was small and she was running out of space to maneuver.

"You come into my house, kidnap my daughter, and here you are again! You got some kind of death wish, boy?" He swung again, and the bat audibly cracked and splintered as it hit the wall when Pagan swiftly ducked out of the way. "Is this the kind of person you like to consort with, Erith? One that hides behind a mask like some carnival clown?" He swung blindly, hitting the wall again as he missed Pagan, and the top of the bat sheared to a rather lethal-looking point.

Pagan tried to steer him away from Erith until she could overpower him and get the weapon out of his hands. She ducked as the bat swung over her head, and she tumbled against a cupboard that dug into her side painfully. The bat smashed into a display case, sending shards of glass everywhere.

"I don't want to fight with you," Pagan yelled at him. "Just let Erith go."

"Go where? Back with the circus freaks you hang out with?" Baylor was panting. "She should be with her family. You took her away from that."

"No, Dad. I walked away willingly from my family because it wasn't healthy for me to stay with you anymore. You were killing me!"

Baylor's eyes flared with fury. Pagan watched as he turned his anger for his daughter squarely on her.

"You set her up to this. You turned my daughter away from me!"

"You did that yourself with your fists and your endless bullying." Pagan kicked him in the chest, spinning him back.

"What would you know?" Baylor spat.

"You'd be amazed by what I know about you."

Baylor roared and threw the bat directly at Erith. He then lurched after Pagan. Pagan managed to deflect the bat away from Erith, throwing herself off balance in the process. Baylor grabbed her roughly by the shoulder and threw her to the floor. Pagan reacted quickly but not quickly enough in the confined space. He straddled her and stared down at her, seething.

"Not so big a Sentinel now, are you?" He ripped Pagan's mask from her face.

"No!" Erith screamed and rushed from her hiding place to Pagan's side.

Baylor pushed her away and threw Pagan's mask at her. "Here's your savior's disguise, girl. Let's see what kind of man he really is."

He looked down into Pagan's revealed face. His jaw dropped slightly and he frowned as he tried to understand what he was seeing.

"You're a woman," he said stupidly.

Pagan just looked at him, trying to predict his next move.

He stared at her as if he had never seen a female before, then touched the aids now visible in her ears. He tapped on them, making Pagan flinch. "Comlinks, eh? Are you wired anywhere else, Lady Sentinel?" He brutally ripped them from Pagan's ears. "Whoever's listening, you won't win!" he yelled down the comlinks, and then abruptly got up off Pagan's chest. He threw the aids to the floor and, although Erith was screaming at him to stop and pulling on his arm trying to unbalance him, he stomped on them, smashing them to pieces.

"Now you can't communicate with your friends anymore," Baylor said.

Pagan got quickly to her feet, snatched up her escrima stick, and moved across the room out of his reach while she got her bearings. She felt more naked without her mask than she did without her aids, as her natural instincts instantly kicked in and she let herself feel the atmosphere around her. She saw Erith snatch up the fallen mask and wave it in her father's face. Baylor backhanded Erith across the mouth. Pagan grabbed him around the neck with her stick and wrestled him down. He struggled, but Pagan held on tightly, this time having the upper hand. She spun him around and punched him soundly in the face. He fell to his knees.

"That's for the last time I saw you," she said. She hit him again. "That is for ripping my mask off." Another blow split his nose across his face. "That is for touching Erith with anything less than love." She went to hit him again, but Erith covered her hand to stop her. Erith moved around so Pagan could see her clearly.

"Don't bring yourself down to his level. You're so much better than he will ever be."

Pagan looked at the bruised and bleeding man before her. She sensed another person enter the room and instantly tensed, her escrima stick poised for action. She blew out a ragged sigh of relief when she saw Rogue standing there.

"Had you waited for me, we might have dealt with this scumbag a little quicker together," Rogue said and went over to where Baylor was bleeding on the floor. She took her Taser, placed it against his chest, and triggered it. He screamed, convulsed, and then collapsed in a shivering heap on the floor.

Pagan read Erith's shock at what Rogue had done. Rogue just looked at them.

"Tell me he didn't deserve that." She bound him tightly by his hands and feet, and when he began to move she threatened him with the Taser again. He capitulated meekly. Rogue moved to check out Pagan. She saw that her aids were gone. "Are you all right?"

"He took my mask off," Pagan said.

"That's not all he did." Rogue looked at Pagan's raw ears, some spots bleeding where the aids were forcibly ripped away.

"I'll be okay, but they were my most comfortable pair," Pagan said and reached for her mask from Erith. She walked over to Baylor, letting him see her face again. "If you ever tell anyone what I look like, I will hunt you down and personally use the bigger Taser that will make what you've just experienced a mere tickle in comparison." She put her mask on, then stopped. "Remember my face, though," she whispered, leaning very closely to Baylor. "It's the face of the woman your daughter loves."

His eyes grew large.

"You ever mess with her again, and I will see to it that you spend the rest of your living days in hell." Pagan fastened her mask back on her face. "She's *my* family now, and we take better care of our loved ones. Remember that and stay away from her if you know what's good for you." She stood and turned to Rogue. "Get someone to come and pick him up, and someone needs to get Erith out of here."

"You could take her back?" Rogue ventured.

"My job's not finished here." Pagan took Erith's hand and brought it to her lips. "I will be back home soon, I promise. You're safe now. The Sentinels will take care of you."

Erith tugged Pagan close and kissed her sweetly. "I knew you were right behind me. I never had any doubts."

"I love you. I'll always do my best to keep you safe. But now I need to go finish the other task at hand."

Are you going to be all right without your hearing aids? Erith signed discreetly.

"It's what I know best," Pagan whispered in her ear. She looked up as another Sentinel popped his head around the door. She signed to him and he nodded and rushed into the room to stand by Erith. "Casper will take you up to safety," she promised. "Take good care of her," she cautioned the young man, who grinned and held out his arm courteously for Erith to take. Erith looked to Pagan with a small frown at his gallant pose. "He's a good guy, I promise. He's one of those strong, silent types you like so much!"

Erith dodged the hand that Casper held out to her. "You're still going to go after Phoenix? Surely defeating him isn't more important than your own safety?" Erith turned away from her father so he wouldn't see the words she mouthed. "You don't have the luxury of sound to help you."

"Defeating him is everything." Pagan began to sign. *Because of him I grew up without parents.*

You had Melina and Rogue. What better parents could you have been given? Erith signed back. She looked down at the man incapacitated on the floor and spoke aloud again. "I had my flesh-and-blood parents, and look how they screwed me up! Going after him in vengeance is not who you are. You're better than that. Remember that, please, and come home to me in one piece."

Pagan felt a war going on inside her. She wanted to assure Erith that she wouldn't be foolhardy, but screaming loudly inside her was the need for revenge. Pagan let out a long breath and stared for a moment into Erith's impassioned eyes. For the first time ever, she saw her future could be held in the hands of someone else.

"I'll be home later. As a Sentinel, that is the firmest promise I can give you."

Erith nodded. "Then that's all I'll ask. But if you don't come back at a reasonable time, with your mentor by your side, I will come and find you and kick your ass all the way back to the lighthouse myself!"

Pagan nodded to Casper, who just grinned at Erith and led her away. Erith didn't take her eyes from Pagan the whole time she was escorted from view.

Rogue looked over at Baylor on the floor. "We could just kill him now," she said. She kept triggering the electrical current so the Taser crackled ominously. Baylor's face twitched in fear as he looked up at her.

"No, let's let him live and just tell Phoenix's men we capture that Baylor here led us straight into their hideout."

"They'll kill him for us," Rogue said. "I like that plan. No blood on our hands, and the end result is the same."

"Fitting for a bully, don't you think? He can only beat up women. Obviously he's not man enough to put that aggression to something more worthy. Pity, because his daughter is so deserving of love. He wasted what he could have had with her."

"Some people don't deserve family." Rogue waved over two Sentinels who came in to take Baylor away.

"I'm sure he'll make lots of friends in jail," Pagan said.

"He's homophobic, though. They might not be the kind of friends he wants."

Baylor's eyes grew huge at her implication.

"Guess he'll learn the hard way that bullies get what's due to them." Pagan watched him being carried away. "He'll have to watch his back in more ways than one."

Rogue laughed. "Our Sighted says we are very cruel."

"I miss her voice in my ear," Pagan said and patted her ears. "I'm going to have to start bringing spare aids out with me at this rate."

"The Sentinels have trapped a load of Phoenix's men in a room not far from here. Seems we caught them all by surprise. Erith is safe. She's being led off the field. Now we need to get back to the matter at hand."

"Settling the score," Pagan said, remembering her sister's words.

"Settling it and then some."

Chapter Twenty-four

P agan and Rogue caught up with the tail end of the tactical team's men. In the pale emergency lighting the team ran through the maze of rooms, picking off Phoenix's men one by one. Pagan punched a heavyset thug who burst from a room, knocking him back on his feet where Rogue brought him to the ground. Pagan high-fived her.

"Quite the tag team against men in bandanas." She chuckled and followed Rogue's lead. She searched her surroundings, all the time looking over her shoulder. She was very aware that an assailant from behind could easily pick her off. Pagan let her other senses reach out and felt the air around her.

"Rogue, something is different down here." Pagan paused to sniff at the air.

"How so?"

"I can smell fuel. Warn everyone, there is the likelihood of fires starting down here." She sniffed at the air once more. "No smoke yet, just that sweet cloying smell of gasoline." Rogue sent out the warning.

"Everyone is being warned. A fire down here would be devastating. Our Sighted says that she has alerted the fire crews and they are on standby." Rogue appeared to listen in again to the information coming through her comlink. "Phoenix's men disabled the sprinkler system. Our fellow Sentinel down here is trying to get it back online again."

"I don't want to be trapped down here, Rogue. I've seen more than my share of destructive fire, thank you."

"I won't leave you down here, Pagan. I promise you." Rogue flicked on her palm computer and scanned the screen. "While the tactical team check down to the right, you and I are being directed to the left. Looks like that's where the main offices are. We should check them out, if only to eliminate them."

Rogue marched off down a corridor, and Pagan followed. She hunkered down behind Rogue when she eased onto her knees to look around a corner. Rogue signed swiftly to Pagan.

All quiet, but there are sounds of movement coming from that top room. She pointed to a white office door with the words Manager's Office on a plaque just visible in the pale lighting. *I can hear more than one in there.*

Phoenix? Pagan asked. *He's the only one who could be this far down in the lair, and if they were planning on setting fire to the rest of the tunnels, he'd need to be away from that and still have an escape route.*

Rogue shrugged. She tapped her ear. *The rest of the police are on their way in. It looks like the whole gang realized they had uninvited guests in the stadium and they are all trying to escape.* She grimaced as cool water began to stream out of the sprinklers above their heads. *And Earl has fixed the sprinkler system.*

Pagan wiped water from her eyes. *Let's hope he can turn it off again, or instead of burning, we'll all drown.*

Rogue carefully cradled her palm computer out of the steady drizzle of water. *They've apprehended several of Phoenix's men, but some have managed to escape.* Rogue eased her way forward toward the door. *Curious. No traps or anything to warn them of our arrival.*

Maybe we weren't expected to ever get this close.

Rogue's head lifted toward the door ahead. *Movement. Let's go see who's up and awake.* She kicked open the door and they rushed in. Two men stood with their backs to the door. They quickly turned at the commotion and fumbled for their guns. Rogue brought her fist down savagely on the first man's wrist, and he dropped his weapon to the floor. She followed through with an elbow to his face, which knocked him back off his feet. Pagan aimed a savage kick to the crotch of the second man and he fell to the floor screaming, his weapon untouched, his priorities elsewhere.

Pagan looked up to catch sight of the third occupant in the room scrambling to get through a door. For a startling few seconds she stared into what appeared to be the face of Xander Phoenix, and she realized this was his son. He flung the door open with a crash as it hit the opposite wall and he rushed into the closet. Pagan reached into a pocket in her uniform and removed a tracker. She quickly flicked it after the escaping man. The button-sized device sailed through the air and landed to cling to the bottom of his suit jacket. Pagan got to see his face before the door closed behind him. He looked furious, his face a blotchy red in contrast to his pale coloring. Pagan read the words from his lips. *Change of plans!*

Rogue raised a thumb at Pagan's quick thinking as Melina confirmed the tracking device was working.

Pagan stepped over the downed man at her feet and carefully eased open the closet door. She peered inside. She pushed aside the line of coats that hung from a rail covering the back of the enclosed space. "There doesn't appear to be anything here." She gave Rogue a sideways glance. "And nothing to kick open either." She gestured for Rogue to join her. "Listen for me, please." Pagan began to rap at the wall.

Rogue put up a hand to stop her. "That sounded hollow." Rogue reached forward and pushed at a panel. Another door opened to reveal wooden steps leading down. "He's back in the underground tunnels again." Rogue's eyes flickered as she listened to the voice in her ear. "And he's speedy too. For a slender guy he can sprint like an athlete, I am reliably informed."

"Did you see him?"

"Between the rain falling inside and the guns aimed at my face, I was a little distracted. But I have a good idea it was Zachary Phoenix himself. Did *you* get a look at him?"

"Yes, I did. I saw him a lot clearer than I did that night at Ammassari's car lot. He's his father's son, right down to the same slicked-back blond hair. Please get our Sighted to confirm that I had a clear view of his face that they can distribute citywide?"

Rogue started to tie up the downed men. She looked up at Pagan and nodded. "His picture is hitting the wire as we speak."

"Excellent." Pagan looked around the room. In all the commotion, she hadn't noticed the large glass trophy case along the wall. She gasped as she took in its contents. "Tito was wrong. Vance Deaver didn't get away in time to be safe." Pagan directed Rogue's attention to the cabinet. Centered in the case was the Chastilian Cobras snake costume, topped with the large cobra head. Dress shoes were sticking out of the bottom of the snake skin. Pagan gingerly reached inside the case and lifted the cobra head off. Underneath were the decaying remains of Vance Deaver. His mouth had been taped shut, his costume nailed into place so he couldn't move. He obviously had been left to suffocate in the mascot suit, all while on display in the trophy case. Pagan gagged at the putrid stench.

"I'm guessing he was killed before Tito," Rogue said, making sure Pagan could read her lips. "Phoenix needed a hideout once he'd started his campaign. I'm guessing he came here and killed Deaver, which also provided him with the perfect base to carry out his plans. There's only one man left now. We need to get to the bank before it's too late. We're too close to him now for Phoenix to stop here."

They turned to leave. Suddenly, they were rocked back by a huge explosion from above. The corridor shook and pieces of the ceiling fell to the floor.

"What was that?" Pagan asked.

Rogue signed swiftly so that Pagan could see.

It felt like a bomb.

❖

The Chastilian Cobras stadium was rocked by missiles that rained down on the field. The explosions ripped open gaping holes in the field and smashed through the tiered seating, sending twisted metal everywhere.

Pagan couldn't believe the devastation. The fierce explosions made her stumble as the earth shook with the terrifying force. Some of Phoenix's men were scattered across the field. Some had been handcuffed by the police. Many were injured or unconscious. She could see others running, fleeing for their own safety as the missiles fell.

"Are Phoenix's men expendable to him?" she asked as the police tried to get the men out of harm's way.

"Clearly, once he was away, nothing else mattered." Rogue faced Pagan so she could read her lips. "We need to go follow him wherever he's headed."

"I read his lips. He said something about a change of plans. I think we upset his carefully choreographed killing spree by turning up at the stadium."

"Then he's got to be heading for the August Dawn Bank." Rogue looked up at the sky. "God only knows what he has planned there, but it's the last piece in this whole plot."

"To the rooftops, then?"

Rogue nodded. "The police are circling the streets trying to find the launchers. The Phoenix won't win, no matter what he does to us."

Pagan followed Rogue's lead out of the stadium. The stadium was ruined, like everything else Zachary Phoenix touched. *Just like his father before him*, Pagan thought. *And just like my father, I will make my stand tonight.* She took out her wire gun and aimed it high into the night to once more take to the towers.

❖

The race across Chastilian's roofs was a race against time. Sentinels swung into the air to travel from building to building. Others sped through the streets on motorcycles. All had one destination in mind: the August Dawn Bank.

With Rogue beside her, Pagan leapt from an apartment building and felt the thrill of the fall before her wires caught her safely and she was pulled high into the night to scramble up onto another roof. She puffed into the blackness of the night, feeling her heart pound, then leapt from the building and landed on the roof below. She just had time to peer over its edge and see the police below capture a group armed with missile launchers. She could see the August Dawn Bank looming closer. They finally took up positions at an adjoining building, and Pagan could see movement on the roof below. She directed Rogue's attention toward it.

"Looks like we have people waiting for us," Rogue said to the other Sentinels. "It's time this Phoenix's fire was doused for good. Put down as many as possible. This is not a rehearsal. Tonight we get rid of this gang for good." Rogue stood on the roof's edge preparing to swoop down on the bank below.

"In memory of our fallen Sentinel Alexis Osborne, tonight we will make the Phoenix family pay the price for taking away those dear to us." Rogue jumped from the roof to prepare for battle.

With her father's name read from Rogue's lips, Pagan added her own prayer to him and leapt from the tower to meet her own fate.

CHAPTER TWENTY-FIVE

Nervous gang members scattered like ninepins when the Sentinels hit the asphalt of the August Dawn Bank's rooftop. Phoenix's men raced for the door that led down into the bank building. Not all of them managed to get away. They were easily grabbed by the Sentinels who sped after them and chased the others down the stairwell. On the ground, other Sentinels arrived by motorcycle and entered the building.

Pagan and Rogue stayed on the roof, scanning the area. Rogue shared her palm computer with Pagan, showing her the red dot that signified where Phoenix was heading.

"He's coming straight here," Pagan said.

"And he has his boys waiting for him, but his thugs are being dealt with as we speak." Rogue spotted Akromon heading her way.

The huge man nodded toward them. "I've just been dealing with a young man who didn't want to stay at the bank for very long. It would seem the men are more frightened by what Phoenix has planned for here than they are of the Phoenix himself."

Pagan found this curious. Phoenix had already proved himself capable of destroying whatever stood in his path. Her mind replayed the threat that Joe Baylor had leveled at her the night she'd rescued Erith. *"This Phoenix will rid Chastilian of you Sentinels. He'll blow you all away."* That was why Baylor had been drafted back into Phoenix's gang. He was the means to the Phoenix's last display of revenge.

"You don't think he has the bank wired with explosives somehow?" she asked Rogue. "Would he really blow the bank up and everyone in it?"

"Everything has been heading to this last showdown, the final piece in his father's puzzle," Rogue said. "No wonder his own men want to be as far away as possible, especially those who just witnessed their own being sacrificed at the stadium." She scanned the building. "The Sentinels are inside the bank, as are the Phoenix's remaining men. Would he really blow up the building and risk wiping out his gang?"

Pagan nodded. "It's a win-win situation. Get rid of everything with one big bang."

"Someone has to have the trigger switch to set the explosives. I bet Phoenix has it. It's too important to him to let someone else have the honor of flicking the switch."

"We're playing his game, by his rules. Seems only natural he would hold the winning card." Pagan leaned over the side of the building. "Many of our Sentinels are now inside the bank. What's Phoenix's position?"

"Melina says he's now in the subway system," Rogue replied. "Seems he has graduated up from the sewers he usually travels in." Rogue shook her head. "And we had police posted at the sewer grates to welcome him out too. Damn it, can he be predictable just once?"

"Why come here? Why not just blow this from a distance?" Pagan watched Rogue's face keenly for her answer.

"I think he needs to dance on the final gang member's grave after making this last play. He's been present at every scene. He's not going to miss the finale. Everything has to play out to his design. I think he has to be here, slap bang in the middle of all the chaos that he alone has created." Rogue looked up. "Sighted, we need to have you check the skies. I think we have an airlift coming to take him away after he's done here." She looked back at Pagan. "Don't worry, we won't stay around long if he presses any button. Just keep your wire gun close at hand."

❖

Rogue watched as the police started to set up barriers around the bank. She knew Phoenix was coming, but they had lost his signal somewhere in the subway system. The sewers were being monitored. Every drain cover was being watched. He'd somehow managed to elude them again.

She was surprised when she heard Melina's voice through her comlink.

"Rogue, this message is for your ears alone."

Rogue's body stiffened. "What's wrong?"

"We have someone else heading to the bank, and I really need you to stop her before she gets herself in any danger."

Rogue closed her eyes and took a deep breath. "Red Fox fleeing the chicken coop again, Sighted?" she said, making sure that Pagan wasn't able to read her lips.

"She told Casper to let her make her own way back to the lighthouse so he could return to the fighting. She never made it here, and now she informs me she has something important to check out at the bank."

"I'm guessing it couldn't wait until *after* the Phoenix's visit?" Rogue caught Pagan's attention and handed her the palm computer. "I'll be back in a moment. Something needs my attention down on the ground."

Pagan nodded. "Be sure to get back before the fun starts!"

Rogue patted Pagan on the arm. "This won't take long. I'll be back before you know it." She attached her wire to the wall and eased herself over the ledge, quickly dropping down the side of the bank's tower. Once on the ground, she detached the wire and clipped her gun to her belt. She searched the dark streets before her.

"Where the hell are you, Erith Baylor?"

"I can direct you right to her," Melina said.

"Please do." Rogue was guided to a position well behind the police cordon. She spotted Erith trying to sneak around the police cars. Rogue stealthily got behind Erith, grabbed her by the arm, and hauled her aside. "What the hell are you doing here?"

Erith looked relieved at the sight of Rogue. "Thank God it's you! I need to get into the bank. My dad has set something up in there."

"And you know this for certain how?"

"Because he warned me. *There's something rotten in the vaults of this city, time's just ticking away on it.*" Erith tugged at Rogue's sleeve. "I have to get in there to stop it."

"Erith, the police checked this bank when they were looking for Menard. They didn't find him or anything suspicious."

"Did they specifically look in the bank vault?"

Rogue sighed and listened as Melina answered them both.

"The vault was on a timer switch. It couldn't be opened at the time of the search."

Erith slapped at Rogue's arm. "See? What's to stop someone from putting a bomb in the vault?"

"Your dad has been watched constantly since he was released from jail."

Erith shook her head at her. "He just has to make the thing. He doesn't have to physically place it somewhere. Someone else can put it in place. They just have to be told what switch to flick or how quick to run."

Rogue regarded her. "And you can do what exactly?"

"You get me in there and I'll try to defuse the bomb before it blows the bank and the Sentinels sky-high."

Rogue pushed Erith in the direction of the bank. "You'll need some kind of disguise. We can't just walk in with you, all red hair flaming, and announce to everyone you're the daughter of the bomb maker."

Erith made a face. "I hadn't really thought of that."

"Then it's a good thing I'm here, isn't it?" Rogue bit back a sigh. "Sighted, we're going to need your help on the schematics of the bank's interior."

"I'm on it," Melina said.

Rogue kept them both to the shadows as they skirted around the police cars. "Like I didn't have enough to contend with tonight," she muttered, looking up to the roof of the bank. She took hold of Erith's hand and ran across the grass. She quickly ducked back into the shadows as she saw a lone policeman walk across the gravel toward the bank's front doors.

"Curious. The police don't usually enter a building alone and unarmed." She edged closer and watched as the man divested himself of his pale blue shirt and cap. When he stepped into an elevator, she got to see a wide smile plastered evilly on his face.

"Sighted, warn everyone. Phoenix has just entered the building and is heading for the roof."

"He was dressed as a cop," Erith said. "Can we get me that disguise?" She yelped as Rogue pulled her out of the shadows and toward the bank at full speed.

❖

Pagan could feel her heart beating out a furious tattoo. The cold night air and the sheer silence she was wrapped in made her highly sensitive to everything around her. She had been informed that the Phoenix was in the building and on his way up. He obviously had something planned on the roof. It was a confined area and the Sentinels were waiting. Pagan looked at the buildings that towered nearby and at the Sentinels poised there. The Phoenix could not escape once he set foot on the roof. Casper and Earl had joined Pagan's vigil. Casper signed that a helicopter had been diverted by Chastilian's Air Traffic Control and a police helicopter was escorting it to a nearby field.

The game was on. The star player just needed to get on the field.

❖

From her vantage point, Pagan watched as Zachary Phoenix boldly stepped onto the rooftop. She felt her breath catch in her throat. He was indeed the image of his father, but he looked strangely nondescript otherwise. Only the coldness in his eyes conveyed his true evil nature. His long black jacket was missing. Pagan realized this was why his signal had been lost. He held a small box in one hand. He was nonchalantly tossing a rather odd-shaped disc in his other hand as he made his way across the roof. He looked into the cold night sky.

"If you're looking for your ride out of here, you might have to wait for a while. Your copter's down, leaving you high and dry."

Phoenix turned to face Pagan, his face full of fury. "Sentinel, you just bet on the wrong man. I have other tricks up my sleeve." He held up the small disc. The moonlight reflecting holographic rainbow colors skated across it.

Out of the corner of her eye Pagan saw the door to the roof open. Sentinels began to march through it. Phoenix just backed up until he was leaning against the roof ledge.

"Stay right where you are," he yelled. "I haven't come this far in my quest to be stopped by Sentinels who won't play by Phoenix rules." He lifted up the small box in one hand. "I press this trigger on this box, and the whole bank is wiped out and you all with it."

"If you do that, you die too," Pagan said.

The Phoenix snorted. "What? Do you goons think you're the only ones who can swing around the city like you own it? You've just left the stadium I destroyed. Didn't you learn that a smart player knows the game plan before he hits the field? But an even better player seizes whatever opportunities come his way." He held up the small disc. "I hate to do this to you." He paused dramatically. "Actually, no, I don't. You Sentinels have been the bane of my existence for years. Maybe tonight, finally, we can be rid of you all." He laughed and pressed a button on the disc.

The Sentinels all fell to the ground in unison, their hands clutching their heads, teeth gritted against the pain. Zachary Phoenix howled with glee as he surveyed the fallen Sentinels.

All except one.

❖

Alarmed, Pagan watched as her fellow Sentinels fell in obvious agony. Yet she felt nothing. It seemed that whatever he had done to the other Sentinels was linked to their comlinks. Her deafness had given her an advantage. It had also left her alone with the man who had brought back the Phoenix's reign of terror to Chastilian. She was unaided, at least until the other Sentinels gained their bearings. She stared at the Phoenix. Everything had come down to this one moment, and Pagan made her choice. He was going to have to pay.

"Now why aren't you on the ground like your playmates?" he asked, pressing at the disc again and sending further convulsions through the Sentinels at Pagan's feet. "What kind of freak are *you*?" he asked incredulously as Pagan walked toward him.

"The kind *your* sort made me," Pagan replied as she smacked the disc out of his hand with her escrima stick. It spun in the air like a coin being flipped to decide the play. Phoenix reached for it, but Pagan snatched it from the air first.

"Tails. You lose." She punched him in the face. He toppled back at the blow.

Pagan eyed the disc and pressed a smaller button on the underside. The Sentinels began to rouse from their fallen positions, shaking their heads and slowly sitting up once more. Pagan quickly tucked the disc in a pocket and rounded on Phoenix again. He held up the trigger device as a warning.

"I'll blow the place up!"

"With you still on it? I don't think so. I'm not much of a betting person, but I'd wager you're too much of a coward to commit suicide because something isn't going the way you planned it." She circled him, all the time watching his face, reading his lips. "I'm guessing you won't just surrender either," Pagan said, clutching her escrima sticks, preparing herself. "I'm also thinking you'll want to fight to the death. Preferably mine."

"You read my mind."

"But you see, a Phoenix already tried that once, and it didn't work. I'm still here, still very much alive, and worse still…I have a debt to repay."

"Who are you?" Phoenix asked.

"Someone your father left for dead after he killed my parents. Don't you just hate it when the past comes back to haunt you?" Pagan flicked out her escrima stick and caught Phoenix's hand sharply with its tip. He lost his grip on the trigger switch. Pagan dove for it, but Phoenix caught it again before the box could hit the ground. He hid it inside his jacket and spun around, his fists balled for a fight.

"You have weapons, yet I am unarmed," he said, splaying his hands from his sides as if to prove his point.

"If I have learned anything from your family, it's that you don't play fair."

She lashed out with her escrima sticks, landing painful blows to his arm and shoulder while moving around him. He yelled out in pain as she cracked her stick across his knees. He fell forward, kneeling on one leg as he clutched the other in agony. Pagan didn't leave him there; she punched him in the neck, making his head spin around. He tried to get back up again, but Pagan kept aiming for his knees, focusing on the weak spot. Knowing where the enemy was vulnerable was the key to taking him down.

Phoenix grabbed for her waist and managed to push her away slightly. Pagan recovered her ground quickly and got close enough to elbow him in the face. He roared with pain as blood poured from his broken nose.

Pagan looked over to where the Sentinels were now getting to their feet groggily. She saw Earl rallying them together as the rooftop doors flung open and the rest of Phoenix's men ran in and began wielding their weapons. She left them to their fight. She had her own war to win.

❖

Escaping from the shadows, Rogue and Erith slipped into the Bank's main foyer, just managing to hide before another group of men entered and started for the stairs. Rogue gestured silently for them to go below and Erith followed after her. They had gone only a few steps when a harsh voice called out in their direction.

"Hey! What are you doing down there, boy?"

Erith spun around at the voice and stood still, her face hidden by a bandana that Rogue had appropriated from a man outside. Her hair was tucked beneath a cap pulled low over her brow.

Rogue quickly moved from her side and worked her way behind the gang member, thankful he'd only seen the one of them.

"We're all supposed to be going to the roof, where are you heading off to?"

The resounding thud that suddenly echoed through the foyer made Erith visibly jump. The man stopped dead in his tracks, his eyes rolled up into his head, and he collapsed like a felled tree at Erith's feet. Rogue put down the heavy bust she had used to knock the man out and grinned at her.

"You disappeared into thin air," Erith marveled.

Rogue placed the bust back in its appropriate place and dragged the fallen man from view. "Come on, let's get out of sight before anyone else sees us."

The door to the basement was locked, but Erith made swift work of it with her lock-picking device. Rogue chuckled at just how skillful Erith was.

"You've certainly got your own way of getting things done," Rogue said as she heard the satisfying click as the last lock turned and the door swung open. "Now let's find the vault."

"Shit!" Melina's panicked voice sounded over the comlink. "Rogue, can you still hear me?"

"Of course."

"Looks like Phoenix has just managed to disable all the Sentinels we have on the roof. Coms are down and so are all our people." There was a pause. "Except for Pagan."

"What's he doing?" Rogue asked, hurrying Erith through the corridors urgently, aware that time was of the essence.

"Thank God the cameras are still working. Sentinels are down, but Pagan is facing off with him. She's taking him on alone."

"Courage, Sentinel," Rogue whispered and led the way down another corridor and then farther still down some steps. She finally found the door to the vault and began to check out the keypad that was flashing on its panel.

"First things first. I think this is where I come in." Melina spoke confidently in their ears. "This is where being a Sighted should make all institutions fear us. Rogue, get a little closer to the keypad for me." There was the distant clatter of keyboard keys echoing through Rogue's ear. "Okay, Rogue, attach the seeker."

Rogue placed a small, square object on top of the pad and they watched as it began to blink. A series of numbers flashed by on the pad. One by one, numbers appeared on its viewscreen, giving the combination to the keypad in the vault. Once the last digit fell, Rogue punched in the numbers manually. The vault door clunked loudly and then hissed open. Erith pulled the huge door back, then reached for the safe-cracking device.

"Do you know how much fun I could have had with one of these before I knew you guys?" she mused.

"Then it's a good thing you're on our side now, isn't it?" Rogue removed the device from Erith's hand and shook her finger at her. She checked the area before them and gave Erith a thumbs-up before allowing her to enter. The inside of the vault was dimly lit and Rogue switched on her flashlights to light the gloom. She pushed forward and saw what lay waiting in the room. The walls were lined with safe deposit boxes.

Rogue took a deep breath when she realized that she and Erith weren't the only occupants in the vault. Jackson Menard was bound with ropes to an ornately carved chair, his mouth gagged by a silk scarf. A copious amount of blood covered his face. His eyes flicked open, and Erith let out a terrified scream.

"He's still alive!" she gasped as he began to struggle. She held up her hands to stop him. "No! You don't want to move. You have a huge bomb in your lap. You keep twitching and we're all going to go up."

Rogue watched Erith trying to calm Menard down as she removed the gag. "You need to just let me think now, okay? I'm going to try to get you out of this, but you have to help me by not moving."

"Someone kidnapped me and left me down here," Menard whispered, his eyes never leaving the elaborate contraption on his thighs.

"Zachary Phoenix, son of Xander, back for some major payback," Rogue said bluntly while looking over the bomb herself. "That's a nasty-looking contraption."

"And I need you to hush too." Erith looked at the device from all angles and then let out a small grunt of annoyance. "Bless him for making my job just that little bit more difficult." She sighed. "Oh yes, that's Joe's handiwork all right." She gave Rogue a wry look. "Now I know what he meant when we first moved here and he said that he was going to be part of something big in the city."

Erith removed a small packet of cutters and pliers from her back pocket and concentrated on the wires. "Sneaky. He's added some extra wiring to confuse the coding, but I know how his mind works." She looked up to find Rogue right by her side, almost crowding over her shoulder.

"You can leave me now. Your friends upstairs could probably use your help."

Rogue shook her head, folded her arms, and planted her feet firmly to make it very clear she wasn't leaving. "I'm not going anywhere."

Erith looked back down at the bomb. "If this goes wrong, you need to be far away from here, so please leave."

"No, so just do your thing and then *we'll* go." She smiled at her then signed slowly for Erith to read. *I'd never leave Pagan's girl on her own.*

Erith snorted. "Damned Sentinel pride. It's going to get you all killed one day." She made a shooing motion. "Then step back at least and give me space to breathe."

Rogue did so and then watched as Erith concentrated on the wiring before her, laid out in a mass of colors all tangled through each other. Obviously making a decision, Erith spared Rogue one last look. Rogue heard her utter under her breath "I love you, Pagan," and then she snipped four wires, naming off the colors—"Red, blue, green, black"—in singsong fashion. She pulled out the two real detonators amid four fakes with a swiftness that made Rogue blink and nearly miss it all. The lights on the bomb blinked out, and Erith finally took a breath.

"The bomb is defused, Sighted. Your Sentinels have nothing to fear from down here."

Rogue stood back and saw Jackson Menard's relieved but embarrassed face. She looked down at the puddle forming on the ground. "It's okay. I nearly had an accident too."

Rogue gathered Erith up in her arms and gave her a hug. "You were brilliant." She felt Erith shake as the realization of what she had just done obviously sank in. Erith clung just a little longer and then patted Rogue on the back.

"How about we find a way to release Mr. Menard and get the hell out of here while you go take out Phoenix?"

Rogue cut away Menard's bindings, then helped the shattered man stagger from the vault.

"We saved one, Sighted," Rogue said.

"That we did. Erith, you are a hero tonight," Melina said.

Erith stood a little taller under the praise. Together they got Menard out of the bank and into the waiting arms of the police.

Rogue rushed back toward the building. "I'd better get back up there now that one threat has been removed."

Erith gripped Rogue's arm and squeezed it. "Be safe, Sentinel, and keep that charge of yours out of harm's way."

"I'll do my best." Rogue prepared her wire gun and then leaned forward to press a kiss to Erith's cheek. "Now, for once in your life, do as you're told and stay out of trouble."

The wire attached high up the tower and Rogue felt the pull lift her from the ground. She saw Erith step back behind the police cordon.

"How's our girl doing, Sighted?" Rogue asked as she traveled upward.

"Pagan's still taking on this Phoenix alone while the Sentinels hold off his men. You couldn't be returning at a more fortuitous time."

Rogue lifted her head so she could see the edge of the roof. "And so it begins again."

❖

Pagan knew she couldn't keep fighting Phoenix until he tired. He seemed blessed with too much stamina. She had landed several blows and he was spitting blood, but whatever injury he suffered, it hadn't put a dent in his determination. She was all too aware that the rest of the Sentinels were otherwise occupied. She could feel the fighting going on around her. She wished she could hear Melina in her ear, telling her what she needed to do.

For the first time in her life, Pagan was a Sentinel alone in a fight to the death. Phoenix lunged for her again and Pagan leapt back, never once losing her footing on the ledge. She balanced like a gymnast on a beam. He sneered at her, wiping the blood from his mouth, then spat it in her direction. Pagan could tell he was talking to her, but she was unable to make out the words.

Pagan vaulted over Phoenix's head to land behind him on the ledge. As he spun around to make a grab for her, she lashed out with a booted foot and again kicked him in his knees. He yelled out in pain. He gathered himself up, then scrambled toward a Sentinel lying prone on the roof, one of the few fallen, hurt in the battle. He moved to pick him up and held the limp Sentinel's body high above his head.

"No!" Pagan yelled, realizing what he was going to do.

Phoenix walked toward the edge of the roof with the body in his grasp. "One by one I'm going to throw the Sentinels off the roof and see if they bounce!" He switched his hold on the man to balance him better. "You're a mighty Sentinel. Do you think you can catch all the ones I throw away? I'll make the game easy for you and let you see which side of the building I'm going to do it from. Makes it more exciting, don't you think? Think you can scramble round the building like a spider catching flies?" He shifted the man again and slowly headed toward the ledge, walking backward, keeping Pagan in his view.

Pagan made her decision quickly. Holstering her escrima sticks, she ran for Phoenix as he turned to hoist the Sentinel above his head to throw him over the ledge. Instead, at the last second, he twisted and threw the unconscious Sentinel straight at Pagan. Pagan stumbled back under the force of him hitting her chest, and they both fell to the ground with a solid thump. Pagan scrambled out from under the downed Sentinel only to catch sight of Phoenix charging her way. Before she could regain her feet, he was on her and lifted her above his head. He carried her to the edge of the roof.

Pagan felt no fear. She was a Sentinel; she leapt from roofs every night. She struggled in Phoenix's arms as he tried to angle her over the edge. Phoenix leaned over the ledge to throw her and slipped on the shards of brick that lay jagged and broken on the roof, pitching them both over the ledge.

Pagan instinctively reached for any piece of wall to halt her flight as she flipped over Phoenix's shoulders. Her fingers just managed to slip around a piece of ornate carving on the building. Phoenix's body was stretched too far for him to get back onto the roof. He dangled over the edge, grabbing for Pagan's shoulders. She looked up at him as he stared down at her, stretched out from the building, only Pagan somehow keeping him balanced.

"You pulled me over the edge!" he yelled.

"Shall we see if *you* can bounce?" Pagan threw his taunting words back in his face.

His eyes widened as he slipped from the ledge, his own weight dragging him over. He gripped hard at Pagan's arms. "If I go, you go!"

Pagan smiled at him. "You forget I swing around the city. You, however, are more suited to setting fires and killing the people who had your father killed." She tried to move out from under his crushing weight. "You need to try to inch back through the hole. I can't hold you up for much longer."

"Are you trying to save me, Sentinel?" He laughed down at her.

"It's my job, whether I like it or not. I'm not a murderer. That's in your family job description, not mine." She tried to inch her way back up the wall, but the added pressure from the man above her wouldn't let her move without him falling. "If you didn't have your men occupying the Sentinels back there, they would be able to grab you and get you back on the roof safely. But you're too far gone to tell your men to stop now, aren't you?" Pagan tightened her grip on the wall. "I think you're going to have to come down off the roof and hold on to me and I'll try to get us to the ground. You're too heavy for me to push back up."

"Yeah, right. And you'll just let me fall once I start moving."

"I could just shift to my right…" Pagan made as if to move, and

Phoenix clenched at her shoulders as the movement made him slip farther off the wall. "If I wanted you to fall, I could have done so by now." She blinked as something hit her face. "You might want to hurry. I think it's starting to rain."

As the words left her lips, the heavens opened and rain poured from the skies. Pagan put her face to the wall to shield her eyes from the stinging water. She tightened her grip on the wall as she felt Phoenix try to move.

"I'll knock you off the wall," he said.

"If you do, we'll fly," Pagan said simply. She braced herself as he shifted his death grip and moved to slide down Pagan's side. He dangled from her, his arm crushing her throat.

"You might want to let up on the choke hold," Pagan said.

"Actually, I like the grip. I figure if I am going to die, I take you with me." He tightened his hold, and Pagan began to see stars as her oxygen was slowly cut off.

"I'm trying to save you." She gasped for air.

"Maybe I'm beyond saving," Phoenix growled. He fumbled at her waist and roughly ripped her wire gun from her belt. He held it up triumphantly in her face. "Now who can't fly away?" He tossed the device over his shoulder and Pagan felt her heart pound as she watched her only hope for escape disappear down the endless side of the tall building.

Phoenix fumbled in his pocket for something else. He drew out a small box with a bright red button on it. He placed it in the hand that was wrapped about her neck so she couldn't miss its importance.

Pagan could feel her grip slipping and cursed the rain for making the brickwork slick. All she could see was the trigger for the bomb before her eyes, and she couldn't do anything about it.

❖

Rogue could hear Melina screaming in her ear, mixed with the screams from the others as they all saw the two bodies disappear over the side of the wall.

"They're holding on to the ledge!" Melina yelled. "Rogue, go get her away from him! I've lost too many to his evil, I won't lose her."

Rogue pushed away the man she was fighting and forced her way through the crowd to try to see what was happening through the broken shell of the wall. She could see Pagan just below, clinging for dear life to a piece of shattered wall with Zachary Phoenix hanging off her side like a huge limpet. She could see the strain in Pagan's face as she tried to keep them both steady. She roared as she watched him pull Pagan's wire gun from her belt and throw it away.

"You stupid bastard!" Rogue screamed. She was suddenly pulled back by one of Phoenix's men.

"Can we save him?" he asked.

Rogue stared at him incredulously. "I think he's beyond saving now." She elbowed him firmly in the mouth and felt his teeth shatter beneath her blow.

"I need Sentinels, *now!*" she ordered at the top of her voice. She could barely hear herself over the pouring rain and Melina's sobbing in her ear.

❖

Pagan looked up at the sky, the rain washing over her face in torrents. "By the way, Alexis and Camillin Osborne send their regards," she said, desperately trying to breathe. She blinked against the water that ran into her eyes and watched Phoenix's lips as he shifted to laugh in her face.

"Who? Oh, the ones my father killed and got caught for? I knew I should have kept my eye a little closer on the Sentinels seeking payback." Phoenix tightened his hold as best he could, but Pagan was slipping slightly every second he cut off her air supply.

"It seems we weren't the only ones who wanted to make your father pay. Guess that's why you've been killing his old gang members, getting rid of the ones who had him killed for his murderous ways."

"I was left with nothing. Nothing! My father was murdered, and I had to grow up without him. They deserved everything they got, the whole stinking lot of them. My father was more villain than they could ever dream of being, and look at them! They all became model citizens instead! Chastilian was theirs for the taking and they gave it all away." Phoenix shifted a little in his hold. "I killed them all, and if you damned Sentinels got taken out at the same time, then good! All I have of my father is a memory. He deserved revenge."

Pagan read every venomous word from his lips. "That's strange, because your father left me with so much more than he did you. Guess he didn't think you'd amount to much, so he left me his lucky coin instead." Pagan fumbled inside one of her pockets. She flicked the coin skyward and Phoenix greedily caught at it. The coin reflected the light from the moon above and shone brightly in his eyes.

"Here's his tip; I hope it brings you better luck than it did my father and mother." Pagan loosened her grip from the wall as she began to lose her hold on consciousness. She whispered Erith's name, her red-haired love the last thing she saw in her mind's eye. Phoenix, too engrossed in the coin in his hand, lost his death grip around Pagan's neck and slipped on the slickness of her jacket. He tried to grab at her, but Pagan was already falling from the brickwork, giddy and almost blind from having her throat crushed. As his grip loosened, Pagan managed to take in a lungful of much-needed air. She instinctively reached for the wall again, but instead was caught by a hand that held her firmly in its solid grasp. She registered the tight grip the fingers had on her, recognizing their familiarity. Pagan squeezed her eyes tight to dispel the rain that nearly blinded her, but grinned as she finally looked up into Rogue's relieved face.

"I've got you, and I am not letting go."

But it was too late for Zachary Phoenix. The shift in position had made him lose his hold and he flailed out of safety's reach.

Pagan made a last attempt to grasp at him as he fell, but the one hand she could have reached was holding on to the coin. In the other hand was the trigger switch which, with one last look of pure evil, he quickly pressed.

Nothing happened.

As he fell he jammed his finger onto the switch again, but there was no explosion. His "No!" echoed into the night. The useless box fell from his hand as he clutched at thin air to save himself.

Zachary Phoenix, son of Xander Phoenix, fell from Pagan's reach, his fate clenched tightly in the palm of his hand.

Pagan clung to Rogue's hand, shaking and gasping for air as she watched him fall to his death on the city street below. Then she was pulled up and back onto the roof and enfolded in Rogue's arms. She was crushed to Rogue's chest and she felt lips kiss her head over and over.

"He's gone," Pagan whispered. "He's finally gone, and unlike his namesake, he won't rise again."

Rogue relaxed her hold a mere fraction so that Pagan could see her face. "It's over."

Pagan nodded. "Erith was right. I may have lost my parents, but I was blessed to be brought up with ones who gave me just as much love and instilled in me their values." She gripped Rogue's arms. "In the end, I couldn't kill him. I was going to try to save him even after all he had done to us."

"That's because you are a Sentinel with love in your heart. You're an honorable warrior who keeps the city safe. You did your parents proud tonight."

"Can we go home now? I have a promise to keep to my girlfriend that I don't intend to break."

Rogue chuckled. "I wouldn't want to get on her wrong side either. Come on. Let's leave this building the old-fashioned way."

❖

Once outside the building, Pagan slowly walked over to where Zachary Phoenix's body lay. His sightless eyes stared up at the August Dawn Bank, his body broken by the concrete he lay on, his hand still clutching the coin that had paid for the deaths of Pagan's parents. She carefully nudged his fingers with her boot and the coin rolled out. It spun drunkenly on the cement, then came to rest. Pagan looked down at it.

"Heads, I win," she said tiredly.

She had taken on the Phoenix and lived to tell the tale.

CHAPTER TWENTY-SIX

Pagan smiled as she watched a familiar black vehicle pull up a short distance from where she waited with Rogue. Melina climbed out of it, dressed in a long cloak and scarf to conceal her face. Pagan grinned at Rogue as Melina neared and tenderly touched Rogue's face.

Pagan was looking around her when she saw someone escape from behind the police line and rush toward them. For all the black attire the smaller figure wore, and the very obvious Phoenix bandana, Pagan was surprised to realize it was Erith beneath it all. Erith launched herself at Pagan, who caught her awkwardly and then relaxed as that all-too-familiar body settled into hers.

"What on Earth are you doing here, dressed like that?"

Erith said something against Pagan's chest.

"I can't hear what you're saying," Pagan said but gathered Erith closer still.

Erith finally drew back and signed to her. *Are you okay?*

"I'm fine, but you're shaking like a leaf." She could feel the tremors vibrating through Erith's body.

"Your girlfriend had quite the adventure herself tonight. She defused the bomb that Phoenix had hidden away in the vault and rescued Jackson Menard in the process," Rogue said, eyeing Erith with a whole new respect and admiration.

"You stopped the bomb?" Pagan was torn between horror and amazement.

I'll tell you all about it when my hands stop shaking!

We saw everything that happened up there through your mask lens, Pagan. Phoenix managed to knock out the Sentinel comlinks for a brief moment until you reinstated them again, but he didn't knock out the one that is connected to the video link, so we saw and heard it all, Melina signed, then pulled Pagan close and hugged her. *Mom and Dad would have been so proud of you tonight.*

"I couldn't save him even though I tried to."

Then he wasn't to be saved. He made his own choices and paid dearly for them. It was not your fault. You were so brave. You fought for all the Sentinels tonight, past and present. That won't be forgotten by the Council. Melina touched Pagan's wet cheek. *I am so very proud of you.*

Pagan finally let go of the constricting breath that was wrapped about her chest, blaming herself for the death of Phoenix.

"The Sentinels were knocked out by some sort of neural emitter?" she asked.

Erith nodded and drew back from Pagan's hold. *Who'd have thought that being deaf would have been such an advantage?*

We're all given abilities with which to perform our duties. You proved yourself today, Pagan. Melina turned to Rogue but signed so that Pagan could read what she had to say. *Rogue, Pagan has always been safe in your care, and tonight you proved it yet again.* She hugged her tightly. *Damn, I hate having to hide! I want to kiss you and I can't!* She tugged at Rogue's hand and gestured for them all to go back to the van. *Let's go. We're done here for tonight.*

Once in the van, Melina threw off her scarf and gave Rogue the kiss she'd promised.

"Hey! Impressionable adults here!" Erith said, removing her bandana. She let go of Pagan and hugged Rogue. "Thank you for saving her, however you did it. I'm sure I'll hear all the details in time. But I will never be able to thank you enough."

"Just love her, that's all I ask."

Erith slipped her arms back about Pagan's waist and nudged at her side to get her attention. "Your family is so cool."

Pagan nodded in agreement. "I am so glad you're safe. I was frightened for you when your dad got his visitor and the whole evening just spiraled out of our control."

"But you saved me. And then I got to do some saving of my own. Guess I showed the city that not all the Baylors are intent on watching it go up in flames." She looked through the windshield over at the crushed body of Phoenix. "He doesn't look much like a guy who could make a man turn away from his family and follow blindly down whatever path was marked. But then my father followed the older Phoenix too, so there must have been something that called to him in that family."

"This Phoenix won't hurt anyone else now, but someone, someday, will come and take his place, and the fight will start all over again."

"But we'll fight them together, side by side. It's what families do. And I'll be your guardian angel like you are mine," Erith said.

"That sounds good to me." She grimaced slightly at her own choice of words. "I need my aids back." Erith tugged on her hand and Pagan looked down at her.

"You did brilliantly without them," Erith told her. "From what I understand, you brought down the city's crime lord."

Pagan cast a small glance back outside the building where the body still lay. "No, he brought himself down. He just couldn't hold on to his father's ghost any longer."

CHAPTER TWENTY-SEVEN

Ronchetti Security with its famed lighthouse was a welcome sight to Pagan's tired eyes as they drove back home. The black van was parked in the underground garage, safe from curious eyes. The four women stood silently in the elevator and then made their way back into the lighthouse's center.

"I can't believe he wiped us out by using our own equipment against us," Rogue growled.

Melina patted her arm. "Look on the bright side. It gives you a new project to work on. You can have the gizmo from Pagan tomorrow. That will be soon enough for you to take it apart and examine it."

Pagan began to remove her uniform, wanting to take off the whole night piece by piece and discard it. She saw Rogue beside her, just looking at her. Pagan raised an eyebrow, wondering what was going through Rogue's head.

"Do you know how very proud of you I am?"

Pagan smiled. "Yes, I do. But in the end, Rogue, you saved *me*. You let the Sentinels dangle you by your boots over the edge of the wall to grab my hand."

"I'll never have you fight alone, not while there is breath in my body."

"I know. Even when you're too old to be by my side in the battle, I'll still know you're there."

"I will never be too old to take you down."

Pagan laughed. "I know that too. Thank you for not letting me fall."

Melina leaned back against her desk and caught Pagan's eye. "All of the Sentinels are accounted for, and all of Phoenix's men are in custody, including the one who kidnapped Erith earlier. The hideouts are being checked out as we speak. The Sighted are back in their rightful places and the wounded Sentinels being cared for. Save for a headache or two, everyone seems to have survived the mental blast without too much damage. Tomorrow we will sit together, watch what happened tonight, dissect it piece by piece, and learn from it all. But for now, you need to go to bed. Pagan, you look dead on your feet."

"I save the city from a madman, and my sister still tells me when to go to bed," Pagan grumbled halfheartedly, removing her jacket. She responded to Erith's touch on her skin and looked where everyone's eyes were firmly fixed. Pagan saw the very clear imprint of a hand that had held her so roughly on the ledge. She flexed her neck. "It doesn't hurt yet," she said. "If he had just listened to me," she began and then shrugged. "But he wouldn't."

"Let's get you in the shower," Erith said "Get a hot spray on those muscles. Try to wash his filthy touch off you."

Pagan lifted Erith's chin and smiled at her. "His father's touch has been something I have felt all my life. He took away my parents, he hurt Melina, and he stole my hearing. These fingerprints are nothing compared to what his father did. These will fade." She brushed at the marks as if they were of no consequence. She moved to hang up her jacket and hesitated. She reached into a pocket and took out the silver disc Phoenix used, then held it out to Rogue. "You might want to have a tinker around with this before I forget."

Rogue let loose a delighted whoop. "You got his gadgetry off him. Melina said you had." Her keen eyes were already looking over the casing.

Melina removed it from her grasp and muttered, "Not now, I said. You and Erith can play with it tomorrow."

Pagan hung up her uniform. "I will see you both in the morning, when I hope I might be able to make more sense of the day's events. I just want to not think about it all for a while. It's overwhelming, and more than a little frightening."

Melina waved to attract Pagan's attention. "You two go get some rest. It's nearly dawn. We'll talk later when everyone is more coherent."

❖

Pagan wandered into her bathroom and started the shower. She stripped out of the remainder of her clothes and climbed in under the water. She closed her eyes against the spray beating on her face. Without warning, she was drawn back to the rooftop when the rain had stung her eyes and she thought she was going to die. She gasped and jumped as she felt slender arms snake around her waist. She was instantly soothed by small hands that reached around and finger spelled *hi* for her to see. Pagan relaxed and began to breathe easier again. Then the reality of the situation dawned on her and her pulse started to race. She could feel Erith's naked flesh pressed against her own. Breasts were pushed against the firmness of her back; hands were now tracing lazy designs on her stomach.

"What are you doing?" Pagan asked with a catch in her voice.

Washing you, Erith signed. She reached around Pagan to grab for the soap and began to lather it up in full view of Pagan's eyes. Pagan tried to turn around, but Erith firmly kept her facing away and smoothed the lather over her shoulders. The soap covered Pagan's back and then Erith soaped along her sides. She twitched involuntarily and looked back to see Erith laughing.

"You're ticklish," Erith said aloud now that Pagan could read her lips. "I'll have to remember that. I might need such a weapon in my arsenal against you."

Pagan turned around slowly under Erith's ministrations. She caught her breath at the sight of Erith naked before her. Pagan's mouth dropped open enough for water to fall into it and she had to spit it out quickly.

"Like what you see?" Erith asked shyly.

"I love what I see." Pagan ran her hand over Erith's collarbone and down to a bright pink nipple that stood to attention.

Erith shivered at Pagan's touch. She went still as Pagan explored further and with both hands cupped her small, firm breasts.

"You fit in the palm of my hand," Pagan said in wonder. She watched as Erith laid down the soap and repeated what Pagan was doing to her.

"You spill out in mine, lucky me." Erith brushed her thumbs over Pagan's darker nipples.

Pagan shuddered at the jolts of desire that burned in her belly. She grabbed for Erith's hands. "Doing this in here might not be the best choice. You're making my knees weak, and I'm liable to slip on the tiles. Hurry!" Pagan quickly finished washing, handing Erith the soap so she could do her own, and within minutes they were both wrapped in towels, drying off as best they could. Pagan took Erith's hand and led her into her bedroom. For a moment she hesitated and looked down silently at her.

"I want you," Erith said. "As I watched what was happening tonight, I promised myself no more waiting, no more hesitating. Life is too short and it can all be taken away so fast. I want to be with you. I *need* to be with you tonight. I need to know you're here with me and safe."

Pagan let her eyes run lazily up and down the length of Erith's naked body. "And I want you so badly I can taste it. No more waiting, no hesitation or shyness any longer."

"And I don't want to wait any longer to show you how much I love you." Erith pushed Pagan onto her back on the bed and leaned into her, kissing her sweetly and then with increasing passion.

"Wait." Pagan pulled back. "I should put my aids in so I can hear you if…I need to," she finished weakly.

"No aids for this time, my love. You do perfectly well without them, and I want this to be as natural to you as anything can be. Just you and me. And don't worry. I'll be sure to let you know everything I am feeling." Her soft mouth captured Pagan's and silenced her in a most effective manner.

Pagan surrendered to the moment. She wrapped her arms around Erith's smaller body and let her hands lazily wander over her flesh, delighting in the sensation, loving how Erith truly looked beneath the clothes she usually hid herself away in.

"You are beautiful," Pagan mumbled around Erith's kisses as her hand tangled in the hair that framed Erith's pretty face.

"I love you, Pagan." Erith kissed her way down Pagan's neck, making her squirm beneath her lips. Erith mapped out Pagan's body inch by inch with kisses and a warm tongue.

Pagan nearly sat upright when that warm mouth latched to her right nipple. Her moan vibrated in her chest. She felt Erith smile against her breast as she tugged a little on the taut bud and sent fiery bolts of electricity coursing through Pagan's body. Pagan's hands did their own exploring, and she reached for a breast and fondled it, marveling at its firmness and the rigidity of Erith's nipple. She grinned smugly when she felt Erith shudder in her hold as she flicked at the tip of her breast.

"I like that," Erith said before sucking more of Pagan into her mouth and lashing a tight nipple with her tongue. She held on as Pagan bucked beneath her. "And I guess you like that." She grinned at Pagan's flushed face.

Erith continued exploring Pagan's body with her roaming hands. She took a leisurely pace, touching Pagan everywhere, learning her body with her fingertips. She finally stopped her torture of Pagan's nipples and lowered her mouth to kiss across muscles that twitched in Pagan's stomach. Pagan took in a deep breath when Erith moved even lower, needy and yet nervous all at the same time. She was bewitched by the sight of bright red hair trailing a path down between her legs. She could feel her control slipping away, and it both frightened and excited her. She gave herself up into Erith's care.

"Let me see you." Erith mouthed the words clearly, expressing her intent.

Pagan complied without hesitation. She spread her legs for Erith, who instantly settled between them. She watched intently as Erith ran a finger through the soft folds that nestled between her thighs. Pagan let out a gasp as Erith's tongue followed the same trail her finger had taken. "God, that feels good," she moaned as Erith ran her tongue over her skin. Pagan began to shake as Erith brushed over one specific spot, gauged her reaction, then did it again more firmly. Erith's tongue felt like concentrated fire, burning through Pagan's most intimate softness.

"You're so hard," Erith said as she looked up briefly at Pagan's flushed face, flicked her tongue once more to catch at her clitoris. "And so very wet," she added and stuck her tongue in deeply where Pagan was the most moist.

Pagan came off the bed, nearly bucking Erith from her. She moaned softly, trying to catch her breath and not miss a minute of what Erith was doing to her. A hand held her back down and then those small fingers began to reach inside Pagan where she had never been touched before. There was a slight discomfort, but Erith's fingers moving in and out soon dispelled the ache and created a pressure that was all pleasure. Pagan began to pant, her head full of sensation, her body no longer her own. She couldn't form words; instead her moans told Erith what she needed to hear. She could feel Erith pushing inside her, felt the muscles inside stretch to accommodate the fingers that mastered her body so forcefully.

Erith shifted position and Pagan felt a hot tongue massaging her clitoris. She marveled at the rising ache that threatened to burst from her. Fingers tugged at a nipple and Pagan gasped as she was flooded with sensations spiraling out of control. She was climbing toward something that engulfed her entire being. She gripped at the sheets to hang on for the ride. Her sudden climax filled her head with bright lights, a kaleidoscope of colors that blinded her in their intensity and then soothed her as she finally came back down. She could still feel Erith inside her, held in place by her pulsating walls, but Erith's head was now resting on Pagan's heaving stomach and she was laying tiny kisses on Pagan's belly, her hand splayed over her breast in comfort. The look in Erith's eyes spoke of such love and devotion that Pagan felt a tear spill from her.

Gently, Erith withdrew and crawled up Pagan's body to lie on top of her. "I love you," she said against Pagan's neck, then moved so Pagan could read the words again from her lips.

"That was amazing." Pagan finally found her voice, her heart still pounding wildly. Her body was vibrating with the sensations that washed over her, sweet aftershocks causing her body to twitch.

"Was it better than flying from buildings with only wires to keep you up?" Erith teased, her eyes drawn to her hand covered with Pagan's juices. She licked at the wetness, savoring the taste and smiling at the sharp intake of breath from Pagan at the erotic sight.

"Infinitely better. And I got to do it with you, which was the best thing of all." Pagan delighted in the feel of Erith in her arms as she snuggled into her and spread her body over as much of Pagan's as she could. She could feel Erith's breath against her neck, and it warmed her all over again. She brushed her hands over Erith's back and down to cup her buttocks. She squeezed them. "I knew you had a cute butt hidden in those baggy jeans you wear," she said, smoothing a hand over the soft curves.

"Have you been checking out my ass?" Erith asked, lifting her upper body from Pagan's chest to stare down at her.

"I've been checking all of you out. But I never dreamed you'd be as beautiful as you are here in my arms." Pagan ran her hand over Erith's breasts, trapping the tips between her spread fingers. She rubbed at Erith, then spread her hands down across Erith's stomach and down over her thighs. "You're so tiny, yet amazingly strong." Pagan dipped a finger into Erith's small belly button and smiled as she wriggled at the tease. "You're gorgeous. I just can't touch you enough." Erith was still straddling Pagan, and Pagan could feel the heat from Erith burn through her. The scent of her arousal made Pagan want to seek out more, and she brushed at Erith's patch of red pubic hair.

"Natural red, all the way." Erith just managed to breathe as she watched with glazed eyes Pagan's adoration of her body. She shifted as Pagan's fingers slipped into her wetness and fondled her with such sweetness that Erith cried out.

Pagan studied Erith's face intently as she felt the textures that greeted her exploration. She was in awe at the moisture that flowed over her fingers, and loved the feel of Erith's intimate flesh against her blunt fingertips. She withdrew her hand, noting the look of instant disappointment on Erith's face. Pagan brought her hand to her face and sniffed the scent she found there, then ran her tongue over the moisture that clung to her finger like honey.

Erith never took her eyes from Pagan's face as she watched the sensual performance. Pagan licked her lips, then returned her fingers to where they wanted to be the most. She sat up a little in the bed, bringing Erith up her body so she straddled her waist. From where she now sat, Pagan could suck Erith's breasts while she pressed farther inside Erith's treasures. Erith held her arms for leverage while Pagan began to tease at her breasts, licking the hard tips, running her tongue around the areolas and then sucking in as much pebbled flesh as she could. Pagan angled her finger into Erith and pushed through the swollen heat.

"Oh God, yes," Erith breathed, her body greedily welcoming Pagan's intrusion. Her nails dug into the skin of Pagan's arms as she gripped her closer.

Pagan waited for Erith to welcome her in more fully, then pressed until she was in as far as she could reach. The vision of Erith impaled on her finger, moving to a rhythm only the two of them knew, was the sexiest thing Pagan had ever witnessed. She could feel Erith's walls tighten to keep her inside, watched her face as the friction they caused together sent her climbing higher still. When Pagan's thumb brushed over Erith's protruding clitoris, Pagan didn't have to hear to know that Erith released a scream to shake the walls. She watched in rapt fascination as Erith shook and shivered as she pumped inside her, all the time touching the sensitive nub between Erith's legs. With one last flick of her tongue over an overly sensitive nipple, Pagan pushed hard into Erith's softness with an extra finger and watched as she exploded on her hand. Erith shivered, and Pagan devoured the sight of the woman she loved finding release at her touch. She relished the feel of Erith's nails digging into her arms as she rode out her climax.

Erith collapsed into Pagan's chest and Pagan tried to carefully remove her hand so that Erith could lie down. Erith's hand quickly clutched at hers, holding it in place.

"No, don't go yet. Let me keep you in there for a moment longer." Erith placed herself at Pagan's side, leaving her fingers still firmly inside, Erith's leg thrown over Pagan's thighs. "It's a good thing you *can't* hear, because I think I may have just shattered all the glass in the lighthouse."

Pagan chuckled and gathered Erith closer to kiss her tenderly on her forehead. She rubbed her free hand over Erith's bare leg that rested on her stomach. "I saw your tattoo finally," Pagan said, trailing her fingers up Erith's thigh. "You have angel wings on your belly."

"My guardian angel watches over me in my most private places." Erith slowly, almost reluctantly, drew herself off Pagan's fingers. She cupped Pagan's hand over her mound to not lose the feeling of her. "You're my first *and* last port in a storm, Pagan Osborne, do you know that?" Erith leaned up and traced Pagan's face. "You were my light in the dark that drew me away from the danger that I was slipping into. You got me to safety and became the one that lit my way to something so much better." She kissed Pagan softly. "Lighting up a future with you by my side, holding me close, loving me."

Pagan smiled. "I feel so different. I feel like I left the old Pagan on the roof of the August Dawn Bank tonight and came home as someone wiser. I faced my past head-on and watched a man intent on killing me die because he wouldn't let me save him. Against all I ever thought I wanted to have happen to him for revenge's sake, I just couldn't kill him. It's not in me." She brushed at Erith's face with her fingertips.

"I've seen my future as well, and it's here in your arms. For all I did tonight, for all that being a Sentinel means to me, my greatest moment was here with you, just sharing our love. Watching you experience pleasure at my touch was the greatest thing I have ever seen. And after tonight, it was *my* shining light at the end of what has been a very long, dark tunnel." Pagan stroked at Erith's bright hair lovingly. "I love you, Erith, and we will guide each other home."

"You're my angel," Erith whispered and pressed a sweet kiss on Pagan's waiting lips.

They snuggled down together, finally giving in to the exhaustion of the day's events and their own more intimate excursions.

Pagan slept soundly, safe in the knowledge that the lighthouse's beam touched upon a city finally free of one of its biggest night terrors. She slumbered dreamlessly, comforted by Erith's warmth beside her and knowing that Erith slept secure in her protective arms, having found the peace she too had been searching for.

About the Author

Lesley Davis lives with her American partner Cindy in the West Midlands of England. She is a die-hard science-fiction/fantasy fan in all its forms and an extremely passionate gamer. When her Nintendo DS is out of her grasp, Lesley is seated before the computer writing. She has been published in *Erotic Interludes 2: Stolen Moments* and *Road Games: Erotic Interludes 5* from Bold Strokes Books.

Books Available From Bold Strokes Books

Lake Effect Snow by C.P. Rowlands. News correspondent Annie T. Booker and FBI Agent Sarah Moore struggle to stay one step ahead of disaster as Annie's life becomes the war zone she once reported on. Eclipse EBook (978-1-60282-068-5)

Revision of Justice by John Morgan Wilson. Murder shifts into high gear propelling Benjamin Justice into a raging fire that consumes the Hollywood Hills, burning steadily toward the famous Hollywood Sign—and the identity of a cold-blooded killer. Gay Mystery. (978-1-60282-058-6)

I Dare You by Larkin Rose. Stripper by night, corporate raider by day, Kelsey's only looking for sex and power, until she meets a woman who stirs her heart and her body. (978-1-60282-030-2)

Truth Behind the Mask by Lesley Davis. Erith Baylor is drawn to Sentinel Pagan Osborne's quiet strength, but the secrets between them strain duty and family ties. (978-1-60282-029-6)

Cooper's Deale by KI Thompson. Two would-be lovers and a decidedly inopportune murder spell trouble for Addy Cooper, no matter which way the cards fall. (978-1-60282-028-9)

Romantic Interludes 1: Discovery ed. by Radclyffe and Stacia Seaman. An anthology of sensual, erotic contemporary love stories from the best-selling Bold Strokes authors. (978-1-60282-027-2)

A Guarded Heart by Jennifer Fulton. The last place FBI Special Agent Pat Roussel expects to find herself is assigned to an illicit private security gig baby-sitting a celebrity. (Ebook) (978-1-60282-067-8)

Saving Grace by Jennifer Fulton. Champion swimmer Dawn Beaumont, injured in a car crash she caused, flees to Moon Island, where scientist Grace Ramsay welcomes her. (Ebook) (978-1-60282-066-1)

The Sacred Shore by Jennifer Fulton. Successful tech industry survivor Merris Randall does not believe in love at first sight until she meets Olivia Pearce. (Ebook) (978-1-60282-065-4)

Passion Bay by Jennifer Fulton. Two women from different ends of the earth meet in paradise. Author's expanded edition. (Ebook) (978-1-60282-064-7)

Never Wake by Gabrielle Goldsby. After a brutal attack, Emma Webster becomes a self-sentenced prisoner inside her condo—until the world outside her window goes silent. (Ebook) (978-1-60282-063-0)

The Caretaker's Daughter by Gabrielle Goldsby. Against the backdrop of a nineteenth-century English country estate, two women struggle to find love. (Ebook) (978-1-60282-062-3)

Simple Justice by John Morgan Wilson. When a pretty-boy cokehead is murdered, former LA reporter Benjamin Justice and his reluctant new partner, Alexandra Templeton, must unveil the real killer. (978-1-60282-057-9)

Remember Tomorrow by Gabrielle Goldsby. Cees Bannigan and Arieanna Simon find that a successful relationship rests in remembering the mistakes of the past. (978-1-60282-026-5)

Put Away Wet by Susan Smith. Jocelyn "Joey" Fellows has just been savagely dumped—when she posts an online personal ad, she discovers more than just the great sex she expected. (978-1-60282-025-8)

Homecoming by Nell Stark. Sarah Storm loses everything that matters—family, future dreams, and love—will her new "straight" roommate cause Sarah to take a chance at happiness? (978-1-60282-024-1)

The Three by Meghan O'Brien. A daring, provocative exploration of love and sexuality. Two lovers, Elin and Kael, struggle to survive in a postapocalyptic world. (Ebook) (978-1-60282-056-2)

Falling Star by Gill McKnight. Solley Rayner hopes a few weeks with her family will help heal her shattered dreams, but she hasn't counted on meeting a woman who stirs her heart. (978-1-60282-023-4)

Lethal Affairs by Kim Baldwin and Xenia Alexiou. Elite operative Domino is no stranger to peril, but her investigation of journalist Hayley Ward will test more than her skills. (978-1-60282-022-7)

Bold Strokes
BOOKS
WEBSTORE
PRINT AND EBOOKS

Romance

Mystery

Intrigue

MATINEE BOOKS

LIBERTY
EDITION

Adventure

Erotica

Fantasy

victory
EDITIONS

Sci-Fi

BS
BOLD
STROKES
BOOKS

ECLIPSE
e

http://www.boldstrokesbooks.com